To LAURA M.

ENJOY!

CROSSING THE BLUE LINE

by R. J. Bonett

M. Bonett

10 - 8 - 21

Credits: Marie Bonett

Editor: Rachel Heitzenrater

Special thanks to: James Raffaele, former co-worker and close friend, also Pat and Gary Ziegler, for their support and encouragement in writing this novel.

Cover Credits: R. J. Bonett, Charlene Lewis – Photography, Karen DeLise – New York Camera & Video
1139 Street Rd., Southhampton, PA 18966

Introduction

Randy Bishop, a veteran cop in the early 70's, chose to remain in a Philadelphia neighborhood he was originally assigned, rather than climb the ladder of promotions. He realized over time, the job of policing became much easier, having gained the trust of the locals. After 18 years of working police cars and a police wagon in the same neighborhood, he was offered a steady day-work assignment on Frankford Avenue, a business district about ten blocks long. It was situated under the loom of the elevated train going to and from center city. His area of responsibility was four blocks in the center of that strip. It was actually open ended if there was something that had to be addressed within a close proximity of the beat. In the center of the beat, there was an elevated train station, a central point, to where the residents from the far North East end of the city would exit buses to take the train to center city. That in itself; would give you an idea of how many people he came in contact with daily.

Randy had a reputation of being objective while dealing with the public. At times, he would be asked by younger cops, his opinion about an assignment. Sometimes, their questions would carry into their personal lives, and they were questions he always tried to avoid.

He had a series of encounters with a police woman named Delores Johnson, whose nickname was Champ. Against his better judgment, he listens to her problem. As he becomes more involved, he's surprised to hear Champ's problems were many. Seemingly not being able to get her life on track, she deepens Randy's involvement. After she goes missing for a few days, she's found dead in a small bathroom in the basement of the district. He wonders whether the coroner's report was correct, suicide by self inflicted gunshot wound of the chest? For the remainder of his police career, it was a question he was never able to satisfy.

Chapter 1

Sitting in his civilian car, Randy Bishop stared up at the communications tower looming over the police cars behind the district. With the rain coming down, he wasn't enthusiastic about beginning the shift. Watching the younger cops in their rain coats checking the oil and a few other responsibilities that go with operating a patrol car, he was happy to be on a foot-beat. Waiting for the rain to slacken, he looked at his watch, realizing the time was getting close to report in. Fortunately, being in the squad he was in, he and a few others with longevity didn't have to stand roll call. They were privileged to be on their honor to check out a hand held radio and get to their assignments on time.

"Hello, David, happy birthday," he said to the corporal behind the desk.

"You too, Randy," looking across the operations room he said, "Happy birthday to you too, George."

"Yeah, that's right. It is our birthday."

Another cop by the name of Don, someone who always bragged about being in the Marines, replied, "It's all your birthdays today? That's funny."

"You were in the Corps; and you don't know what today is?" Randy asked.

"Yeah, it's November 10th," he replied.

David, George and Randy looked at each other then looked at Don. David said, "If you didn't know today's the Marine

Corps birthday, you were never a Marine. You're full of shit! Every Marine knows what today is."

Embarrassed he was discovered, Don quickly checked out a radio, then headed out the door. The corporal asked, "What do you think of that asshole Randy?"

"I don't," Randy replied, as he looked in the cabinet that stored the hand held radios. He asked, "Hey corporal. Is there a strap for this radio?"

Pointing to several cops working in the operations room, the corporal jokingly replied, "Yeah. There's a strap sitting over there, and there's another one over there in the corner typing that report."

Everyone looked at him and laughed. Walt, who was making out the report, had a rebuttal to his claim, by crumpling up a piece of paper and hurling it across the room, landing on the corporal's desk.

"Hey, Randy."

"What's that corporal?"

"I received a few phone calls from girls this morning asking whether you were on duty today. What the hell are you running for, mayor or something?"

Turning before he walked out the door, Randy replied, "No, I'm just a lovable kind of guy."

Randy always tried to keep in some sort of physical condition, and at almost 40, the trips to the gym were getting harder. That was one of the reasons he preferred walking a beat. Daily exercise, and let's face it, being in uniform helps with the opposite sex.

He worked the same neighborhood for 18 years, from 1967 thru 1985. First, in a police car, which were always one-man, for the exception of his assigned sector, then a police wagon which were two-man. He had a black partner named Jesse for about 8 years, from 1968, to 1976, covering the same sector in a patrol car from 1968, until 1972, then a police wagon. The area they were assigned was part business, a large part residential, and a public housing project. The makeup of people who lived in their assigned area was about 60% black, 10% Puerto Rican, and a mixture of whites and Orientals.

Unlike Jesse, he chose not to go up in rank, thinking he was going to cure some of the ills of the world. They had that discussion several times, and he pointed out on more than one occasion, they were in the best position to help John Q Public. Looking back on it, he questioned whether he was right. After 18 years, to his dismay, he realized with few exceptions, his contribution to mankind would have been the equivalent of standing on a pier and pissing in the Pacific Ocean.

Getting back to his private auto, he headed south on Frankford Avenue to the beat. Parking on a small intersecting street, he picked up his radio and walked out on his assigned area. His beat was commonly referred to as "the avenue." It was under the elevated train-trestle that serviced about 12 stops in different areas, on its route to center city, and the noise, as it passed overhead, was deafening. The beat consisted of all businesses: five banks, two savings and loans, four jewelry stores, four shoe stores, three bars, and the rest a mixture of women's and men's clothing stores. A restaurant was at each end, and one was conveniently located in the center of the beat. That in itself will give you an idea of the foot traffic he encountered daily.

An added responsibility, at the center of the beat, was a major intersection. It was also an elevated train stop. Margaret-

Orthodox station was a hub where busses and trolleys deposited passengers. The majority came from the northeast section, traveling to center city to work, and at the end of the day, traversed the same route. Several businesses were also on Oxford Avenue, an intersecting street, which wasn't a part of the beat, but as he said, he was a public servant. There was also a high school several blocks away on Oxford Avenue, and being visible, deterred more than one fight between students after dismissal.

A small coffee and sandwich shop was located between Frankford Avenue and the high school. Alma's restaurant was more or less a small order take out sandwich shop, with five stools for patrons who chose to have breakfast or lunch. It was in a prime location, being next to a news stand that took daily numbers. That was before the state moved in with daily lotteries, which robbed a lot of people from making a living. Alma was in her late fifties and worked side by side with a woman a little older, named Sadie. They were proficient, and turned out a sandwich that was so packed full of lunch meat, it was difficult to span with one's mouth. It was also a stop where Randy usually began his day.

"Good morning, Alma. How's the coffee?"

"You know; same as usual," she said, pointing to a sign prominently hanging over the coffee urns. Looking at it, he laughed. It read, "Don't complain about the coffee. Some day you'll be old and weak too."

Outspoken, she had the kind of demeanor that was brash, but one of those people that could say something offensive, and you automatically knew she wasn't serious, and Sadie was a perfect accomplice when it came to backing up Alma's statements. The restaurant was open from 6 a.m. until 3 p.m., and he always tried to make it a point to be there early when the students were on their way to school, and at dismissal, so they wouldn't take advantage of her, by stealing candy from an open display-case.

"Thanks, Randy. Sometimes they rush the store and steal half the candy in the cases when my back's turned," she said.

"That's okay, Alma," jokingly adding, "I'm here to serve."

He always played sort of a game with Alma. She never knew how old he was, and he kept her guessing, by reminding her of things associated with the neighborhood, such as establishments that had been gone for years, places he was told about in general conversation by older people familiar with them.

She asked, looking over her shoulder as she poured his coffee, "What do you think of the police department hiring female cops?"

"Alma, the police department always had female officers, but they were always assigned juvenile aid, or sex crimes unit. If they can handle the job, I say more power to them. Personally, I was tired of working different shifts. When the chance came to walk a permanent day-work beat Monday through Friday, I took it."

"When do you retire?" she asked, trying to trip him up on how old he was.

"I don't know when I'll pull the plug. The job's not the same as when Dumont's was around the corner," he said, knowing Dumont's was a night club that had been long gone, even before he became a cop.

Turning to face him, she replied, "Damn it! "That's what I mean. If you're old enough to remember Dumont's, you have to be in your 50's. If you are, you preserve well. If I was your girlfriend, I'd have to follow you with a damn baseball bat," pausing for a moment to refill the small cream pitcher on the counter, she continued, "Every morning when I wake up, I look in the damn mirror and wonder who in the hell's the old lady staring back at me? I always open the medicine cabinet door hoping someone else was there, but no, it's just me."

Sadie remarked, "Ain't it the damn truth."

He laughed as he walked out the door.

The rain slacked off, and he decided to make "the run." That's what he called walking from one end of the beat to the other, checking stores. Part of his duties was signing a log-book kept in all the banks, savings and loans, and the two drug stores, morning and afternoon. He knew most of the people who were tellers, and bank personnel, from when he worked a car. Amongst the radio assignments, which dealt directly with the beat, on occasion, he had a school crossing at one of the elementary schools, just off the beat, when one of the crossing guards was absent.

While passing one of the bank parking lots, he saw what looked like the female cop assigned to the high school. There were two cops assigned, one male and one female. Champ was her nickname, and he didn't know how she came by it, unless it had something to do with her kick boxing ability. He saw her demonstrating her skill once to a few other cops in the roll room. Champ was a young, beautiful, well-built light skinned black girl, in her late 20's. From rumors surrounding her personal life, apparently she was separated from an abusive husband, and trying to raise a young daughter. The other occupant of the car was a dark skinned black male he didn't recognize. He stood watching for a few moments, just to make sure if it was her husband, she wouldn't have a problem. It could just as well been someone else she knew, or even a teacher she may have been dating. After watching for about 10 minutes, he decided she didn't look like she would have a problem, and continued on the beat.

Entering several stores where he was familiar with the owner, he always asked if they had any complaints. Most of the time, it was about the meter maids writing parking tickets. The meter maids would walk the avenue checking parking meters, writing tickets for the ones that were displaying the little red sign reading *VIOLATION*, the dreaded little logo warranting a $6 parking ticket. He would always remind the store owners it was for their own benefit. If it wasn't for the meter maids, people who took the elevated train would park all day, avoiding the parking lot fee in town of $15. The store owners would grumble some, but realizing he was right, never pushed the issue.

This particular Monday, he was approached by a well dressed, young white female, who identified herself as Cheryl Freeman. She asked, "Officer, is there a store that sells baby clothes and related items in the area?"

"Yes, there is. Ginsberg's in the next block," pointing in that direction.

"Is this a safe neighborhood?" she asked.

"That's a strange question. What made you ask that?" he replied.

"I have a friend who's 7 months pregnant. We were supposed to have a baby shower for her on Sunday, but she never showed up."

"Where does she live?" he asked.

"We were originally from the Ogontz section of the city, but moved out to a small town called Glenside, just over the city line 5 years ago."

"How do you know she was here?" he asked.

"My friend gave her a gift certificate for an expensive baby carriage from a store. The store is called Ginsberg's. They're supposed to be the best in the city for that sort of thing."

Walking in the direction of the store, he asked, "Are you trying to tell me you suspect she's a missing person? Maybe she just hadn't picked it up yet."

"I spoke to her on Thursday. She said she was picking it up the next day, and asked if I could go with her. I was busy Friday making preparations for the shower, and told her I couldn't. I asked if she could postpone it until Saturday. She said she couldn't, and told me she was going by herself. I was supposed to take her out for lunch on Sunday so we could surprise her with the baby shower when we got back that afternoon," she explained.

"Well, Ginsberg's is in the next block, let's go and ask if he remembers seeing her."

Walking into the store, Mr. Ginsberg said, "Randy, what's new and interesting on the beat today?" as he turned on the lights in the display counter.

"Mister Ginsberg, this young lady wants to ask you a question."

"What is it, young lady?" he asked.

After describing her friend, and the circumstance of why she was asking, he thought for a moment then replied, "Yes, I remember her. She had a gift certificate to pay for the coach. My son-in-law Allen carried it out to her car and put it in the trunk."

"Do you by chance remember what time that was, or have a receipt Mr. Ginsberg?" Randy asked.

"Let me see," he replied, as he thumbed through a stack of receipts. "Randy, I can't seem to find it," pausing for a moment wondering why it wasn't there. "Wait a minute! While she was here, she bought a few other things. I remember she paid for them with a credit card."

"If she did, the copy would have a time of purchase. Can I see it?" Randy asked.

"Sure, here it is. It was 3:45 p.m."

Looking at Cheryl, he said, "Well, she was definitely here. That was almost three days ago. Does she have any other children?" Randy asked.

"No, this is her first, and she was really excited about it too."

A worried look came over her face, "It's not like Bernice. We've been friends since elementary school. I don't like this at all," Cheryl said.

"You said you gave her a gift certificate too. What was that for?" he asked.

"It was for a baby store in the mall at Cheltenham and Ogontz Avenue. Why?"

"Did she mention whether she was going to that store when she asked you to accompany her?" Randy asked, with Mr. Ginsberg listening intently to their conversation.

"She said she wanted to go to both places. I wonder if I should go there and see if she went there too," Cheryl replied.

"That mall is across the city line. It's in Cheltenham Township, out of the city's jurisdiction. I assume she has a husband or boyfriend. Did you call him, maybe he knows where she is?" Randy asked.

"I called him, but he said she hasn't been home since Friday."

"Why didn't he report her missing?"

"I don't know. She told me several months ago they weren't getting along so well. She suspected he was having an affair with his hygienist."

"That means he's a dentist. Did she tell you about any arguments they may have had?"

"No, she only mentioned it casually. She thought it began after she got pregnant. I don't think he wanted children. He was always more into the sports car and yacht kind of life style."

"You mentioned you lived in the Ogontz section of the city. What street was that?"

"It's a small street west of 75th and Ogontz, Windam Street. All of our friends grew up in that neighborhood."

"What's the name of the store in the mall, maybe we can look up the phone number and ask them if they remember seeing her?"

"Wait, I have the receipt from buying the gift certificate, it should have the phone number on it," she said, frantically searching her handbag. Finding it, she handed it to Randy.

"At one time, that neighborhood was predominantly Jewish. I use to live in that neighborhood too," Mr. Ginsberg said.

"Mister Ginsberg, can I use your phone?" he asked.

"Certainly, come around the counter."

After dialing, Randy identified himself, and asked the person who answered if the gift certificate number was cashed. After a few minutes, the person replied, "Yes, officer, it has been."

"Could you tell me when, and what time of day that was."

"Yes, officer, it was Friday at 5:30."

"Do you remember whether she was alone at the time?"

"Yes, she seemed to be in a rush to leave too."

"Thank you. Oh, one more favor if you will. Could you save a copy of the receipt for me?"

"No problem. Is there something wrong?" she asked.

Avoiding any conversation about the incident, he said, "No."

Wringing her hands, anxious to hear what he discovered, Cheryl asked,

"Officer, what did they say?"

"They said she was in the store at 5:30."

"I heard you ask if they could save a copy of the receipt. You must suspect something."

"It's just precautionary, in case there is foul play. Do you know what kind of car she drives?"

"Yes. It's a silver color Buick LaSabre. She has a Temple University sticker on the back window."

"Mister Ginsberg, may I use your phone again?"

"Certainly, Randy."

Calling the 37th district, which covers her former neighborhood, he asked for the lieutenant in charge. After filling him in on what he was trying to do, Randy gave a description of the car, and asked if the patrol cars covering that area would keep an eye out for it. After his conversation, he called the homicide unit, and asked to speak with the captain.

After being paged, the captain answered the phone.

"Jerry, this is Randy from the 13th."

"How you doing Randy, still walking the beat?" he asked.

"You know me, Jerry. I like to keep a low profile."

"What's on your mind?" he asked.

After giving him a description of the incident, Jerry said, "How do you know if it's not out of our jurisdiction? I can't take a missing person on someone that lives outside the city. It's up to the police department where she lives."

"I realize that, but Jerry, something's definitely wrong here. I have a hunch that car might turn up in that neighborhood. I already called the 37th, and told Lieutenant Monfort. He's going to have the sector cars take a look."

"Well, you went as far as you can. I guess if it turns up and it looks like foul play, he'll let me know," Jerry said.

Randy had known Jerry from the time he was a patrolman in his district, and they trusted each other's judgment. He knew by his reputation, Jerry would do everything in his power to help. After hanging up, he told Cheryl, "That's about all I can do. I hope your friend is fine. You'll just have to sit tight and wait."

"Thank you, officer, I think I'll take your suggestion and drive over to that neighborhood and take a look too."

After a parting gesture, he resumed walking the beat. Other than a few minor adjustments of complaints, the day was pretty much normal. The funny thing about being a cop, is working with all kinds of personalities. When he was assigned to this district, there was a sergeant with a lot of years on the job. He seemed to enjoy being a philosopher and Randy discovered over the years, his description of being a cop was pretty accurate. He remembered him saying, 'Kid, being a cop is 98% boredom, and 2% sheer terror.' He never gave it much thought, and I guess the reason for it, is when you're caught up in a situation, your instincts become keener. He never feared the street, and being raised in a rough section of the city, he enjoyed the challenge. He liked the people, and got quite a bit of respect from the locals, and the feeling was mutual. After a last pass on the beat, he headed for his vehicle and drove to the district.

Chapter 2

They walled off a section of the locker-room for female cops, and as Randy walked in, Champ was just leaving.

"Champ, I saw you in the bank parking lot. I hope I didn't disturb you. I just wanted to wait for a few minutes to make sure everything was copacetic."

Looking away she replied, "I saw you too. Thanks for not disturbing me."

"No problem, prospect from the high school?" he asked.

"Not really, husband."

When she turned, he could see she was sporting a black eye, something he didn't notice that morning as they passed in the hallway.

"I didn't notice the black eye this morning. Get that kick boxing?" he asked.

As she turned, he noticed a frustrated look. She didn't answer, and he realized he must be treading on tender ground, and didn't pursue the conversation.

Going up to the operations room to hand in his radio, he met the cop that shared the high school assignment with her. He said quietly, "Hey, Jimmy, I saw Champ down stairs. She's sporting a black eye. What happened?"

Looking bewildered for a moment, he replied, "I didn't notice anything this morning. She had a court notice for Juvenile-Court. She only checked in at the high school to tell me I'd be alone today. She wasn't wearing it then. She never did get back to the school though, so she had to have gotten it during the day."

"While I was checking the bank at Unity Street, I saw her sitting in a car with a dark-skinned black guy."

"What kind of car was it?" Jimmy asked.

"An older model Buick 225, painted black. Do you know who it may have been?"

"I've seen her getting out of a car like that. I just assumed it's her husband."

"When I saw her in the lot, I waited about 10 minutes to make sure she wasn't going to have a problem. She seemed alright, so I left. When I saw her downstairs a few minutes ago, she said she saw me watching, but didn't elaborate. When I asked her a question about it, she blew me off like it was none of my business. I heard she had an abusive husband. If it was him, why doesn't she file charges?"

"Maybe when we're back at the high school tomorrow, I'll ask. She won't be able to hide it from me."

"Try and find out if there's anything we can do to help," Randy said.

"I will."

Standing in the doorway, about to leave the building, Randy looked up at the sky. The rain clouds had dissipated, and the air was considerably cooler than when he was on the beat. Zipping up his jacket, he walked across the parking lot to his vehicle. Getting in, he thought, "Well, Monday's in the history book, four more to go."

Before pulling out of his parking space, he looked across the parking lot and saw Champ getting into the same car he saw her in during the day. His first instinct was to confront the driver, but on second thought, not knowing whether he was the person that gave her the shiner, opted to wait in his car. From where he was, he could observe what was taking place. There was a lot of hand gesture from both, and it was obvious the discussion was becoming heated. At one point, Champ started opening the passenger door to get out, when the driver pulled her back by the arm. That was it. He wasn't going to sit idle for her to get another black eye. Getting out of his car, he began walking in their direction. Champ, seeing him coming, took advantage and quickly exited. The driver, seeing Randy walking toward them, put the car in drive and sped off, making it necessary for Randy to jump out of the way.

"Champ! What the hell's that all about? That asshole almost hit me. The next time I see him, he's getting locked up."

"Randy, I'd appreciate it if you wouldn't."

"Why the hell not? He's probably the one that gave you the black eye too."

"Can we go somewhere and talk?" she asked.

"I'm going home to change. You can come along or we could go to a restaurant, your choice."

"I don't mind going to your apartment. It will be a little more private. I don't know where your apartment is. I'll have to follow you."

"That's alright, I'll drive you there, hop in."

Getting to his apartment complex, he parked, and they went inside the building. Opening the door to his apartment, she said, "I knew you lived in the northeast end of the city somewhere, but didn't know quite where."

After stepping in, he closed the door. Looking around with approval, she said, "Nice, real nice."

"It's only an apartment, but it's what I call home. Can I fix you a drink?" he asked.

Sitting on one of the leopard skin bar stools, she replied, "I'd love one."

Looking in the cabinet behind the bar he asked, "What's your pleasure? I have scotch and scotch, there doesn't seem to be anything else. I've been trying to cut back, so I haven't replenished the bar lately."

"Scotch with water will be fine."

"Ice?"

"Please."

"Okay, Champ, what's the story with that asshole?"

"He's my ex-husband. Well, almost my ex-husband. He keeps pushing to get back with me."

"It looks like he's pretty forceful," he said, pointing at her eye.

Putting her fingers to her black eye she said, "Oh, no. He didn't do that. He was abusive, but since he's been trying to get back with me, he's laid off the rough stuff."

"Then how did you get it?"

She paused, looking at the drink he handed her, "Do you have a coaster? I don't want to leave rings on your bar top."

He realized she was hesitant to answer, and excused himself heading for the bedroom replying, "I think the coasters are under the counter. You don't mind if I slip out of this uniform and get out of these wet shoes do you?"

"No, go right ahead. My feet are a little wet too," she said.

Opening the door of the bedroom, he tossed out a pair of slippers. "Here, they might be a little big, but at least they're dry."

"Thanks."

Coming out, he looked down at her feet. Her small foot seemed to be lost in it, and looked circus-like when clowns wear an oversized shoe. Looking at her feet, he laughed. "Ok, Champ, father Randy's here to take your confession."

Looking up from her drink, she replied, "Can I ask you something personal?"

"Sure, why not?"

Looking back down at her drink, she hesitated for a few moments, and he realized she was wondering whether or not she should ask.

After a few moments, he said, "Well, are you going to ask?"

Looking back up, she seemed to find the courage. "Why are all white guys so nice?"

Shocked that she asked such a question, he could feel his face turning red, and quickly replied, "Well, not all of us. What brought on that question?"

"No reason. I just haven't met anyone that wasn't. They seem to be a little gentler with their women."

"If I didn't know better, I would have thought you just made a pass at me."

Looking up from her glass, "Suppose it was; what would you say?"

"I'd say we're here to discuss your problem, now what is it with this guy? What's his name?"

"His name's Eric. The reason I left him, he was always asking me where I was going and what I was doing, really possessive. He began with the rough stuff and it got so bad, it was affecting my daughter's nerves. She just didn't want to be around him."

"How old is your daughter?"

"She just turned 9 last week."

"You must have had her pretty young?"

"Yes, I was 18. She hates her father, and I try to let her stay with my mother whenever he's around."

"That sounds like a wise thing to do. What were you discussing today before he tried to run me down?"

"I don't think he was trying to run you down. I don't think he even realized you were there. He's just pissed at me for not wanting to give him another chance."

"Did he ever confront you on your detail at school?"

Looking at him, she realized he knew that would be the only way she was with him earlier. "Not in our office inside the building. But he did see me outside, that's how we met today."

"Why don't you get a restraining order from a judge? Like me, you know a few from the job. It wouldn't be that hard."

"I thought about it. Maybe you're right."

Noticing her shifting back and forth on her stool, he asked, "Champ, something else is bothering you. Remember, I'm a cop that can read people. What else did you want to discuss?"

Looking at him, she replied, "What do you know about Jimmy?"

"Jimmy, Jimmy Bryan, your partner?"

"Yes."

"I know he's married, or I think he's still married the last I knew. Why, or shouldn't I ask?"

Looking down again, she confessed, "We've been sort of seeing each other."

"You say sort of seeing each other. That's like saying I'm almost pregnant. You either are, or you aren't. How long have you been sort of seeing each other?"

She smiled, realizing he had thrown in that pun on words.

"It's been almost 3 months."

"Then it's been going on since you two were detailed together?"

"Yes, it started out innocently enough. He was having a bad time at home and told me about it. We would talk mildly about his relationship during school hours, but then we started driving to the detail together, and joined a karate class," pausing for another moment, she looked up, "The next thing I knew, we were intimate. I guess being without a man, and him having the problems with his wife, it just happened."

"Look, Champ, I don't want to bust your bubble, but I believe his married life isn't what he says it is. I never heard anyone say it was anything but amicable. Jimmy's a good looking guy and very personable. But I'd have second thoughts about anything long term with him, it just isn't happening, understand. Now, how did you get the shiner?"

Passing off his question, she replied nonchalantly, "I got it at the gym."

"If you say so, I better get you back to your car. Did you want to call your daughter and explain why you're late?"

"No, that's alright. She's at my mother's."

Putting on his coat, she grabbed his arm. With a concerned look she said, "Randy, do me a favor. Don't tell Jimmy I was here."

Looking at her, he replied, "It's not my secret to tell. My lips are sealed."

Arriving at the district parking lot, they saw Jimmy leaning against the open doorway.

"Champ, there's Jimmy. Were you supposed to meet him?"

"Shit, I didn't want him to see me."

"Well, it's too late now. What do you want me to do?"

Replying nervously, "I'll make some kind of excuse."

"Well, before you get out, you better tell me, so I don't fuck up and say the wrong thing."

"Ok, I'll tell him you went with me to a used-car dealer on Harbison Avenue, to look over a car I was thinking about buying."

"That sounds reasonable," he replied.

As she was getting out of the car, Jimmy was approaching. She said loud enough for him to hear, "Thanks, Randy, I won't buy anything until I let you see it first."

"Champ, what do you want Randy to look at before you make a decision to buy?" Jimmy asked.

Turning to look at him as if she just noticed his presence, she replied, "Jimmy, what are you still doing here? We've been off duty for several hours."

"I was waiting on you to ask about that black-eye. Now, where did you get to?"

"I had Randy give me his opinion about buying a used car from the lot down Harbison Avenue. He told me to forget it."

Randy realized by her response, she was involved with Jimmy far greater than she confessed.

"What's the matter, don't you trust me to do it?" he asked.

"Sure, but I thought you were already gone, so I asked Randy."

Jimmy looked as though he was annoyed, and wasn't quite buying her excuse.

"What's the big deal Jimmy? She asked, and I said ok," Randy said.

"Oh, it's not that. We were supposed to stop for a bite after work."

"Jimmy, I forgot. Don't start acting like my ex. He always did that shit. 'Where you been? Who were you with?' I don't like being preached to."

"Sorry, Champ, I didn't want to sound pushy. But when Randy told me he saw you with your ex today, I thought you might have had a problem."

Randy thought, *"He just gave away our conversation in the locker room, when he told me not to mention seeing her on the bank parking lot. Why?"*

"Well, Champ, I'll see you tomorrow," Randy said.

After getting back in his car, he watched through his rear-view mirror as Jimmy walked her to her car.

Driving back to his apartment, Randy thought, *"Something didn't sound right about the exchange of words. If he was so concerned about her abusive husband, why didn't he ask about the black-eye? It was plain to see?"* Realizing Jimmy's forcefulness, it sounded like the relationship on his part, was stronger too. Randy thought, *"Oh well, that's between them."*

Getting back to his apartment, he opened the freezer and looked over the menu, trying to decide which frozen dinner to throw in the microwave. He thought, *"There are several divorced women that live in this building, maybe I should get friendly enough to have a different kind of meal once in awhile."*

Sitting at the table eating his now steamy T.V. dinner, he couldn't keep from thinking about Champ's personal life. For such a young kid, she seemed to have a major problem getting it in order.

After dinner, he tuned into Monday Night Football, and listened to the familiar beginning of the broadcast. 'Are you ready for some football? And a Monday night party,' as the song goes. Yes, he was ready. Leaning back with his feet on the Hasek, he was about to get into the game, when the phone rang.

"Hello, Randy."

"Who is this?" he said, pretending not to hear the teletype clicking away in the background along with the police broadcasts.

"This is Corporal Mark Silverstein. I got a call when we came on duty at 4 p.m. It was from homicide unit. Did you have a job today that involved a homicide?"

The words stunning him, Randy replied, "Yes, but it wasn't a homicide. It was a woman that was trying to find a friend."

"Well, it's a homicide now. The captain of homicide, Jerry Cramer, wants you to call him in the morning."

Hanging up the phone, he stood there looking at it for a few moments thinking, *I'll be damned, they found her.* Nothing he can do about it now; it will have to wait until tomorrow.

Getting back to the game, he wasn't enjoying it as he would, knowing the call to homicide in the morning wouldn't be pleasant.

***

Arriving at the district the next morning, he walked into the operations room.

"Hey Randy, here's a message for you to call homicide. What's it about?" Corporal Tyler asked.

"I know. Corporal Silverstein called me at home last night. I was involved in a job yesterday where a woman was looking for her friend. The friend had been missing since Friday."

Thumbing through yesterday's paperwork, the corporal said, "I didn't see a missing persons report. Did you file one?"

"No, she lives outside our jurisdiction."

"Well, what's with you having to call homicide?" he asked,

looking bewildered.

Picking up the phone and dialing, Randy said, "I'll let you know in a few minutes."

"Detective Brown, homicide unit, how can I help you?" the voice on the other end asked.

"This is Randy Bishop from the 13th. Is the captain there? He wanted to speak to me."

Randy heard him say aloud, "Hey captain, there's a cop named Bishop from the 13th calling, he's on 2."

"Randy, that missing person you called about yesterday, well, she's not missing any longer. They found her car in the 37th in the neighborhood you told them to look. She was in the trunk. How did you guess where the car would be?"

"The woman that was looking for her is her friend. Her name is Cheryl Freeman. She said that's the neighborhood they were originally from. She told me her friend asked if she could go with her to pick up a baby carriage at Ginsberg's on Friday. It's a children's store on my beat. She also told me she gave her a gift certificate for a children's store in the Cheltenham Mall."

"Was it for her, or someone else?" Jerry asked.

"It was for her. Cheryl and I went to Ginsberg's. She described what her friend looked like to Mr. Ginsberg, and he said he remembered seeing her. He told me she cashed the gift certificate for an expensive baby carriage on Friday, and told me his son-in-law, Allen, put the coach in the trunk of her car. The time stamped on the receipt was 3:45. "I asked Cheryl if she knew the name of the store in the mall, and she handed me the gift certificate receipt. I called the store, and gave them the number. They said she was there around 5:30."

"Do you have any paperwork on the job?" he asked.

"I have the receipt from Ginsberg's, and I told the store in the mall to hold the receipt for me. Do you want me to get them and come down?"

"Yes, I'll see you when you get here."

Corporal Tyler, listening to the conversation, asked, "Well, what's the story?"

"They found her dead in the trunk of her car in the 37th. I have to go to homicide and give a statement. Can you get me a ride?"

"No problem."

Just then, a cop named George Simmons, a fellow ex-marine walked in.

"George, when you're finished with your paperwork. Take Randy down to homicide unit. I'll put you out of service with police radio from here," Corporal Tyler said.

"No problem. I'll be with you in a few minutes Randy. I just have to finish this accident report."

After retrieving the receipts from Ginzberg's and the store in the mall, they headed for homicide. Walking into homicide operations room, Randy saw Jerry sitting at his desk in his office. Looking up, he waved for Randy to come in.

"Hi! Jerry. Long time no see."

"Yeah, I'm not sure that you didn't make the right decision staying in the district, as you said, 'keeping a low profile,' Jerry said. Turning his attention to the case, he asked, "What else can you tell me about this job?"

"I told you about all I know," thinking for a moment, he continued, "There is one thing. When I asked Cheryl, why didn't her husband report her missing? She told me the deceased and her husband weren't exactly hitting it off. That's where you might start the investigation. You said she was in the trunk of her car. Was it a robbery?"

"We don't know. We didn't find a purse, and the keys to the car were on the floor."

"How did she die?"

"She was stabbed multiple times; it wasn't pretty," Jerry replied.

"I'm sure it wasn't. Was she stabbed in the vehicle?"

"It doesn't appear so. There was no blood inside the car, only in the trunk."

"Did anyone see anybody get out of the car?"

"Yes, there's a woman who lives in the second house from the corner where it was recovered. She was coming home from food shopping Friday night about 7, when the car pulled up almost directly in front of her house. She said a black guy who looked to be in his late 20's got out and went around the corner. She couldn't identify him as one of the people who lived around there, and just thought he was visiting someone."

"Could she give you any better description than being black and in his late twenties?"

"She said he was about six feet tall and thin, real thin. He was only wearing a dark sweat suit and pull over knit cap. That's it."

"Well, since I can't do anymore, I'll be shoving off. Happy Thanksgiving," Randy said.

"Yeah, you too," Jerry replied.

Getting back to the district, he went directly to the beat. He thought about what Jerry said, "Happy Thanksgiving!" to him, it was like any other Thursday. Maybe he'd go out to a turkey dinner at a diner somewhere instead of a microwavable turkey dinner from Swanson's, but that's about it.

Chapter 3

The avenue was beginning to come alive, with windows being dressed for the upcoming holiday season. Even the pillars supporting the overhead elevated trains were adorned with plastic garland and lighted stars. Piped-in music was played from loud speakers gifted to the businesses by a local music shop. It was done to make shoppers feel a lot better getting into the holiday spirit, so they would lose track of how much they were spending.

There was a men's clothing store mid-way on the beat Randy would go into on occasion to get warm and fill out his daily log. The three Kramer brothers that owned it were young guys, and he got a kick out of some of the things they did or said. One of the people who worked for them was a black guy named Barry. He was around 30, short and thin, but was the sharpest dresser Randy ever knew. Barry racked up probably more clothing sales with his appearance and smooth salesmanship, than all three brothers, and the other two salesmen combined.

Walking in the store, he was greeted by one of the brothers.

"Hey Randy, are you in the holiday spirit yet?" he said, with a sarcastic smile.

With all the preparation for the holiday season that would make even the hardest scrooge succumb he replied, "Bah! Humbug!" which brought a laugh from everyone.

Barry said, "Now all we need is a little dusting of snow, just a little dusting to make my holiday a little brighter." He too, realized it would bring out more shoppers, and give him a pretty good commission over his regular salary.

As Randy was leaning on the counter filling out his log, he looked up. Through the front window, he saw Champ's car pull into a parking space on a small side street. She got out of the car with a guy dressed in plain clothes. Randy recognized immediately, it was Sergeant Howard. He was recently assigned from another district, but since he was new, Randy hadn't had any conversations with him. Being in a steady day work squad, Randy worked with all the other squads that rotated shifts. Champ was still in uniform, and off her assignment at the high school.

Curious, he watched as they entered the restaurant across the street. He was about to walk across to join them, when Champ exited the restaurant, hurrying back to her car. Sergeant Howard briskly followed, and before she could unlock the door, he pushed her against the car. Apparently, what Randy thought was just a normal gesture going to lunch, wasn't. It had to be something more. He thought, *"What is it with white guys she seems to be attracted to? Maybe the offer at his apartment wasn't just a grateful gesture being concerned for her safety. Maybe she was serious?"* he watched as she got into her car and drive away.

When he left the store, he knew Sergeant Howard saw him, but made no attempt to acknowledge the fact. Not knowing whether Randy saw them together, Sergeant Howard opted to do the same.

At the end of the shift, he drove back to the district. After turning in his log and radio, he was about to leave the operations room when Sergeant Howard entered. He was on the 4 to 12 shift and just finished his squad's roll call. Again, Randy made no attempt at mentioning he saw him with Champ earlier. Not knowing for sure whether Randy did see him and Champ together, Howard tapped him on the arm.

"You're Randy, Randy Bishop, the beat cop from the lower end, aren't you?"

"That's right, Sergeant."

"I just wanted to know. I'd like to get acquainted with all the cops in 5 Squad. We'll be working together at some point every month. Who else works the lower end from your squad?"

"In the lower end of the district, there's the mounted cop, Joe Kelly, the high school detail, Jimmy Bryan and Champ, oh sorry, Delores Johnson, and me."

"I'd like to get to know them too," he said, trying to hide the fact he obviously knew Champ, and was expecting Randy to say something about seeing them together. Instead, Randy played his game and didn't comment.

Going to the locker-room, Randy saw Champ and Jimmy in the hallway talking. He remarked, "Didn't you two see enough of each other today?"

Jimmy answered passing off his comment as a joke, "No, we're secret lovers."

He noticed Champ's approving smile, and attempt at a little humor by making a fist and gesturing punching Jimmy's stomach. He responded to her action by saying, "See what I mean, Randy. I'm into sadism too, it's our secret."

She replied jokingly looking at Jimmy, "I told you not to tell anybody. You just can't trust a man to keep his mouth shut," pretending to punch his stomach again, but this time accidently making contact.

Before entering the locker-room, Randy said, "I'm the kind

of lover you wouldn't approve of. I'm the gentle type. Oh, by the way, the new Sergeant, Sergeant Howard, said he wants to get to know everyone in 5 squad. Have you met him yet?"

To Randy's surprise, they both said "No," and wondered why Champ was lying, but passed it off, and continued to his locker to hang up his gear.

Getting to his car, he waited a few minutes until the engine warmed. He saw Sergeant Howard come out of the building and walk toward his patrol car. To his surprise, Champ got out of her private auto and approached Sergeant Howard. He walked her back to her car, and what Randy thought was going to be the confrontation he saw earlier, to his surprise, through her open window he saw them kiss. Whatever the problem was, had obviously been resolved, but why did she lie about not knowing him? It was obvious she must have been in a relationship that went on before he was assigned here, and watched for a few minutes until Champ drove away.

On the way home, he stopped at a supermarket to get a few things. He looked over the frozen food section, trying to decide what to buy, as if there was somehow going to be a magical change from last week, and all the other previous weeks. No luck, same old, same old. On the way to the check out, he smelled something good. Following the scent, he saw a rotisserie. It was the supermarket's first attempt to offer pre-cooked ribs and chicken. He thought, *They must have read my mind.* Looking at the selection, he said to the girl at the counter, "I'll take one of those ribs."

"Certainly, sir, will there be anything else?"

"No, that's it. Thank whoever's responsible for this. I'm sure I'll be a regular customer."

Driving into the apartment complex parking lot, he saw Champ's car, and thought, *"What the hell's she doing here?"*

Exiting the car, he asked, "What' going on Champ? Why are you here?"

"Don't sound dumb, I came to see you," she shockingly replied.

"Well, that was blunt, but I'm not going to stand out here and let my dinner get cold. You can come in if you want."

"I'm sorry for the remark. Thanks for the invite. Here, give me the key, I'll open the door," she said.

After putting the grocery bags on the table, she commented, "Smells good. What are we having?"

"Ribs, they're starting to offer cooked ribs and chicken at the supermarket. I thought I'd give it a try, but I want to get out of this uniform first."

While he was changing, she yelled out, "What do you want me to heat up for you? You only have frozen peas and carrots. Wait a minute, here's some frozen mashed potatoes too. Which one should I heat up?"

"I guess this means you're staying for dinner. If you are, it's your choice."

"Mashed and peas sound good," she replied.

She began to speak again in a loud tone as he entered the room. "Not so loud. I have neighbors, and these walls are paper thin," he said.

Putting her fingers to her lips, she replied, "Sorry, I wasn't thinking."

"Care for a drink? I only have__"

Before he could finish, she said, "I remember, scotch and scotch."

"That's right. Now what can I attribute this visit to?"

"I didn't want to say anything in front of Jimmy about Sergeant Howard, but I knew him before I became a cop," she said.

"Well, that's between you three. Why would I say anything?"

Moving her food around with her fork, she replied, "I'm having a difficult time with him."

Putting down his glass, it aroused his curiosity, and asked, "With who, Jimmy? What sort of difficult time?"

Hesitating again, she said, "Not with Jimmy, with Sergeant Howard."

He realized she probably didn't see him watching them, and Champ asked, "You never saw my daughter, have you?"

"No, I haven't."

Taking a picture from her purse, she handed it across the table. "This is my reason for living. She's gorgeous isn't she?"

"Yes, she's quite beautiful. But that doesn't tell me much about your relationship with Jimmy and Sergeant Howard."

Looking down at her plate, she was silent for a moment, then looked up sending a shock to his system, "That's Sergeant Howard's daughter."

"Is he married?"

"Yes, it was before he was married. We had an affair when he was a cop in the 37th district."

"Were you married to that asshole that tried to run me down at the time?"

"Yes. Sergeant Howard, I mean, George, came to my house several times when I was being abused. You know, domestic disturbances and all that shit. He seemed really understanding, and sometimes when we met we would talk about my problems.

Eventually we began talking about things we had in common, then we began seeing each other after he was done his shift. We would go for coffee, or just sit in his car and talk."

Randy, so intent at what she was saying, didn't realize his dinner was beginning to get cold, but had to make it known he saw them together today.

"Champ, I was in Kramer Brother's Clothing Store today, and saw you go into the restaurant with him. I also saw you when you came out and he followed you to your car and pushed you against it. Now, what was that about?"

"It's about helping me pay for my daughter. He was giving me money out of his small business he has on the side, but wants to stop paying."

"Well, if you were married at the time, why would it be his responsibility?"

Looking down again at her now cold dinner, she replied, "I made the mistake of telling him I'd tell his wife. That's what it was about today. I wouldn't be unbelievable. I know things about his married life only someone intimate would know."

"Why does he want to stop paying?"

"He said he's tired of the second business, and his wife's a hairdresser who wants to close down her shop. He said there wouldn't be any way he could hide paying me."

Randy lashed out unintentionally, "How the hell does a kid your age get into so much shit?" pausing, "I just hope you can come out of this still smelling like a rose."

Smiling, she replied, "I hope so too, father Randy!"

It brought a smile to his face and a response, "For your penance, it will be 5 more Hail Mary's, and 500 our fathers."

She laughed.

"My dinner's cold and so is yours, I'll reheat them," he said.

"Don't reheat mine, I had enough. Besides, talking about this shit makes me lose my appetite. I had better be going; I have to pick up my daughter."

"Is she at your mother's?"

"Yes, my mom's a real life saver. I couldn't imagine what I would have done without her."

After helping her with her jacket, he walked her to the front door of the apartment building. Before stepping outside, she suddenly stopped, pushing back to him.

"What is it Champ?"

"The asshole, as you call him. He just drove out of the parking lot. He must have followed me from the district."

"Well, wait till I get my jacket. I'll follow you home to make sure you're safe."

Randy couldn't help but notice how nervous she was from the experience, and asked, "Do you carry an off duty gun?"

Opening her purse, she pulled out a Walther PPK, pretty accurate at close range.

"Remember, it's better to be tried by 12 than carried by 6. They print obituaries in the newspaper free," he said, as they headed to their cars.

Smiling, she said, "I'll remember that father Randy."

He followed her to her mother's and watched until she picked up her daughter, then followed them to the apartment complex where she lived. Walking them to her door, he waited until she was safe inside. Her daughter kept looking at him suspiciously, and when her curiosity finally got the best of her, she asked, "Mother, who's he?"

"I'm sorry baby, this is Randy. We work together. Randy this is my precious, Lea."

"I'm pleased to meet you Lea. Champ, if you don't need me I'll leave."

Holding onto his arm, she walked him to the door.

"Thanks, Randy, I'll be alright now. I'll see you tomorrow."

After leaving the building, he waited in his car for 15 minutes making sure the asshole didn't show up.

Returning to his apartment complex, he noticed a black Buick 225 parked on the street. The same kind and color car Champ's ex drove. After looking it over, he went into his apartment. After an entertaining night of reading, he fell asleep sitting at the end of the couch.

It was still dark when he was awoken by the telephone ringing. Looking at the wall clock, it was 2 a.m., stumbling to the phone, he answered, "Hello, who is it?"

"Randy, it's me, Champ."

She sounded very upset and calling at this hour, he knew she must be having a problem.

"What is it Champ, what's happening?"

"My ex came back and tried to break in. I wound up threatening to shoot him, but one of the neighbors must have heard all the noise and called the police. A scuffle ensued when they got here, and he had to be restrained, so they gave it to him pretty good."

"That's good news isn't it?"

Still nervous, she replied, "Not really, when they searched him, they found a knife. If the neighbors hadn't called the cops, I don't know what he might have done."

"Well, he's away for the night. You should take off tomorrow and get that restraining order I mentioned to you."

"I will now. He's totally lost it."

"If you want me to be a witness to the judge of how he acted at the district parking lot, let me know."

"Thanks Randy. Sorry for disturbing you."

Wide awake at this point, he decided to take a shower and go to bed.

***

When he got to the district, he went into the operations room. The squads had changed from the previous day, and one squad was now on day work. Corporal Silverstein said, "Randy, here's a court notice for a homicide. It's from Montgomery County, what gives?"

"I had an investigation that begun on my beat. They found the body in the 37th district. I guess they made an arrest. When is it for?"

"It's for the 5th of December. Here, sign for it."

After signing, he put it in his pocket and went to the locker room. Walking in, he saw Jimmy getting into his uniform, "Jimmy, I don't think you'll have a partner today."

He didn't seem surprised, and Randy knew Champ must have already told him what happened last night. Turning to Randy he said, "I didn't know you knew about last night. Why is it, all of a sudden she's confiding in you?"

Looking at him, Randy sharply replied, "Maybe it's because I'm not personally involved in her life. You know; a neutral party."

He looked embarrassed for a moment replying, "I guess she told you about us too?"

"Yes, she did. I think she has some sort of expectations that you two will wind up living together. You're still married and living at home aren't you?"

"I believe that's nobody's business but mine and hers," he said.

"You're right! I just hate to see her imagining something that isn't real. Her life seems fucked up enough without it. If it's only a sex thing you're having, why not tell the truth? This way, she can make up her mind whether she wants it to continue."

Looking up from tying his shoe, he replied, "I guess you know more about her private life than I know?"

"Yes, she told me quite a bit. That's why I'm mentioning it to you."

After closing his locker, Jimmy slowly turned saying, "Maybe you're right, but she's more than just a 'sex thing,' as you call it. I really enjoy being in her company."

"Well, if you're really concerned like you say, why not ask for a different assignment?"

"You mean give up a steady day work job and go back to rotating shifts? That's something I'll never do," he replied.

"As I said, it's up to you. If you continue to work together, then you should try to let her know where she stands."

"Maybe I will," he replied.

Leaving the conversation in the locker room, Randy walked out into the hall. Seeing Champ he asked, "I thought you were taking off today to get that restraining order?"

"I am. I just came in to tell Corporal Silverstein I wanted the day off."

"Don't disappoint me," Randy replied, waving his finger.

"I won't. After pulling that shit last night, I'm not taking any chances."

"Good, glad to hear it. Now all you have to do is straighten out the rest of your relationships. I had a discussion with Jimmy in the locker room. You can start there."

The day began as any normal day, with the exception of handling a burglary of a business on the beat. One of the jewelry stores had a break in from a sky-light on the roof during the night. Frank Grace's Jewelry Store has been a fixture on the avenue for about 40 years. Randy knew him quite well, and advised him in the past about being vulnerable from that sky light. Frank was living in the past, when stores on the avenue didn't need iron gates in front of the windows, and he refused to acknowledge the neighborhood, the people, and the times had changed. He was lucky though. Apparently the burglars hadn't had time to grab much before tripping the silent alarm.

Later in the day, Randy walked into one of the savings and loan to sign the log, and noticed everyone standing still, but no one was speaking. He also noticed a guy standing by the back door that led to the parking lot, and another standing in front of a teller. Two people were standing at the counter, convenient for people to fill out deposit slips, but they weren't writing, and Randy quickly surmised he walked into a holdup taking place. Being in a bad position for everyone involved, he decided to act as though he didn't realize what was going on.

After signing the log, he walked out the front door. Getting out of sight, he radioed what was taking place, and as soon as the first patrol car arrived they went in together. One of the males tried to escape through the rear door to the parking lot, but there was already another police car and police wagon there. They had apprehended the males that exited, and the driver of the getaway car.

The male still inside was about to exit the front door, when

Randy grabbed him by the neck, and threw him to the floor. After cuffing him, he patted him down and found a gun with some of the bait money given to him by a teller.

After putting him in the wagon with his cohorts, they took them to the district. Having to fill out the paperwork for the arrest, Randy got a ride with one of the police cars to headquarters. When he walked in the building, he met Champ.

She said, "Good job Randy. I heard it over police radio. I'm glad you didn't get hurt," remarking again, "Good job!"

"Thanks! But never mind me. Did you get that damn restraining order?"

Holding up an envelope she replied, "I sure as hell did."

"Good, that's another thing off my mind."

After handling the paperwork on the holdup, he called Jerry at the homicide unit.

"This is Randy Bishop from the 13th. Is the captain there?"

"No, Randy, he's at a commissioners meeting. I'm the detective that you met when you came down to homicide to give me the paperwork on the missing woman. I guess you're wondering about the court notice?"

"Yes, I guess you made an arrest on it?" Randy replied.

"Yes, believe it or not, it was a paid contract by her husband."

"How did you tie him in with it?"

"A cop in the 37th remembered hearing the corporal in his squad talking about Ginsberg's, where she picked up the coach. He used to live in that neighborhood, and bought their first baby's coach there too. Someone reported finding a brand new coach in their backyard and called the police. He picked it up and brought it to the district. The corporal on duty thought enough to call us, and we sent the crime unit to dust for prints.

They came up with several, and one of the sets matched a set found on the inside of the deceased's car. They belonged to a junkie by the name of Anthony Butler. He has a string of priors, almost two pages long. Like most junkies, he doesn't have a permanent place to live, but was caught burglarizing a house. He was shooting up two bags about every 8 hours... really strung out. He lived in your district, do you know him?"

"I know him, but never had a run in with him as I recall. What did he tell you?"

"At first, he wouldn't say anything. But with the habit he has, after holding him for almost 24 hours, he was ready to talk. I told him we not only had his prints from inside the car, but on the coach too. He knew at that point it was no use lying about it, and told us the whole story."

"How did her husband know someone like Butler?" Randy asked.

"Apparently, Butler lived in the neighborhood where he had his first dental practice. When he moved, Butler went to his office to get treated for a broken front tooth. While he was being treated, the deceased's husband asked him about doing the job on his wife."

"Did he say how he knew where she would be?"

"Apparently, she told her husband what her plans were for the day, and Butler followed her from the time she left her house. He said he followed her to Ginsberg's, but it was still daylight and there were too many people around. She stopped at another store, and by that time it was getting dark. He followed her to the Cheltenham Mall and waited near her car. When she returned, that's when he put a knife to her back and forced her in the car. He drove to a secluded spot then forced her out. After rifling her pocketbook, he stabbed her multiple times then put her in the trunk."

"Did he say anything else?"

"He said he drove around awhile trying to find a street that was kind of dark in the 37th. That's where he took the coach out and went down the alley and tossed it over a back yard fence. After he got rid of the coach, he drove a few blocks away and parked the car a few spaces from the corner."

"Did you ask him about her purse?"

"Yes, he said he took everything of value then tossed it in a trash can. We notified the Cheltenham Police and told them what we had. She was murdered in their jurisdiction."

"What about the husband?" Randy asked.

"After they picked him up, they took him to their headquarters and warned him of his rights. He knew he was had, and wouldn't talk. He only asked for a lawyer."

"Then he's not officially charged with the murder?"

"No, but he is the accessory before and after the fact. It will be determined by the district attorney of Montgomery County I'm sure. Ultimately, his guilt will be determined by a jury."

"I hope all I'll have to stay for is the beginning of the trial. I hate that shit anyway," Randy said.

"We all do, but you're actually the beginning of the case, so you're necessary. Oh, by the way, Jerry told me if you call, to tell you you're not bad, even as an old timer."

"Tell Jerry thanks. I guess I'll be meeting you again in court?"

"That's right. I'll see you then."

As Randy was standing in the hallway, the captain of the detective division, Tony Girardo, stepped out of his office. Randy knew him from being a street cop too. Tony said, "Hey

Randy, you're knocking them dead this month. Aren't you getting a little old for that?"

Turning to him, Randy replied, "Other than a few gray hairs, I don't think I've changed much... prick."

Tony laughed then went back in his office.

Randy went back downstairs to the operations room, and told the corporal, "It's almost 3:30 now. I'm off duty at 4: I think I'll call it a day."

"Go home Randy, you deserve it."

Going down to the locker room, he saw Champ. She seemed upset and he asked, "What's wrong?"

"Nothing really Randy, I guess it's for the better."

He already surmised Jimmy had told her where their relationship was, but asked anyway, "What's for the better?"

Looking at him she realized he must have said something to Jimmy.

"You know what it is. I shouldn't have mentioned it to you."

Offended by her thinking somehow it was his fault, he bluntly said,

"Look Champ; that was your decision. I was only giving you my opinion. I told Jimmy if he doesn't have any long term plans with you, as I suspect you want, he should tell you, and let you decide whether you should still maintain the relationship."

Putting her head down like a kid being scolded, she replied, "I'm sorry. I didn't mean to take it out on you."

"That's alright, you'll owe me 200 more our fathers. At this rate, you'll rack up so many penance you won't have time for a relationship."

It brought a smile to her face, and she replied, "Thanks for being concerned."

In the lockerroom, he stopped to have a conversation with the cop that relieves him on the beat for the 4-12 p.m. shift.

"Hey, Charlie, it was busy as a bitch today. Be careful. You know Ho! Ho! Ho- and all that Christmas shit. The holdup men and purse snatchers will be out in force for the next few weeks."

"I know, the sergeant told me they put on another beat cop, and another mounted man. I don't know his name, but I'll probably see him tonight."

"Did he tell you we have the Thanksgiving parade this year, instead of the Father Judge- Lincoln High School Football game?" Randy asked.

"No, shit. That sucks! That means it'll be a late day. The football game usually ends by 11 11:30, and it's a hell of a lot closer to home than going all the way to center city. The parade's till noon, then the traffic post getting the spectators out is another 2 hours."

Randy replied, closing his locker, "Yeah, that's a real bummer. It's not nearly as bad as the New Years Day parade though. That's really a fucked up detail, cold as a bitch too."

"Yeah, I'm not looking forward to that either," Charlie said.

"Well Charlie, be careful out there."

"Thanks, I will."

Randy stood in the doorway and zipped up his coat before walking out the door. Going to his car, he noticed a few snowflakes began to fall. He thought about Barry from Kramer's. He must have called on the snow gods for this, remember Barry saying, *Just a little dusting of snow, a little dusting to make my holiday spirit a little brighter.* laughing, he got in his car.

Waiting for the engine to warm, he looked over at Champ standing in the open doorway of the building. He was about to pull away, when he saw a civilian car pull up. It was Sergeant Howard. After she got in, they drove away. Pulling out onto the street, he headed for home. The comfort of his meager abode was still the tonic after a day like today.

Taking out a T.V. dinner, he popped it in the microwave. Before it was finished, there was a knock at the door. Opening it, he was surprised to see Jimmy, and asked, "What's up Jimmy? Nothing I did wrong I hope?"

"No, Randy. Can I come in?"

"Sure, why not. If you'll excuse me, I have my dinner heating, care for a drink?"

"No, I'm still on the wagon. I haven't touched a drink for three months. I don't want a repeat of what I went through."

"Yeah, I heard you had a little bit of a problem. I'm glad you straightened it out though. I went through that after I got out of the service years ago, before I became a cop. Can I get you anything else, a soda or something?"

"No, I'm fine."

"Well, I don't want my dinner to get cold. Why don't you sit at the kitchen table and tell me what's on your mind?"

"It's about Champ," he said.

Before he went any further, Randy said, "I assumed that. I saw her in the locker room. She was upset and mentioned to me you told her you called it quits."

Looking surprised at his statement, he said, "We didn't call it quits. I just let her know there was no future in it, just like you told me. She said she was fine with that."

"I know she was upset when I spoke to her. If she agrees to it, that's on her. Is that all you wanted to say?" Randy asked.

Jimmy seemed transfixed on the revolving tray on the table,

and after giving it a slight spin, looked up and asked, "How much of her personal life did she tell you?"

"Jimmy, I don't know how much she told you, but she asked me to keep what she said in confidence. I won't break that pledge."

"I'm not talking about her life before the department. Just about how she got the black eye," he asked.

"She said she got it at the gym."

"No, she didn't. I was there. Is she seeing someone else?"

"If she is, she didn't tell me. What's your reason for asking?"

"It wasn't the first time I saw marks on her. I just don't want you to think I was responsible."

"I wouldn't worry about it if I was you. She showed me a restraining order she got from the judge," Randy said.

"That's not what I was referring too. Her husband's been locked up since yesterday. She went out for lunch today, and after she got back to school, we had an unruly girl in one of the classrooms. Champ got ink on her long sleeve shirt and changed. She only had a short sleeve in her locker, and I noticed a pretty big bruise on her arm when she came back in the office. It was beginning to turn black as the afternoon progressed, so I knew it was fresh. That's why I'm asking."

Not wanting to tell him about Sergeant Howard, Randy responded, "Did you ask her about it?"

"Yes, I pointed it out, but she just blew my question off. I thought since she's been confiding in you so much, you might ask her."

Putting down his fork, Randy replied pessimistically, "Now, how would I ask about a mark I wouldn't be able to see?"

"I guess you're right. I'm just desperate to know whether

she's having some sort of other problem."

"Jimmy, excuse me for saying it, but I think you're full of shit about your relationship not being serious. Now, why don't you tell me the truth?"

Randy and Jimmy had known each other for quite awhile. Jimmy, as well as other younger cops, sort of looked up to Randy, and the experience he had dealing with the people in the lower end. They would ask from time to time, about a certain person that lived in the neighborhood they had contact with, and Jimmy was one of them when he was a rookie working a police car. He looked offended Randy would refer to him as being, 'full of shit!' and finally opened up.

"Randy, you're right. She does mean more to me than that. But how do I go forward having a wife and two kids at home?"

Finished with dinner, he put the serving tray in the trash can. Thinking for a few moments how to respond, Randy replied, "That sounds like a question you should ask either a lawyer, or a marriage counselor. Being a cop, you already know we don't take sides with a domestic problem, not unless it turns violent. If you're looking for me to make a decision, you're asking the wrong person. Have you talked about it with Champ?"

Going to the bar, Randy poured himself a drink, and was shocked at Jimmy's next statement.

"I haven't told Champ, but I think my wife's seeing someone from where she works. Until I find out what my wife's intentions are, I don't want to build up Champ's hopes."

"Is that why you questioned so severely about her confiding in me? Is it some sort of insecurity from what your married life's like?"

"That's not the only reason. She's black and so is her daughter.

How would it be, living together? You know that doesn't resonate too well with other cops we work with."

Randy said replying annoyingly, "Oh! Fuck everybody else. It's whatever makes you happy that counts. Do you think I really like living alone? I'm divorced too! Jimmy it's something I can't resolve for you. You have to do it yourself."

"I guess you're right. Just keep it private, what we discussed."

"You know me, I don't tell tales out of school," Randy replied.

After putting on his jacket, Randy walked him to the front door of the building. He never noticed from the inside of his apartment, but the dusting Barry was hoping for, had already turned into two inches of snow, with more still coming down. Returning to his apartment, he put on the local news to listen to the weather forecast. The prediction was for three to five inches, depending on where you lived in relation to the city. He thought, *"Shit, I was dreaming of a white Christmas, but not a damn white Thanksgiving. I hope that weather man is right. Let me get my galoshes and rain coat out of the closet, and put them by the front- door, so I won't forget them."*

Chapter 4

When he got to his car the next morning, he took the snow brush from the trunk and began clearing the snow from the windows. After he finished, he looked at a neighbor's car parked next to his and cleared the windows too. She was coming out of the building just as he was finishing.

"Thanks for the favor. I'm really in a rush today. I should have left 20 minutes ago. I'll have to return the favor sometime. You're Randy Bishop right?" she asked.

"Yes, how did you know?"

"I saw your name on the mail box. Mine's Charlotte Yard: *YARD,* as in back yard."

"I got it. Be careful. According to the TV, driving is pretty slippery. There are a lot of fender benders."

After getting in the car, she rolled down the window, "I'll be careful. Thanks again."

Traffic was slow going, but he managed to make it to the district on time. Walking into the operations room, he saw Sergeant Howard. His squad had taken over the day work shift, and as Randy was checking out a radio, the Sergeant said, "Bishop, I'm putting you on a car today. We're short a few people."

The corporal on duty looked up from his paperwork and said, "Excuse me Sergeant, but the captain ain't gonna like that idea. He doesn't want the five squad people reassigned unless you get his permission." He took down a clip board, and showed

Sergeant Howard the directive.

Sergeant Howard appeared to be annoyed that he couldn't make the decision on his own authority, but after reading the directive, frustratingly handed the clip board back to the corporal. Looking at Randy with contempt, as though it was his decision instead of the captain's, he walked by him grumbling something Randy or the corporal couldn't quite hear. After he left the room, one of the operations room personnel said, "He's a grumpy bastard. What did we do to get that bone-head assigned here?"

The corporal replied, "Fuck him, if he can't take a joke! Randy, when the captain comes in, I'll ask him to straighten out that asshole."

"Thanks corporal."

The corporal said, "Randy, you know you have the Thanksgiving Day parade tomorrow don't you?"

"Yeah, I've been told. Who else has it from 5 squad?"

"Champ, Jimmy, George O'Mara from 2 Squad, and one of the mounted guys."

As Randy checked out a radio, he asked, "Who's in charge of the detail?"

Looking up from his paperwork, the corporal replied, "That asshole that just walked out."

Laughing to himself Randy thought, *"This ought to be interesting, the love triangle on the same detail."*

Going to the locker room, he saw Jimmy in the hallway. "How come you're not at the school?" he asked.

Jimmy replied, "They're opening one hour late because of the snow. I don't know why they bother; it's an early dismissal anyway."

"If I was you or Champ, I'd steer clear of the sergeant. He's looking for bodies to man police cars parked on the back lot without drivers. He wanted to grab me for one a little while ago."

Jimmy replied, "She called off sick this morning. She didn't look like there was anything wrong with her yesterday, other than the bruise she had."

Randy asked, "Have you met Sergeant Howard yet? He seems like a real prick."

"I haven't had a chance to talk to him other than introducing myself, but I'll take your word for it. It's funny though," after hesitating, he said, "I think Champ must know him from somewhere."

Randy was about to go out the door, then stopped. Turning to look back at Jimmy he asked, "What makes you think that?"

"The way he looked at her when we introduced ourselves, something I felt. Did you ever get the feeling that something's going on between people without really knowing what?"

"What kind of feeling?"

Passing off his previous comment Jimmy replied, "Never mind; forget it. Maybe it's my imagination."

Randy replied, "Well, I'll see you later. If I don't, I'll see you at the parade detail."

Driving to the beat, he thought about what Jimmy said. "*Yes I've had that feeling before. It's like an extra sense you pick up being a cop.*"

Around 9:30, the avenue started to come alive with shoppers trying to beat black Friday sales. He walked by Kramer's and tapped on the window, then looked inside. Seeing about six or seven customers, Barry was all smiles and gave him a wave. The brothers were busy too, so he opted not to disturb the sales, and continued on the beat. Suddenly, a radio call came out of a holdup at the bank on the south end of the beat. Being only two blocks away, he started in that direction when the captain pulled up in his unmarked city car. Rolling down the window he yelled, "Hey Randy, get in."

Quickly getting in the car, they sped off to the scene, with police radio giving out the description. There was a small side street adjacent to the bank, and they saw two men fitting the description running from the bank in that direction. Randy quickly said, "Hey boss, there they are. Let me out here and go to the other end of the block."

When he stopped to let Randy out, the holdup men looked in his direction. Seeing him, they thought it would be better making their escape on foot rather than driving fast on a snowy street. The captain hastily drove to the other end of the block and exited his vehicle.

The holdup men trapped between Randy and the captain with their guns drawn, quickly gave up. Putting up their hands, Randy pushed them against the wall in the frisk position. After patting them down while the captain held his weapon on them, Randy found a small hand gun. After putting the handcuffs on the prisoners linking them together, a patrol wagon came down the street and they were put in.

The captain said, "Good job Randy, this deserves a commendation."

"No, thanks boss, but I have to tell you something."

"What's that?" he said looking at Randy inquisitively.

"I'm glad you didn't have to use your gun."

"Why, don't you think I can shoot?" he replied.

"No, it isn't that. Your gun isn't loaded."

Looking surprised, he opened the weapon and looked at the cylinder, "Shit, you're right!"

Randy opened the car the holdup men exited, planning to drive it to the district. Putting the key in the ignition, he turned it. As the battery labored trying to start the engine, he said to the captain standing next to the vehicle, "Boss, I thought they were smart enough, not making their getaway driving fast on the snowy streets. I guess I was wrong. You don't have to be a genius to be a stick-up-man, but these guys have to be pretty stupid. I'll go back to the bank and let them know we have them, and the money. The teller that got held up will have to get to the district. Are you going to take them?"

"No, I just happen to be driving down the avenue checking things out. I'm on my way to a divisional meeting. Get a patrol car to take you and whoever it is, up to detective division. I'll call the tow squad to pick up the car."

"Ok, boss!"

Getting into his car he added, "Oh, by the way."

With an annoying look he continued, "The corporal told me about Sergeant Howard wanting to reassign five squad people. Don't worry, I'll straighten his ass out."

After getting in his car, he commented again, "I'll make sure the corporal types up the commendation. I'll see you later. Have a Happy Thanksgiving."

Randy watched as he drove away thinking, *"Stick the commendation, let me skate and not have to go on that New Year's parade detail."*

With all the years he had in the department, he was only able to avoid one. He was on the 4 to 12 shift when he was on a patrol car. He was backing up another officer on a disturbance, when he saw someone getting ready to hit the other cop from behind. Randy quickly reacted, by punching him in the back of the head, and in doing so, broke his hand.

The captain of the 13th was Gene DeGragorio. Everyone always referred to him as "Mean Gene" for some reason, but Randy never understood why. Gene was around 5'10", with an olive complexion and stocky. He would yell like hell at something not done right, but five minutes after he chewed your ass out, it was as though it never happened.

After taking care of business back at the bank, he continued walking the beat. With the early dismissal at the high school, he wanted to make sure he was at Alma's. The school apparently let out even earlier than was expected with the temperature dropping, and the snow that turned into slush earlier, was now beginning to crust under foot.

After signing the logs once more on the last run, he was walking across Orthodox Street, when he saw a few youths at the end of the next block. There were only three businesses on that side of the street, but he decided to take a look to see what they were up to. Seeing him coming, they walked away. Whether he averted anything was something that would have to remain a mystery. He did recognize the one kid, and mentally made a note to speak with his mother when he returned to duty on Friday.

Walking back to the avenue, he had to pass a bar. The Knotty was more or less a bar for locals. It was generally loud with music, and activity, and from time to time, he was called to handle anything that might go wrong, fights and that sort of thing.

When he walked past the bar to where he saw the youths, he could hear a loud familiar voice from inside. Even with the door closed, he could hear Pauline talking loudly and laughing. She had a combination that let you understand she was the life of any party. She was big boned, and on the heavy side, with dark skin in her late 40's. He knew Pauline well, and several times when he was called to an assignment where she was present, she would always say out loud with a smile, "Hey, ya'll knock that shit off! Here comes my man Randy."

On his way back to the avenue, he was about to walk past the bar when suddenly the door burst open, and out came Pauline. She had obviously been in the bar drinking for several hours, and wasn't aware of the temperature change making the sidewalk icy. Her second step out the door sent her face first to the ground. Quickly helping her to her feet, he looked at her then went in the bar for a towel. Her lips were bleeding profusely and he radioed for a patrol car to take her to the hospital. She was still laughing as if it never happened, and Randy asked, "Pauline, why do you drink so much and almost always have something like this happen?"

For the first time she became quiet, and moved his hand with the blood soaked towel away from her face, replying, "Randy, I'll tell you a secret baby," she said, drawing closer as if there was someone present not privy to their conversation, "I'm gonna enjoy this life as long as I can suck fuckin' breath." Continuing in a whispered tone, "You know something else Randy. I see you almost every day walking your beat. You be struttin' like you be the cock of the walk," getting quieter still, she continued, "Baby, I'll tell you what. If I had the chance, I'd fuck the hell out of you, you know what I mean__ you just the wrong color."

He laughed, and when the patrol car pulled up, he helped her in then returned to the beat.

After the last pass on the avenue, he headed for the district to turn in his activity log and radio. The operations room was bustling with activity with all the reports of auto accidents coming in, and after doing what he had to do, he went to the locker room. Seeing Jimmy as he entered, he said, "You were right this morning when you said they should have just suspended school today. It wasn't worth the effort for only three hours. I didn't get the chance to get to Alma's at dismissal. I hope they didn't hit her too hard."

He replied, "When I heard you call for a car at the Knotty, I followed the kids to the El stop. I checked on her; she's fine."

"Did you see Champ today?" Randy asked.

Leaving the locker room he replied, "No, she didn't get back to school. I'll see her tomorrow at the parade detail," he said, pausing for a moment, "And you too."

"Yeah, see you in the morning," Randy replied.

***

After arriving home, he parked in the lot and headed for the apartment. He thought, *"What's this envelope taped to my front door?"* Reading the note, it was from Charlotte Yard, the neighbor he brushed the snow from her car windows. It was a request for him to knock at her door when he got home. His apartment number was B-12 and her apartment number was B-16. Going down the hall, he knocked at her door. After answering, she invited him in. He asked, "Were you late getting to work this morning?"

"Luckily, no. I just made it on time, how about you?"

"I'm in a uniquely different position. I don't drive a patrol car. I walk a foot beat, so I'm more or less on my own."

"That must get pretty cold at times."

"Yes, it does, but the businesses are open, and I can always duck in somewhere and get warm. What did you want to ask me?"

"When I was coming into the building, I saw a black guy outside your door. He was trying to turn the doorknob, but after seeing me, he walked out of the building. By the look on his face, I know I startled him. I just wanted to ask if he was a friend, or is it some kind of problem?"

Concerning Randy, he asked, "Can you give me a description?"

"He was about your height, maybe not as built, but he was very dark skinned. He seemed to be dressed pretty well, so I thought he may have been a detective or something. I just wanted you to be aware of it."

"Did you happen to see where he went after he walked out of the building?"

"Yes. I looked out the front door, and watched him get into a dark colored two door Buick, then drive out of the lot."

She must have read his facial expression of concern and asked, "I hope that isn't a problem?"

He only knew one person that drove that kind of car, Champ's ex, Eric Johnson. Still waiting for an answer she asked again, "Well, is it a problem?"

Her question snapped him out of thinking about what Eric could be up to, replying, "No, it's a problem a female cop in the district has. I'll take care of it. Thanks."

"Is that the female cop you left your apartment with last week?"

He curiously asked, "How did you know that?"

"I was coming home from work late that night and saw you leaving the building with her. Come to think about it, that same Buick I saw today looked like the one I saw that night too."

He realized she meant the day Champ was there. Eric might be a problem knowing where he lived, but never expected him to have the balls to confront him. He knew better than to take a chance giving Eric the element of surprise, and made a mental note of carrying an off duty gun. Getting ready to leave, she asked, "I hope I didn't upset you. Would you like a drink or something?"

"Can I get a rain check on that? I have to make a few phone calls," he replied.

"No problem. Oh, I don't know what your plans are for tomorrow, but Happy Thanksgiving."

"I have the parade tomorrow. I'll probably treat myself to a turkey dinner at a diner somewhere, how about you?"

"My family lives just outside Scranton, a little town called Throup, to be exact. I have to work on Friday, so I opted to do this," opening the freezer door, she pointed to a Swanson's Turkey Dinner. He laughed replying, "Well, we can always make it a twosome, how about it?"

Surprisingly, she quickly replied, "That sounds good. What time should I be ready?"

"I won't be home from the parade detail until 3, or 3:30. By the time I shower and dress- how about making it 5?"

"I'll be ready," she said with a smile.

Returning to his apartment, he quickly looked up Champ's phone number. After dialing, he got a busy signal. After getting into more comfortable clothes, he redialed again, another busy signal. He dialed every 10 minutes, but no luck, and thought, *"Did she leave the phone off the hook on purpose? Did she inadvertently not cradle it?"* His mind suddenly went to Eric being at his apartment door, and the more frequently he dialed the number, the more impatient he was becoming without her answering. After a half dozen more tries, he realized he would probably be taking a trip to her apartment. Being unsuccessful he thought, *"Fuck it! I might just as well go."*

While driving to where she lives, he had to pass her mother's house on the way, and decided to stop there first. He knocked at the door, and to his relief, Champ opened it.

"Randy, what are you doing here?"

He had a chance to give her back her exact words when she surprised him at his apartment, "Don't sound stupid. That asshole was at my apartment complex this afternoon, and the neighbor said he was trying my door knob. I thought you might be having a problem too, so I tried calling. After trying for an hour, and getting only busy signals, I decided to go to your apartment and see if you were okay. I remembered you picking up your daughter here, and it's on the way, so I decided to stop here first."

"I'm sorry, Randy. I didn't think I left the phone off the hook. Wait a minute! Come to think about it, I didn't use the phone at all today. You should have heard it ringing."

After stepping inside, he could smell the odor of pies being baked and other food being prepared for tomorrow's feast. Her mother came from the kitchen with Champ's daughter in tow, Lea wearing an apron, with a smudge of flour on her chin. Champ introduced him to her mother and he said hello to Lea.

Her mother asked, "Delores, is there something wrong?"

Covering what might be a potential problem, she replied, "No, mother. I have to go to my apartment with Randy. I have to give him a report I forgot to turn in. I'll be back soon."

Lea asked, "Can I stay here with grand-mom?"

"Yes, baby. I'll be right back."

Her mother and Lea returned to the kitchen, and after Champ put on her coat, they left.

Arriving at her apartment, they noticed the door was slightly ajar. They saw immediately the lock had been jimmied and he pushed Champ behind him. Pulling out his gun, he slowly opened the door. The place had been ransacked, and the reason for the busy signal was the phone was lying on the floor. After surveying the damage, she said, "I hope that mother fucker didn't do this. Let me take a look in my bedroom."

Randy checked the rest of the apartment then joined her. She was sitting on the bed crying, holding a framed picture of Lea. Whoever had been in there, apparently knocked it on the floor, checking the drawers of the bedside tables, inadvertently stepped on it. Randy remembered, *seeing a picture of Champ and Lea together in the center of the living room floor. The glass on that was also smashed. It couldn't be a coincidence. It had to be on purpose.*

"Champ, is there anything missing?"

"There's some money and a few pieces of jewelry. Other than that, I don't really have anything of value."

"Why don't we call the police and get them started on the paperwork. Then I'll take you back to your mother's."

Still upset, she asked, "What am I going to do about this mess?"

"Nothing for now, why not leave it alone until we finish the detail tomorrow. Leave Lea with your mother for a few days, and we can work on getting it back in shape over the weekend."

"Thanks, Randy. Do you think it might have been Eric?"

"I wouldn't put it past him, if he had the balls to go to my apartment. Maybe it was."

After the police arrived and made the report, Champ packed a few items of clothing for herself and Lea- then he drove her back to her mother's. After arriving, he saw her to the front door and asked, "Champ, if you don't mind me asking, where's your father?"

"He died two years ago. That's why I stay here as much as I can. I was really thinking about leaving my apartment and just moving back home. My brother and two sisters are on their own, and I think my mother would enjoy having Lea around on a full time basis."

"That sounds like a good idea. I'll see you on the parade detail tomorrow."

After returning to his apartment, he settled in for the evening. Around 8, there was a light knock at the door. Opening it, to his surprise, Charlotte was standing there.

"Randy, I saw you leave the building after our discussion. Is everything okay?"

Happy that she was concerned enough to ask, he replied, "A co-worker had a problem, but we took care of it."

Looking at him, she candidly asked, "Did it have anything to do with the man outside your door today?"

"I don't know for sure. Why do you ask?"

"It's none of my business really, but the girl I saw you leave your apartment with was black, and the guy that was trying your door knob was black. I just thought they might be connected."

Surprised at her perception, he replied, "It has something to do with it, if it's the same person. At this point, it's only speculation, but I'm glad to know you're concerned."

Changing the subject, he asked, "Can I offer you a drink or something?"

"I'll pass on the alcohol, but if you offer me a cup of coffee I wouldn't mind." When he went to make it, he remembered he didn't have any. He had forgotten he spilled it on the floor while in a rush trying to make it this morning, and forgot to stop on the way home to pick up more.

"No sweat. I'll get some from my apartment. I'll make it," she said.

Returning with the coffee, he began to set up the pot. With his back turned to her, he asked, "You said you were from the Scranton area. What brought you to Philadelphia?"

"I graduated from Temple University and liked the area. While I was in college, I majored in accounting and held down a part time job. After graduating, it became a full time position."

"I take it you work somewhere in center city?"

"For now, yes, but the company's moving to the suburbs. I can't wait until they do, the commute will be a lot shorter. In fact, with the company moving outside the city, I was looking into relocating too. This way, I wouldn't have to pay the city wage tax. That's money in my pocket."

When the coffee was finished he asked, "Cream and sugar?"

"I use both," she replied.

After setting out the cream and sugar, he sat down and asked, "What area have you been looking for an apartment?"

"There's an apartment complex behind the Neshaminy Mall. It's pretty pricey, but the convenience and area is well worth the price."

After taking a sip of coffee, he asked, "How soon will this move take place?"

"I think I'll do it right after the first of the year. I want to get past the holiday. Enough about me, I take it you're a native Philadelphian?"

"Born and raised. I've lived here all my life for the exception of four years in the Marine Corps, a pretty drab life."

Blowing on her hot cup of coffee, she looked up with a smile, "With your job, I can imagine it's anything but drab. Have you always lived in this area?"

"No, I originally lived in North Philly. I settled here after leaving the Corps."

Getting up from the table, she looked at a mechanical drawing he had framed hanging on the wall.

"This is unusual. I see your name at the bottom. What does it represent?" she asked.

He said with a smile, "That's my first mechanical drawing. I took mechanical arts when I was in high school, and even did a stint in a junior college. I keep that to remind me how I became a cop."

The bewildered look on her face at his statement sent her curiosity into high gear, "What do you mean by that?"

Looking down at himself, he replied with a hand gesture. "I never thought about being a cop. When I got out of the Marines, I applied for a job at a local company. The Budd Company was founded in Philadelphia over a hundred years ago. It came into existence making wagon wheels. As time progressed, the company expanded making railroad cars. At the turn of the century they began making major parts for automobiles, hoods doors and other parts. I was in the drafting department of the rail car division. Small assignments at first, but after the corps, I felt uncomfortable sitting at a desk. My desk was next to a window, and one day, I watched as the lawn maintenance men cut grass and trimmed hedges. I looked around the room, and noticed almost everyone wore thick glasses, and were stoop shouldered. I said to myself, "This isn't for me." The boss I had at that time was a guy named Mister Shore, the head engineer of the department. His drawings were so grand, you thought you could pick the railcar off the paper and roll it down the track. One day he noticed me looking around and approached my desk. He said, 'Randy, you and I are going on an extended lunch together.' I thought he was going to tell me about my lack of attention to my work, and I was canned. To my surprise, he gave me a lecture of why I shouldn't be in the mechanical drafting field."

"What was the lecture?" she asked.

Toying with his empty cup, remembering something that happened years ago, he looked up smiling at her interest. Continuing he said, "He told me if I didn't like the drafting trade, to make a clean break, and get away from it. I thought he was being polite by telling me privately they didn't want my services, but it was just the opposite."

"What do you mean?"

"He told me he hated every day of his life for becoming a mechanical engineer. He actually wanted to be a forest-ranger, but explained to me his father was a draftsman and pushed him into being an engineer. He said he only had a third of his stomach after several operations for ulcers, and it was all do to stress from the job."

She asked, "Did you quit then?"

"No. I was already getting tired of going to work every day, and being threatened with the employees in the manufacturing department, calling a strike. Everyone with a little longevity would get some kind of small compensation, but on the other hand, I was just beginning to start out on my own. I didn't have that option. At that point, I didn't even have furniture. Only a bedroom and kitchen set."

Interrupting, she said, "That must have been rough. But how did the drawing make you become a cop?"

"Sorry, I ran off on a tangent. With the looming of a strike every week, and the conversation I had with Mister Shore, I decided to re-enlist."

"How long had you been out?"

"If it was still under 60 days, they let you come back with your current rank. I would have still been able to advance from being a sergeant to being a staff sergeant, and I wouldn't have lost anything."

"That still doesn't tell me how you became a cop."

"I'm coming to that point. I was on the subway heading toward 30th, street train-station, when I looked up at the advertising marquee to join the Philadelphia Police Department. I thought, *'What the hell. Why not give it a try?'* I got off the subway at city hall, and filled out an application. After taking a test, I passed with a pretty high mark and the rest is history."

She seemed mesmerized by his story, and after a few moments staring at his drawing, said, "That's one hell of a story. I can see why you framed it."

He jokingly replied, repeating a statement from an old T.V. series, "There are 8 million stories in the naked city. This has been one of them."

She laughed, as she got up and put her cup and saucer in the sink.

"I better get back to my apartment. I guess you have an early morning. What time does the parade start?"

"On T.V. it begins at 9, but we have to be downtown by 7."

Walking her to the door he said, "Goodnight."

Chapter 5

Arriving in center city where the detail was scheduled to meet, Randy saw Champ and Jimmy coming in his direction. He suspected they drove to town together, but chose not to comment. After Sergeant Howard gave them their assigned area of the parade route, they dispersed. Champ and Randy were assigned the same intersection for traffic control, and Jimmy was sent to a different location. Before he walked away Randy asked, "When are we getting together to help Champ?"

"Help her with what?" Jimmy asked.

"Didn't she tell you what happened last night?"

"No, is it something I should be concerned with?"

"You better ask her," Randy replied.

"I will, but why is she confiding in you all of a sudden? Is there something between you two?" Jimmy asked.

With hostility in his voice, Randy said, "Why don't you ask her?"

As he walked toward his assignment, Jimmy grumbled in a low tone, "I will."

While waiting for the parade to reach the intersection, Randy asked Champ, "Why didn't you tell Jimmy about your burglary last night?"

She looked down at her feet for a few moments, like a kid who was just discovered doing something she shouldn't have done. Impatient for an answer Randy said, "Remember Champ, I'm a cop that can read people, what's on your mind?"

Making eye contact, he could see she was having a problem with telling him her inner feelings, and finally had to pry an answer from her, "Come on, Champ, let it out."

"I didn't say anything because I think it was Jimmy that did it."

"Why do you think it was him?"

"He said he came to my apartment last night, but didn't mention it was broken into."

"Maybe he was there before it happened. Did you ask him what time he was there?"

"No, I didn't think to ask, maybe you're right."

"When I mentioned it to him a little while ago, he seemed surprised. I assumed you rode in together and would have told him. He was actually pissed that you've been confiding in me lately."

"That's what I'm talking about. Remember how he acted when he saw me getting out of your car several weeks ago? That's the bullshit he's been doing lately. I was talking to a gym teacher the other day, a young single guy, the football coach. We stopped to talk about the upcoming Thanksgiving game with North Catholic, and I was just wishing him good luck. Jimmy must have seen me talking with him several times, and came up to us handing me a bullshit line that he had something important to talk about. After he broke up the conversation, I asked what he wanted to tell me, and he said, 'Oh, I guess it wasn't really that important.' He just wanted to break up the conversation. That's the kind of shit he's been doing."

Randy replied, "That sounds like a lot of jealousy on his part. When I mentioned the burglary to him, he seemed really surprised. I can read faces pretty well, and by his expression, he was definitely shocked."

"Did you ask him if he was going to help me move?"

"No. I thought I'd leave that up to you. Whatever you decide, you know I'm available."

The head of the parade was about to pass the intersection, and they separated to different sides of the street. It was moving along pretty quickly, and looking at his watch, Randy realized it would probably be over by noon. He didn't have a chance to talk with her for the first two hours, but when there was a break in the parade, he started across the street.

He saw Sergeant Howard speaking to her and what it was about he couldn't tell. Whatever it was didn't seem police related, it looked as though she turned away from him while he was still talking. Sergeant Howard followed, and she turned to continue the conversation but when they saw Randy approaching, they ceased.

"Sarge, it looked like we were going to get away from here early, I wonder what the holdup is?" Randy asked.

"I think they're having problems with those damn balloon characters. With this wind and cold air, some of them lost control of the guide ropes," he replied.

In a little while, Jimmy approached, and Sergeant Howard asked, "Jimmy, why aren't you on your detail?"

"I was relieved by the sergeant down there. One of his men took over my spot. He told me to report to you."

"Ok, you be the relief for Champ and Randy if they have to take a break."

Just then a woman approached with two young children, "Here you are. We've been trying to catch up to you," she said, addressing Jimmy.

Hearing the familiar voice, Jimmy quickly turned. "What are you doing here?" he asked.

Surprised at his bluntness, she replied, "I thought it would be nice to bring the kids to see you. Aren't you going to introduce us?"

"I'm sorry dear, you just surprised me. Champ, Sergeant Howard, Randy, this is my wife Donna and my two boys, Jimmy Jr. and Joey."

Donna was 5' 5" and very attractive. The boy's looked to be, 6 and 8 respectively and were well dressed. Sergeant Howard said, "Pleased to meet you Mrs. Ryan," looking down at the boys shaking their hands he asked, "Are you anxious to see Santa?"

Jimmy Jr. replied enthusiastically, "Yes, our daddy helped us write this letter to Santa," pulling it from his coat pocket. "He told us to put it in his mail bag when the parade ends."

Champ saw the embarrassment on Jimmy's face, at a family scene he obviously been lying about. Swallowing her pride, she extended her hand and cordially shook Donnas, "Pleased to meet you, Donna. Jimmy often speaks about you and the kids," looking at Jimmy with contempt.

Donna said, "Jimmy, don't forget. You promised the boys you'd take them into Gimbles to see Santa."

The parade resumed, and they returned to their assigned side of the intersection. Donna and the children faded into the crowd, and Sergeant Howard walked away to check the rest of the detail. Randy saw Jimmy and Champ in conversation later; and it looked like she walked away from him while he was still talking.

After the parade ended, everyone gathered together before dispersing. Jimmy and Champ were standing together, when

Jimmy decided to ask what her plans were on making the move. After putting their heads together, they decided on doing it Saturday.

As Randy was about to walk away, Sergeant Howard approached and asked, "Aren't you guys going home to that turkey dinner?"

Champ sarcastically replied, "We know what Jimmy and his family are doing. Why doesn't he invite all of us to his house for dinner? My apartment is a shambles. Some mother-fucker broke in last night and wrecked the place."

Looking at Sergeant Howard's face, Randy noticed he didn't seem surprised or concerned as he should have been. If Randy had to bet on him having some prior knowledge about it, he would have probably won the bet. He didn't ask whether she needed any help, or if she needed time off. Most supervisors would have asked that question immediately. He just didn't seem like he cared. Randy wasn't going to let it interfere with his plans with Charlotte for dinner and headed straight home to change.

He rarely wore his uniform to and from work, but didn't want to waste time going back to the district. As soon as he got home, he called Charlotte to ask what time she would be ready. While her phone was ringing, there was a knock at the door. Answering it, Charlotte was standing there. Before he could speak, she looked both ways down the hall before stepping inside.

"Charlotte, what's wrong?"

Excitedly, she replied, "That black guy I saw at your apartment door, I saw him again in the parking lot about 10 o'clock."

"What was he doing?"

"I don't know whether he was coming from the building, I was just coming back from the store. I know he saw me, and maybe he remembered me seeing him at your apartment door. Whatever it was, he quickly got in his car and drove away."

"Where was his car parked?"

"I'll show you. Let me get my jacket."

Meeting at the front door of the building, they walked out on the parking lot to where she saw his car. Looking at the ground where the driver's side would be, there were about six cigarette butts that were the same brand. It was an indication he'd been watching for awhile, *but why me?* Randy thought, *"Did he think by following Champ and him here, they were physically or emotionally involved?"* Walking back to the building, he thanked Charlotte for being so attentive, and made up his mind. One way or another, he was going to confront him.

Getting back to his apartment she asked, "How did you enjoy the parade?"

He didn't know whether she meant that as being a joke, but answered sounding like a kid anticipating Santa Clause coming to town, "I put my letter to Santa in his bag. I'm sure he'll read it!"

Her thought that he was there to be entertained, brought a smile to her face.

"I guess that was kind of dumb asking that question," she replied.

"No harm done. What time are we getting together?"

After looking at her watch, she replied, "How about 5?"

"That's fine. I'll see you then."

At 5 he knocked at her door. When she opened it, she already had on her coat, and they proceeded to his car. Driving to the restaurant, she looked at him then asked, "What's the problem you seem to be having with that guy; is it police related?"

"In a way, yes, but it has more to do with one of the female cops I work with. That's her estranged husband. He followed us here, and I guess he thinks we're having some kind of relationship. The next time I get a chance, I'm going to confront him. Let's not talk about that, I don't want to spoil my dinner," he said.

"I'm sorry for bringing it up," she replied.

Pulling into the restaurant parking lot, they found an empty spot, and went into the building. The Hofbrau Restaurant is a German-American establishment, just outside the city. He chose it over the Greek style restaurants, because those would probably be crowded with older people. The menu is a little limited, but being Thanksgiving, as most restaurants, they offered the traditional holiday dinner. Not only that, the atmosphere's a little more serene. Instead of booths, they have candle-lit tables and the holiday decorations with the Bavarian Decore' added a little extra.

"This place is really neat; I've never been here," she said.

"I come here once in awhile for their roast beef. They make the best I've ever eaten. On Saturday night they have a Bavarian Band. You know, the kind that plays the Ump, Pha, Pha kind of music."

"Is it the kind you're able to dance to?" she asked.

"I guess. I never tried it."

Looking over the top of her menu, she replied, "We'll have to try it sometime."

Without looking up, he said, "That's a bet! Would you care for a drink?"

"I think I'll have a glass of wine," she said.

Looking around the room, he said, "Since I'm in here, I think I'll have a Heineken. It goes with the atmosphere."

She smiled, "Are you always so nonchalant about things?" she asked.

"Why get upset? Life's too short," he replied.

"I could never be a cop. I just wouldn't have the patience to deal with some people."

"You get used to it after a while. Let's not spoil our dinner over talking about cop stuff?"

All of a sudden she went quiet. Examining her face, he realized he may have been too brash with his comment. "I'm sorry Charlotte. I didn't mean that the way you may have taken it. I just more or less would like to change the subject. Why don't we talk about you, and what you do?"

Looking at him she began to apologize, but he cut her short, "You don't have to apologize. It's just that when most people find out you're a cop, they seem to want to talk about it. It's like having to work another shift you don't get paid for."

"I never thought of it that way. I guess you're right. Okay. It's a deal. We won't talk cop stuff."

When they finished dinner, the waitress handed them a desert menu. He asked, looking over the selections, "I think I'll go for the traditional pumpkin pie, how about you?"

"That sounds good. I'd like mine with whipped cream on top."

Looking at the waitress, "That will be two. I'd like a coffee with mine, how about you Charlotte?"

"Make that two!" she replied.

While enjoying their desert, she asked, "What do you want

to do after dinner?"

Toying with a match book, the complimentary kind in most restaurants, he looked up. Not wanting to intrude on her entire evening, he had an alternative excuse. He said, "You told me you have to work tomorrow, and I don't want to keep you too late. I was thinking about going back to my apartment and watch the Dallas, Detroit football game. It should be about halftime by the time we get back."

Expecting a response something like "Well, if that's more important, so be it."

Instead she remarked, "That sounds like a great way to end the day."

Looking at her, he asked, "You mean you like football?"

"I love it! My two brothers played for Syracuse in college. I know all about the game."

Looking at his watch he replied, "Well, its game time," he said, after helping her with her coat they left.

Returning to the apartment building he asked, "Your apartment or mine?"

"If you don't mind Randy, I'd like to use mine. Give me a few minutes before you come over. I'd like to slip into something a little more comfortable. I'll leave the door unlocked."

"No problem. I'd like to do the same. Oh! By the way, I should have said it earlier. You really look great."

Entering her apartment, he made himself comfortable on a large throw pillow on the floor, with his back against the sofa. Coming out to the living room she said, "Now that's letting your hair down. You can sit on the couch or a chair."

"I'm fine with this floor pillow. I always meant to get one, but never got around to it."

R. J. Bonett

Tuning into the game, it was almost half-time. She asked, "Can I get you a drink or something?"

"After that meal, I don't think so. I never thought to ask, but what's your favorite team?"

She loudly proclaimed from the kitchen, "Dallas!"

"Ahhh! Not the Cowboys!"

Coming back to the living room in a quieter tone she said, "I'm only kidding. I know how the people in Philadelphia seem to have a vendetta against America's team."

"Okay, what is your favorite team?" he asked.

"Since I'm from Scranton, the people up there only have two preferences. One is the Buffalo Bills or the Pittsburg Steelers."

Adjusting himself on the pillow, he said, "I'll have to go up there someday and straighten them out."

She laughed, and when halftime was over, they settled into the game.

During game breaks, they had mild conversation, and he discovered amongst her other interests, she liked to fish. He considered himself lucky to have, for a lack of better words, someone he can really get in tune with.

"Where did you pick up all your very masculine interests?" he asked.

"I get it from my father and brothers. I also hunt."

Turning in her direction, "You're kidding me, right!"

"No, I'm very serious."

Surprised, he said, "I would have never believed it."

Getting up from the sofa, she went to the bedroom and retrieved a framed picture. Returning, she pointed to two tall well-built men standing on either side of her. The three were dressed in hunting clothes, with an antlered buck lying on the ground. She said pointing at the picture, "These are my two brothers. This was my first deer."

"I can see why they played football; they're pretty big."

"Yes, my dad's the one that took the picture. He's a hunter and fisherman too."

"If I would have had to guess what you were like, I could have never done it. You just seem to be, to be, so city oriented."

"Can I tell you a secret?" she said.

"Sure, why not."

"Living down here, and working in center city, scares me to death."

"You certainly don't act like it."

"Well, I am. With Thanksgiving coming, I was looking forward to getting back home for a few days. You know; a pause from being frightened every day. When my boss told me I had to work Friday, I had to excuse myself and go to the ladies room. I actually started to shake and became nauseated, that's how nervous I became."

She had his full attention, and he propped himself up on his elbow. Looking at her, she actually looked as though she was experiencing the same fear just relating her story. He never realized, something he took as being so ordinary, could have such a profound effect on a person. Whether it was just masculinity, he didn't know. He just never encountered a woman with that kind of unprovoked fear.

"Maybe inwardly you're just a little homesick. Why not try thinking past working tomorrow, and focus on heading home after work, or early Saturday morning?"

"If I have to work tomorrow, that means I'll have to bring work home to do on the weekend. To be very honest, having the problem with that black-guy only heightened my fear."

"I'm sorry it added to your problem. Maybe city life's just not for you. Why not try another place of employment, say outside the city? If you can't do that, maybe you should try another type of work altogether," he said.

"That's easier said, than done. I work in a high-end bank, where depositors have to maintain an account of more than $500,000. They just don't have that kind of facility anywhere else, not to mention the money I make. So I'm more or less stuck with it."

He replied, "Do you remember the story I told you, the one about my boss at Budd Company? He said it wasn't worth his health, and by your reaction, it seems to be affecting you the same way. That's my best advice."

After a little more conversation about her predicament, he excused himself and left.

Getting back to his apartment, he kept thinking about Champ's estranged husband having an effect on Charlotte's already troubling situation, and it only hardened his resolve to confront him. After taking a shower, he went to bed.

***

When he awoke, he rolled over and looked at the alarm clock. It was already 8:15, and knew he'd be late getting to the district, so he picked up the phone and called. It was picked up on the second ring with a voice responding, "Corporal David Tyler: 13th District, how can I help you?"

Trying to mask his half awake voice he said, "Dave, this is Randy. I had a flat tire so I'll be a little late."

Replying sarcastically, "Sure, I'll call my grandmother to change it for you. Who do you think you're bullshitting? You must have had a little too much last night."

Randy replied, "If I told the truth, would you have believed me?"

"Probably not, get in as soon as you can. I think the captain wants to have a meeting with five squad people. If he asks, I'll make up a better excuse than the flat tire story."

"Thanks Dave, I'll see you in a little while."

Getting out to the parking lot he saw Charlotte getting in her car.

"Good morning, I'm running late. You too?" he asked.

"Yes, after our conversation, I had a hard time getting to sleep."

Trying to ease her tension, he replied, "Just think about getting home tonight. Well, see you later."

She rolled down her window before pulling away, "Thanks Randy, and thanks for the dinner."

He began to say a few words, but didn't get the chance, as she rolled up her window and drove away. He had entertained the thought of taking her to Lawn Wood Gardens on Saturday, a botanical paradise that's an exclusive landmark. The holiday decorations and floral displays are magnificent, and he knew it would have a positive effect on her nervousness. Since their conversation last night, he realized her family would probably be a better tonic for her nerves. He'd have to postpone asking her to go on a trip to Lawn Wood Gardens, for another time.

When he got to the district, he went into the operations room. Corporal Tyler quickly remarked, "You better get into the captain's office. Everyone else is in there."

"What excuse did you give him?" Randy asked.

Chuckling, Tyler replied, "I told him your grandmother had

the flat and you had to change it."

Randy laughed, "Thanks!"

As he was about to go into the office, the door opened and the squad began filing out. He saw Champ, and asked quietly, "What's the big meeting all about?"

"The captain told us we'd have to work tomorrow. He thinks the avenue could use the extra coverage. It looks like I'll have to postpone the move to my mother's. He did say you guys walking the beat can be off Monday. School's open, so that leaves Jimmy and me out. I think he wants to give us time off later, maybe during the week, but it will have to be separate. One of us will have to be at the school."

Stepping into the office, the captain asked, "How did you make out with your grandmother's problem?"

Bending down, pretending to tie his shoe, it was all Randy could do to keep from laughing. Regaining his composure, he straightened up, "Fine boss. Thanks for being understanding."

"No problem. I told the rest of the squad they'll have to work tomorrow. I want the extra coverage on the avenue. I gave them the option to take off Monday or another day they choose. What do you want to do?"

"I'll take off Monday boss. The avenue won't be that crowded."

"That's fine," adding, "Randy, I received an anonymous phone call this morning. The caller said Jimmy Bryan and Champ are having an affair. I know Jimmy's married. Do you know if having an affair is true?"

He knew the captain could read his face, but told him, "No."

Randy asked, "Do you have any idea who the caller could have been?"

With a bewildered look, the captain replied, "No, but

whoever it was, had to be near the elevated train. I could hear it in the background."

Randy thought, *"Maybe it's Eric? On second thought, could it be Sergeant Howard? His squad's off today, maybe he was hanging around the avenue hoping to see Champ?"*

After getting to the beat, he made the run of the avenue. With the extra help, the beats were overlapping. He saw Champ later that morning and asked, "Champ, the captain told me he had an anonymous phone call this morning. The caller told him you and Jimmy, are an item. Do you know who it could have been?"

Looking surprised, she asked, "Did he say if it was a male or female voice?"

"I didn't ask. I assumed it was a male. He said whoever made the call, was near the El. He could hear it in the background."

She replied, "I'll ask the captain when I get back to the district." As she was walking away, she suddenly turned, "Fuck that! I'll call him now."

"Don't do that, I don't know whether he wanted me to mention it to you. That puts me in a bad position."

Smiling, she said, "Okay, father Randy. I won't. How was your Thanksgiving?"

"Pretty good, I took a neighbor out for dinner."

"It wouldn't be that good looking woman I saw leaving the building the day I was waiting for you, would it?"

Surprised she made the connection, he replied, "You know me, I don't tell tales out of school. But if I were you, I'd cool it for awhile with Jimmy."

During the day, he handled an attempted shoplifting assignment, and one disturbance in a bar. Other than that, things were pretty quiet. Walking back to his vehicle, he saw

Sergeant Howard in his private auto, slowly moving along with traffic. He looked in Randy's direction, but made no attempt to let him know he was there. Standing just off the avenue, Randy looked toward Orthodox Street and saw Sergeant Howard pull to the curb. Champ hurriedly exited a store on the corner and got in his car. Randy thought, *"I don't know what the hell her problem is, but she should begin by scrapping the pretend relationships she has."*

Getting to the district, he turned in his radio and headed for the locker room. Passing the section partitioned off for the police women, he could hear someone crying, and stopped to listen for a few moments, trying to figure out who it was. It sounded like a frustrated cry. A cry of someone who desperately wanted to control something they had no power over. Suddenly, he heard a bang as if whoever it was, took that frustration out on the door of their locker. He knocked lightly asking,

"Champ, is that you?"

"Yes, Randy. I'm fine. I'm just pissed at someone, but I'll be alright."

"Do you want to talk about it?"

"No, really, I'll be fine."

"You're the boss."

Getting to his locker, he saw Sergeant Howard getting dressed for duty. Sergeant Howard asked, "How was the avenue today, it must have been pretty busy?"

Randy realized he knew it firsthand, but still opted not to say he saw him; replied, "It wasn't bad at all." He threw in a dig to make him wonder whether Randy did see him, "You know how the avenue always is on Black Friday, crowded with slow moving traffic."

Crossing the Blue Line

Pausing briefly, he looked at Randy, "Yeah, I guess so. I was down there. I had to pick up something at Ginsberg's."

Looking at him as he closed his locker, Randy asked, "What was it?"

"I had to pick up a few baby clothes."

"Do you have small children? Randy asked.

"No, this is our first. I never had any children from my first marriage. It was just as well; we were only married for several years. I remarried two years ago, and the wife's 5 months pregnant. She's so excited about it; she's buying everything now, even before she knows whether it's a girl or boy."

With his statement, he inadvertently told Randy why his wife was giving up her hair dressing business; she's pregnant. Randy thought, *"That's good, but I know it's not your first,"* and wondered whether that was why Champ was so upset. Did she just find out?

Putting on his coat Randy said, "Take it easy out there. I think with the temperature dropping, the streets will be a little slick."

"Yeah, I know. It was beginning to ice up as I was coming to work."

Getting to the parking lot, Randy looked at the gas shack. What they called the gas shack, was actually that, a shed attached to the rear of the building. It looked like an afterthought that was built when the building was completed, and someone suddenly realized it was something they forgot to add. In the gas shack was a set of stairs leading to the basement locker rooms. They too, looked like they were an afterthought. They were about 15 stair steps and very steep. Although they were closer to the locker-room, for some reason, they were rarely used by anyone.

Waiting for his car to warm, Randy saw Champ coming from that section of the building. She was parked two spaces away from his, and he rolled down his window. "Hey Champ," he yelled, "Come here a minute."

After getting in, she still seemed very upset, and asked, "What's on your mind father Randy?"

After a few moments of examining her frustration he said, "You know, I have your best interest in mind, don't you?"

Looking up, her eyes began to fill, and he realized she knew he was about to strike on a point she would rather not talk about.

"I saw you get in Sergeant Howard's car at Orthodox Street. Would it be a good guess on my part, that you saw him coming out of Ginsberg's?"

Looking at Randy she couldn't hold back the tears. He wasn't sure whether they were tears of sadness, or anger, and asked, "What's wrong?"

After studying his face wondering what his reaction might be, she said, "Randy, I think I'm pregnant again."

"Is it by Sergeant Howard?" he asked.

"Oh no, I haven't had anything to do with him that way for several years. It's by Jimmy. What am I going to do?"

He replied, "You're going to have a baby, that's what you're going to do. Are you worried about not having enough money to support them?"

"That's one of the reasons I'm so upset. Another reason, Jimmy said he was going to get a divorce and we were going to get married. After I told him I was pregnant at the parade detail yesterday, he said he made no such promises. Seeing his reaction when he introduced me to his wife and kids, I know

now he was only lying. I really love him and trusted him. That's why I was a little careless. He told me to get an abortion, but I'm not only afraid, I'm religious and don't want to violate that part of my belief."

Thinking for a few seconds of how to respond, he said, "There doesn't seem to be a way out of your predicament without hurting yourself physically, or mentally. I don't see many options for you. You're going to have to make some hard decisions. You're lucky your mother's there to help."

"I know, but she doesn't have much income. My father was really sick the last few years he was alive, and it almost drained my mother financially. In a way, my apartment getting wrecked, gives me a perfect excuse for my daughter not to know my personal problems. Are you still in for helping me make the move? Jimmy backed out. It's like I'm being abandoned by everyone," she said, breaking down with anger, she continued in a frustrating voice slamming her small fist down on the dash board, "Randy, what the hell am I going to do?"

Angry at the position Jimmy put her in, he replied, "Hey, take it easy. Fuck Jimmy! We can do it without him."

She replied, "I don't want anyone from the district to help, that news will be all over the squad."

"I'll tell you what, I can take off Monday. I know someone else that might be able to help. I can ask her if she could get the day off. Give me your key. We can clean up and put everything in boxes. I'll rent a van so all you'll have to do when you get there is help load it."

Volunteering his services and possibly Charlotte's, made her feel somewhat better. Looking at him, she smiled then gave him the key.

"Thanks Randy."

Arriving home, he didn't want to waste any time contacting Charlotte. If she was agreeable to help, he wanted to give her enough time to ask her boss for the day off on Monday. After entering the building, he went straight to her apartment and knocked at the door. After waiting several minutes, he knocked again. He was about to walk away, when the door opened slightly. Peering out from behind the partially opened door, he was surprised to see Charlotte with a towel wrapped around her head. Apparently catching her at a bad moment, perhaps coming from the shower, he said. "Charlotte, it looks like I caught you at a bad time. I'll come back later."

"No, that's okay. Come in."

Opening the door to admit him, she said, "I just got home about a half hour ago and wanted to take a quick shower. Have a seat, I'll be right out."

"Thanks!"

Waiting for her to return, he began surveying the room. He noticed how much more homey her apartment was than his, something he didn't take into account when he was there Thanksgiving evening. His place brought back an older cop's opinion from years ago.

At the time, he was still pretty much a rookie with only two years on the job, and lived in an apartment similar to the one he had. In those days, when the circus came to the city, it would set up at the race track parking lot in the northeast. As usual, the older cops got the easy detail and for some unknown reason, another rookie cop by the name of Tony and him were assigned with them. It had rained most of the week prior to the circus' arrival, and was forecasted to continue for several more days.

After reporting to the detail, it was supervised by a sergeant that looked like he'd been in the department for 50 years.

Sergeant Frances Farrell was distinguished looking, with snow white hair and light complexion. With the older cops, it was reassuring he wouldn't want to keep a detail in place when the circus was postponed for the day. After holding roll-call, he looked around at the puddles of rain on the parking lot surface, and the circus tents with their flaps closed. One of the older cops by the name of Louie said,

"Aw, come on Franny. What the fuck! There ain't gonna be a circus tonight."

All the older cops laughed, and Sergeant Farrell smiled at Louie's remark. Sergeant Farrell asked,

"Do you guys have a place you can hide for the next few hours?"

They looked at each other pondering his question. They all lived in Kensington, or Fishtown, closer to the inner city. Randy said, "Hey Sarge, They can stay at my apartment. I live right down the road."

"Thanks kid! Now listen you guys, don't get drunk and make sure you get back here at 9 to check out," Farrell said.

One of the older cops named Frank added comically, "Yeah, you bunch of alcoholics, don't get drunk!"

As we dispersed, Lou asked, "Hey kid, where do you live?"

"I live at the end of Academy Road. It's the Ivory Court Apartment's. Building B, apartment B-12."

"Thanks kid, we'll see you in a little while."

Tony and Randy headed for Randy's place, and within a few minutes, the older cops entered. As they entered the apartment, Lou looked around commenting, "Hey kid, what's with the red flocking wall paper? This apartment looks like a fucking whore house."

Remembering that day then laughing to himself, Randy looked around Charlotte's apartment. Comparing it with what his looked like back then, he realized Lou was right. He needed to get a little less bachelor, and a little more home like décor.

When Charlotte returned to the living room, she asked, "Can I fix you a cup of coffee?"

"That sounds great. How was your day?" he asked.

"As I said before, I would have rather had the four days off and gone home for the holiday."

Smiling, he said, "So you didn't think going out with me was at least something to take the edge off?"

"No! I didn't mean it that way. You know what I mean," realizing he was kidding, she smiled.

After pouring the coffee he asked, "Charlotte, can I ask a big favor?"

"Sure, what is it?"

"The woman you saw me with, the cop from my district. She has a problem."

Stopping from making the coffee, she looked up asking, "What kind of problem?"

"Her ex wrecked her apartment and she has to move. She asked, or rather I volunteered to help her pack her things and move most of it to a storage shed. Some of it has to go to her mother's where she's relocating. There was another cop that was supposed to help, but he backed out at the last minute."

Stirring his coffee with a spoon, he looked up. Hesitating for a moment he asked, "I hate to impose, but could you possibly get a day off to help?"

She didn't instantly reply, and he thought he was going to get a resounding *"No."* Instead, he got a *"Yes."*

"I'd be happy to help, when are you going to do it?" she asked.

"I was thinking about Monday. Is that enough time for you to arrange a day off?"

Looking at the clock, she replied, "No, it's too late now. I can call first thing Monday morning though. I don't think it will be a problem."

Happy she was enthused, he racked up another quality in her he liked. She didn't appear to be selfish.

"That's great. Now what's your weekend going to be like?" he asked.

"I was thinking about taking a drive to my parents. I missed the dinner Thursday, but I'm sure there's going to be leftovers. I called them, and two of my brothers are staying until Sunday afternoon. I'll at least get a chance to see them before they leave."

Randy replied, "That's good, just be careful driving. There are still some slick spots on secondary roads."

"Thanks, I will."

Chapter 6

Afyter returning to Philadelphia Sunday evening, Charlotte knocked at Randy's door.

"Come in, how was your weekend?" he asked.

"Short, but enjoyable. It felt good to see my parents and two brothers again.

"Did you have leftovers?"

"Yes, it wasn't as good as Thanksgiving dinner, but I enjoyed it. I see you're watching the football game. I don't want to disturb you."

"That's alright, its half time. Do you think you'll be getting the day off tomorrow?"

"I don't foresee any problem. What time are we leaving?"

"If it isn't too early, how about 9 o'clock- Care to watch a little football?"

"I don't think so. I'll see you in the morning."

Seeing her to the door he said, "Good night."

***

At 9 a.m., there was a knock at the door. He already had his jacket on and they promptly left.

He asked, "Have you had breakfast?"

"No, I was a little late getting up."

"There's a small restaurant around the corner. I sometimes eat breakfast there. You'll enjoy the atmosphere."

Looking at him, he could tell she was confused at his statement, probably wondering, "How can a small restaurant have an atmosphere worth commenting on?"

After pulling into the small parking lot, they entered the establishment. The owner and cook was a short heavy set man. Smitty was a person from an age gone by. His real name was Joe Salamone, and was part of the Italian immigrant population that once inhabited the Frankford section. Smitty, like most of the older Italians who lived in that neighborhood back then, had nick names. They were at one time heavy into the numbers racket or other gambling enterprises, like horse betting and card games. Some of the names were actually part of their make-up in one way or another. Smitty was actually called, Fat Smitty, obviously for his size. Then there was, No Coat Joe, Joe Vergaglioni, who never wore more than a sweater, even in the winter. Another was called Deep in the hat, because he had such a small head, he never seemed to have a Jeff hat that wasn't supported by his ears. There were a few others Randy couldn't relate as to how they got their titles, but most certainly had something to do with their makeup. Mummy, Spaggs and Dracula Gino.

Gino was another interesting guy. He owned a pizza shop at the south end of the beat. He controlled the illegal card games, and had on occasion, high rollers from as far away as Cincinnati, Chicago, Boston and a few other cities.

Tony the barber was another prominent character. Tony was a numbers man that never wrote a number down on paper. He kept several hundred of them in his head daily, and was well known to have never missed remembering a face of who won a number, and could have probably been a genius in any other field or profession.

They would gather at Smitty's in the morning reminiscing

old times, and some of the run-ins with cops they encountered years ago. The stories were hilarious to the point they would have made a great book. Their activity was illegal, but something Randy always considered harmless. The gambling habit was hard to break with these guys. It wasn't out of the ordinary for them to watch a pigeon on the sidewalk pecking at a few discarded crumbs, and bet on whether it would hop off the curb within a few minutes, or on a cloudy day, what time it would begin raining. They would even bet on which way a person would walk after coming down the steps from the elevated train.

Randy's entry to the restaurant was acknowledged by Smitty. In a loud tone, "Hey Randy, aren't you walking the beat today?"

"No Smitty, this young lady and I are going to help a friend from the district move. We just stopped in for breakfast."

"Tell me what you want, I'll make it."

"Eggs and toast will be fine for me, how about you Charlotte?"

"That sounds good, how about some coffee first?"

Smitty replied as he broke the eggs putting them on the grill, "Sure thing."

Putting down the coffee in front of Randy, he appeared to have something on his mind. Randy asked, "Smitty, you seem to have something to say. What is it?"

Hesitating for a moment, in a quiet tone, he leaned toward him and said, "I don't want to get anybody in trouble, but when I was in Frankford a couple weeks ago, I saw one of the female cops get into a private car. She was in uniform, but I didn't recognize her. I don't know whether she's even in your district."

"What's so unusual about that?" he asked.

"As I walked by, I saw the guy in the car hit her in the face. I was going to say something, but thought it might be wiser not to get involved."

Putting down his fork, Randy asked, "What kind of car was it, do you remember?"

"I think it was a dark green Chevy, but I'm not sure. I was more interested in who would hit a woman in a cop's uniform."

"Was he a white guy, or black guy?"

"He was white."

"Was she a white person?"

"No, she was black. Light skinned, but she was definitely black. Why are you asking?"

Not wanting to get into what he was thinking, Randy replied, "No reason, just asking."

"That would probably explain the black eye Champ had," he thought. He remembered when he saw Sergeant Howard in traffic that was the kind of car he was driving, and wondered whether the guy in the car was him.

After breakfast, they said goodbye and left.

Driving to Champ's, Charlotte commented, "That is a colorful group in Smitty's. You seem to know them pretty well."

"I've had a few run-ins with them, but nothing out of the ordinary, quite harmless. The biggest problem is with No Coat. I think he's getting senile. Sometimes, I have to pull him aside when he starts cursing out loud on the avenue. He always seems to make Dracula the focus of his hostility. It's something I believe from the past."

She seemed to enjoy her introduction into city life as it actually exists, and not an outsider's perception, so he related the story to her.

"I'd been in the district for less than a year, and in those days, older cops always steered clear of any conversation with newer cops, until proven. They just didn't trust us not to be internal security."

"What's internal security?" she asked.

"A plant in districts at times, to observe what might be going on illegally. It was primarily to find out where numbers rackets or card games existed, that higher ups in the department weren't getting a cut from. Everyone knew it for what it was, and until proven otherwise, new cops were considered an outsider."

"I wouldn't think there would be that sort of distrust between cops," she said.

Passing on her comment, he continued the story.

"Like all newer people, I was assigned a foot beat. In warmer weather, it wasn't bad, but towards winter, it gets damn cold and windy under the El. The underside of the trestle, being rooftop level of three story buildings, has a tunnel like effect beneath it. At times, the wind whips down the avenue strong enough to take discarded newspaper pages to flight. On day work, or 4-12, it wasn't bad. You always had an open store to get in for a few minutes. Something we call '*Catching a heat.*' After 9 p.m. all the businesses would be closed. The only place open was Gino's Pizza Shop. Remember, I mentioned, he was the guy who ran the card game in the back room. A quiet guy, like most of the other older Italian's, they always tried to kept a low profile. He always tried not to rile the cops, or embarrass them by doing his side business in the open. After being on the beat for awhile, he gave several of us rookies a key to the store. We were able during the midnight to 8 shift get in out of inclement weather."

"That was pretty decent of him," she said.

"It was."

By Randy's story, she began to realize, although the criminal element was on the other side, it was a mutual respect. Getting back to his story, he said, "Beginning the 4-12 shift one day, one of the members in my squad, said 'Randy, I just heard the inspector's men talking about raiding a card game at Gino's. Try to get down there to warn him.' I was working a police wagon at the time with Jesse, and said, 'John I can't. We're stuck in the gas line out back. I'll have to wait until I'm refueled. We're running on fumes.' Heading back to the operations room, John took the phone number of Gino's from his wallet. After dialing the number, he got a busy signal. Thinking the line was busy with people ordering, he hung up and waited a few minutes, then re-dialed. The phone was picked up and a voice on the other end in a heavy Italian accent said, "Ello! This a Gino's. Whata you want?"

John replied excitedly, "Gino, this is John. Stop playing cards, the inspector's men are coming to raid the game."

"I'mma no understand. Watta you want?" the voice on the other end demanded.

John said in a slower tone of voice, "Break up the game! The inspector's men are coming!"

Without a response, he realized he couldn't make Gino understand, and headed for the pizza shop. Not giving up hope to warn him, he stopped at the emergency room at the hospital on the way, to try once again. After dialing the number, he heard the same announcement, "Ello! This a Gino's. Whata you want?"

Desperately, he tried once more to explain. "Stop playing cards! Break up the game. The inspector's men are coming to raid the joint."

Going back to his police car, John heard the call for a police wagon to go to the Pizza Shop. Realizing he was too late, he gave up. After fueling, we headed to the assignment, to transport the gamblers. Our sergeant at the time was already at the scene, and after pulling up, he asked to sign our log."

"What's a log?" she asked.

"It's a sheet for the tour to log radio calls, and activity you performed during the shift. The sergeant signs everyone in the squad each day. When we got to Gino's, John drove up to see what was going on. When the Sergeant saw him, he waved, motioning for him to bring his log to be signed. Standing next to the open window of the Sergeant's car, he handed my log back, and took John's. Looking up at John, he asked, as he signed his log, "Hey, John, who's side are you on?"

"What do you mean Sarge?" John replied.

Looking up as he handed him back his log, the sergeant paused for a few moments. Pointing to himself he said, "This a Gino. This a Gino, A, watta you want?"

Charlotte laughed almost hysterically remarking, "That's funny, do you have any more stories?"

"I have plenty. It'll take forever to tell you all of them."

She sat back and if he had to bet, she couldn't have imagined what a cop goes through in a normal day.

Arriving at Champ's apartment, he unlocked the door and they went in. Surveying the room, Charlotte asked, "What the hell happened here?"

"Champ's been having problems with her life, and someone wanted to make it a little worse. I have a bunch of empty boxes in the trunk. I'll get them, and we can start in the bedrooms packing stuff."

As he walked to the door, he turned to look back. She seemed to be upset at seeing someone's personal belongings strewn about, and he asked, "If this is too much for you to handle, I understand. I can take you back home."

It seemed to snap her out of her private thought of how someone could be so cruel to do this to a person they had a relationship with. She replied as she began to pick up a few things from the floor, "No, I'll be fine."

Coming back with the boxes, they proceeded to Champ's daughter's bedroom first. Gathering the clothing, Charlotte folded them neatly, and began packing them away. There were a few stuffed animals on the floor, and as she picked each one up, there seemed to be feeling of sadness for what happened. When they finished, they went into Champ's bedroom. It was more of a mess and it was obvious the person that did it, had more of a vendetta against her. The strong odor of a mixture of perfumes spilled on the carpet permeated the air. Whoever it was, threw the bottles against the wall.

Charlotte asked, "What's Champ going to do about cleaning the smell out of the rug?"

"She's obviously going to have to hire a carpet cleaner," he replied.

While Charlotte was gathering the clothing and neatly folding them on the bed, something interesting caught Randy's eye. Amongst the photographs lying about, the ones of her ex were only torn in half. As he was picking them up, he noticed there were some that were torn in smaller pieces, and began to put them together on the bureau like a jigsaw puzzle. The picture that emerged was a photograph of Sergeant Howard and Champ in a compromising position, obviously taken during a party of some kind, by another person. Wait, there seemed to be too many pieces. Looking around, he found a few more. Putting them together wasn't easy, but it began to give him an understanding why Champ made the gesture toward him the first time she came to his apartment. She obviously liked men, and it didn't seem to matter who they were. Claiming anyone in particular she was interested in was beginning to get a black eye, and he wondered whether she was telling the truth at all. Finding an empty shoe box, he put the torn photos in it. After packing her bedroom, they went to the living room.

Charlotte picked up a large throw pillow, and stuffing began to spill out. When she turned it over she dropped it.

"Randy, Look at this. Somebody has a real hatred towards this woman."

He noticed a kitchen knife lying next to it and realized whoever did this, took out more of their frustration stabbing and slashing the pillow. Could they have been imagining it was Champ? That would have been the logical conclusion. Seeing it, he remembered Champ saying her husband had a knife in his possession when the police came for the disturbance, and it seemed to make Charlotte lose her concentration of gathering Champ's personal items. Seeing it bothering her of how violent a person could be, he said, "Charlotte, if this is too much for you, perhaps you should go to the kitchen and gather the stuff together that's strewn on the floor."

Looking at his watch, he hadn't realized it was almost 1:30, and said, "After you finish in the kitchen, maybe we should take a break for lunch?"

"That sounds good. I think we're pretty much finished packing the personals."

As they were about to leave, they heard someone putting a

key in the door lock, and motioned for Charlotte to be quiet and stand behind him. After hearing the lock open, he drew his revolver and stood at the ready. The door slowly opened, and through the open space behind the door, Randy could see a black guy, who he recognized immediately as Champ's ex, Eric. Surprising the intruder, Randy grabbed him by the jacket and flung him across the room onto the couch. Putting his knee on his chest and his revolver to his face, Randy demanded,

"Ok, what the fuck do you want?"

Eric's eyes were wide with the shock of being surprised, and couldn't find the words to answer. Randy quickly asked, "Do you have a weapon on you? You mother fucker!"

"No, who are you?" Eric nervously replied.

"Don't act stupid. You've been hawking me since you saw Champ leaving my apartment. Now what the fuck do you want?"

Randy let him up, and for his personal protection, frisked him. Randy looked at Charlotte, who seemed to be having a hard time digesting what was taking place. Looking around the room for Champ, Eric said, "Where's Delores?"

Randy had to think for a few moments then realized he was using her proper name.

"Champ, I mean, Delores, isn't here. She couldn't get off work today, so my fiancé and I are packing for her. What do you want?"

Eric looked at the packing boxes but didn't answer. He picked up the pillow and more stuffing poured out. Seemingly surprised, he put it down. "What happened to the throw pillow, how did it get torn?" he asked.

By the look on his face, Randy could tell he really didn't

know how it was damaged, and his intuition told him he wasn't the person who wrecked the place. With continued hostility in his voice Randy told him, "There's an old saying in the police department that goes, 'I'd rather be tried by 12, than carried by 6.' Do you get my fucking meaning? You almost ran over me in the parking lot at the district. If it wasn't for Champ telling me who you were, I would have taken care of your ass a long time ago. The next time you stalk me, is going to be your last. Understand, mother fucker?" Randy said, as he holstered his weapon.

"I'm not interested in you. I saw Champ with a black eye awhile ago. I thought you might have had something to do with it," Eric said.

Taking him by the coat collar, he walked Eric to the door. After shoving him out, he repeated himself, "Just remember what the fuck I said," then closed the door. Going to the window, Randy watched as Eric looked back at the building, then get in his car and drive away.

"Are we ready to go to lunch now Charlotte?" he asked.

She seemed to be mesmerized at the event. "I can't believe you're so nonchalant about what just happened. Excuse the expression, but to quote a vulgar phrase from my brother when he was confronted by a bear while he was hiking through the woods. 'I was shittin' in my shoes.' Yes, I'm ready for lunch."

After helping her with her coat, he surveyed the room. Satisfied with their accomplishment, they left.

Randy wasn't familiar with the diners in the area, so he opted to go back to Frankford Avenue for lunch. On the way, she remarked, "When you drew your gun and shoved it in his face, you said I was your fiancé. Why did you say that?"

"I wanted him to think twice about bothering me or you. I think it will work. You, or rather we, won't have a problem with him anymore."

Arriving at the avenue, it was hard finding a parking space on the street, so he parked on the bank parking lot. They were familiar with his car so he knew it wouldn't be a problem. Walking the two blocks to the Riviera Restaurant, he saw Sergeant Howard in traffic. He was on duty and when he saw Randy, he pulled to the curb.

"Hey Randy, aren't you used to having a day off during the week?" he said.

"I'm here strictly as a civilian. We're going to the Riviera for a late lunch."

"Well, enjoy, I think most of the lunch crowd will be gone," Sergeant Howard said.

After entering the restaurant, they found an empty booth as far away from the front door as possible. Randy didn't want people who knew him disturbing them during lunch. When the waitress, Eleanor, came to their booth, she recognized him immediately and in a somewhat embarrassing statement, said, "Randy, I didn't recognize you with your clothes on."

Charlotte looked shocked at the statement, and Randy had to clarify it before she got the wrong impression.

"Charlotte, she means she didn't recognize me in civilian clothes instead of in uniform."

Smiling she replied, "I assumed as much."

"Well, at least it wasn't in a place that I didn't have some measure of control," he said.

"What do you mean?"

"I was on a crowded elevated train once heading for city-hall for a court appearance, when someone at the far end of the car recognized me in civilian clothes. They yelled out the same thing, and it brought the attention of almost everyone in the car."

"Why?" she asked.

"I guess because he was a man."

She laughed, and it seemed to calm her from the incident at Champ's apartment. Although he thought the temperature in the restaurant was comfortable, she pulled her coat tight together and shivered.

"Are you cold? If you are, we can move to another booth."

"No, I'm still cold from walking the couple blocks from where we parked. I'll be fine. I don't know how you can stand being out in this weather all day. I don't think I could handle it."

"You get used to it after awhile."

Randy was facing away from the front door, and Charlotte looked past him. Someone tapped him on the shoulder, and turning to look, it was Champ. He stood up to let her slide into the booth, and introduced her to Charlotte.

Champ asked, "How much were you able to get done? I know the place was a mess."

Charlotte replied, "We got most of it packed in boxes, there's not a whole lot left to do. I didn't know what you'll need as far as kitchen utensils or dishes, so I didn't pack them."

"That's okay. I'm going to my mother's and she has everything. I'll just put them in storage. Oh, by the way, Charlotte, thanks for helping."

"That's okay. It was just that I'm not used to seeing someone have a gun shoved in their face."

"Gun, what the hell happened?" Champ said looking at

Randy.

"Champ, I wasn't going to say anything, but Eric showed up while we were there. I hid behind the door and waited until he was inside. After I surprised him, I told him in no uncertain terms that he would pay a severe price if he comes around Charlotte's or my apartment again. I don't think he'll bother us anymore."

"You mean he had a key to the apartment?"

"Yes. Why?"

"I never gave him one after we separated. I can't imagine how he got it."

After the food order came to the table, Randy asked, "Champ, do you want anything?"

Still wondering how Eric got the key, he had to repeat himself. It seemed to snap her out of her deep thought and she replied, "No Randy, I have to report off. School was let out early. I can go back to the apartment with you. Why don't you wait for me here?"

"We'll be finished before you get back. Why not meet us at the apartment?" he replied.

"After telling me he had a key, I'm worried he's going to come after me. He must have gone through an awful lot of trouble getting it."

"I took it off of him. Here it is." Handing it to her, he asked, "Are you sure your daughter didn't give it to him?"

"She wouldn't have done that without asking me first. She's afraid of him."

"Well, hurry up and report off. I'm parked on the Second National Bank's Parking Lot. We'll wait for you there. You can follow us."

Getting up, she quickly exited the restaurant. After finishing lunch, Charlotte and Randy headed back to the car.

Walking back, Charlotte asked, "How is it she has so many personal problems? I would think if anyone, a police officer would know how to straighten out her own life."

"You're right. She just seems like everything overwhelms her. All I can do is suggest and be as helpful as I can."

Looking at him with an approving smile, she said, "I'm glad I met you."

Taking his focus from the parking lot entrance he replied, "Me too! Finding a woman as attractive as you that likes football, hunting, and fishing, is probably every man's dream."

Realizing he was focused on the parking lot entrance, she asked, "You seem to be looking at something. What is it?"

"I saw Sergeant Howard looking in the lot. He must have been watching Champ and saw her go into the restaurant. He probably assumed she went in to speak with me. Maybe he thought she was here at the parking lot too, and when he didn't see her, he's wondering why I haven't left yet."

"Is there something going on between him and Champ?"

She's been having problems with him not sharing the expense of raising her daughter."

Looking more bewildered than ever trying to read his mind, she decided not to pursue any more questions.

Putting the car in gear, he pulled up to the parking lot entrance. When Sergeant Howard saw him coming, he drove away.

Within 15 minutes, Champ pulled up, and Randy motioned for her to continue, and pulled into traffic two cars behind her. At the end of the block, the car in front of Randy stopped for the red light. Champ didn't notice, and continued ahead. Randy saw Sergeant Howard who must have been parked on a side street facing the avenue, pull into traffic behind her. When the traffic signal turned green, the car in front of Randy made a left and he quickly accelerated getting behind Sergeant Howard's car. Sounding his horn to distract Sergeant Howard's attention, he pulled to the curb allowing Randy to pass. There was no doubt in Randy's mind, had he not been there, Sergeant Howard would have confronted her.

Pulling up in front of Champ's apartment, they went inside. Entering, Champ looked around, surprised at the work they were able to accomplish.

"You guys really did a hell of a job. Now all I have to do is take the clothing to my mothers and store the rest of this stuff."

"Is there anyone that can help me move the furniture into storage?" Randy asked.

"Since my mother doesn't have a place to put it, I was thinking about selling it. I have a cousin that might want to buy it. She's just graduated college and starting out on her own. I'll call and ask."

"Okay, what do you want me to load in my car?"

"If you'd start taking the boxes marked clothing, that'll be a big help. I don't think you'll be able to get it all in, so I'll put the rest in my car."

While Randy carried the larger boxes, Charlotte and Champ carried out the clothing on hangers that were still in closets, laying them on the front and back seat. After securing the front door, they headed to Champ's mothers.

Arriving at her mother's, Champ introduced Charlotte to her mother Angelique, and daughter Lea. Angelique, a small woman with light features, still carried a slight accent from the Caribbean Island, Barbados, where she came from at the age of 20. Perfectly ladylike, Lea said, "I'm happy you helped my mother. I heard her in her room last night, she was crying."

Randy couldn't help but notice the look on Charlotte's face. The words had a profound effect of concern for a child whose mother seemed to have a multitude of problems. After unloading the vehicles, Champ's mother invited them to the kitchen for some tea and a piece of sweet potato pie.

Lea asked, "Mommy, may I have a piece too?"

"Yes, dear, you were a big help. Charlotte, I don't know if you've ever had sweet potato pie, but it's a southern tradition rather than pumpkin. I'm sure you'll like it."

"I'm sure I will," she replied.

Angelique asked, "Charlotte, are you and Randy just friends, or are you living with each other?"

Champ was about to take a swallow of her tea, when she suddenly coughed, and put down her cup. "Mother, that's an embarrassing question."

Looking at her, Angelique replied, "Well, you young people seem to do things differently these days. How was I supposed to know?"

Champ was about to apologize, when Charlotte interrupted, "No, Angelique, we're not living together, we're just neighbors. Randy's been helpful a few times though."

Angelique didn't seem to want the conversation to die without relieving her personal thoughts. "Well, you two seem to be a good couple. Charlotte, there don't seem to be too many men that's good these days, not like my husband. He was a really good man."

Randy could tell immediately what Angelique had to say, was only to bring out the goodness of a husband she once had. After she said it, Angelique picked up her spoon and began stirring her tea. Randy saw her eyes begin to water, and was sure if it wasn't for their presence; she would have let her emotions go. Champ got up from the table and embraced her saying, "Mother, we all miss him very much. You'll be alright though. You'll be taking care of Lea."

Angelique looked over her shoulder smiling, a reassuring smile, Lea would be well taken care of. Feeling a little uncomfortable in that sort of environment, Randy said, "Champ, I think Charlotte and I better get going."

Getting up from the table, Charlotte quickly remarked, "If there's anything else you need, just give me a little advance notice."

Turning to look at Angelique she said, "Angelique, the pie was delicious. I'll have to get your recipe."

Champ came around the table and gave Charlotte an embrace. She said, "I don't want to embarrass you, but my mother's right. There aren't many men like Randy these days."

Cutting the compliment short, he said, "I'll see you at work tomorrow."

Walking them to the front door, Randy turned and could see Angelique still sitting at the kitchen table. He said in a loud tone, "Goodbye Angelique. I'm sure I'll see you again."

"Thanks guys. I don't know how I would have gotten it done without you," Champ said.

"Just remember, lock the door after we go out."

"I will, Randy."

On the drive home, Randy said, "Charlotte, I hope Angelique

didn't embarrass you too much."

Turning to look at him, she replied, "Not at all, I do think she's right about one thing."

"What's that?"

Hesitating for a few moments, she looked at him to evaluate his response to what she was about to say, "You are a good man."

Smiling, he said, "No, I'm just a good listener."

Countering his remark she said, "No, you really are a good person."

Pulling up to the apartment complex, he took a chance moving closer to her. She didn't fight the issue, and they looked into each other's eyes. Letting their emotions take control, they kissed, and after the kiss, he said, "I've wanted to do that all day."

Sheepishly she replied, "I've been waiting for you to do it."

After entering the building, they went to their respective apartments, but before going in, they said goodnight.

Chapter 7

The following morning, Randy saw Jimmy in the locker-room. Jimmy asked, "How did you make out with the move?"

"What the fuck do you care? Where was all your concern yesterday when we were doing it?"

Looking at Randy, he replied, "I wanted to, but I had something else really important to take care of."

"Jimmy, don't bullshit me. I'll bet if you wanted to get laid, you would have found time. When you told me you thought your wife was having an affair, I believed you. When she showed up at the parade with your children in tow, she couldn't have portrayed anything better than a concerned family-oriented person," he said, closing his locker. Walking by Jimmy, he said, "Remember the old adage Jimmy, what goes around comes around."

He didn't respond, and Randy knew he was wondering how Jimmy would face Champ at the school security office.

Randy hadn't had time for breakfast, so he began the day sitting at the counter at Alma's.

"What will it be Randy?" she asked.

"French toast and a cup of that weak coffee," he replied.

"No problem. What's with this new sergeant?" she asked.

"You mean, Sergeant Howard?"

"Yeah, I was at Teddy's newsstand next door yesterday putting in my numbers when he walked in. I didn't hear what he was saying to Teddy, but I believe he's shaking Teddy down.

He seems like an arrogant prick."

Randy replied, "For someone that's new in the district, he's not starting off on the right foot. After I'm finished, I'll ask Teddy."

With her back toward him, she said in a lower tone. "If he is giving Teddy the strong arm, I hope he gets transferred."

"I'll talk to Ted and find out. There are ways to handle a person like that."

Alma was setting up another pot of coffee when she turned, "Oh, by the way, that woman cop from the school, she was in yesterday morning to have a bite. She didn't get three bites down, before she had to use the bathroom. I heard her throwing up; then I heard her crying. When she came out, I asked her if there was anything I could do."

Randy jokingly asked, "Was the food that bad?"

"Smart ass," Alma replied before continuing, "If I had to bet, she has morning sickness. What will the police department do in that case?"

"I really don't know. If she is, I'm sure there's a point where they'll reassign them until they have it."

After finishing, he went next door to the newsstand. Teddy, a big man in his late 50's, has been a fixture in the neighborhood long before Randy was ever a cop. Almost blind, he had a way of being able to identify people by their voice. As Randy walked in, Teddy said, "Hello Randy. Want a newspaper?"

"No, Ted. I was just in Alma's. She told me you had a visitor yesterday, the new sergeant. What did he want?"

Hesitating for a moment, Teddy replied, "He just wanted to introduce himself."

"Ted, don't bullshit a bull-shitter. Was he trying to shake

you down? If he is, you don't have to worry about me telling him I got it from you. I was just telling Alma he's creating a lot of problems. I think half of my squad would like to see him transferred."

Coming closer, Teddy said quietly, "He wants $20 a week, and from what I understand, I'm not the only one he wants it from. He's trying to tap No Coat for the numbers too, and Gino's Pizza for a cut of the card games. I don't know for sure, but you might check with Simmy at Dale's Bar too. I think he's breaking his balls about Black Harry taking numbers in there."

"Thanks Ted. I'll see what I can do."

"Remember Randy, you didn't hear it from me."

Before closing the door, Randy looked over his shoulder, "No sweat."

After making a run of the beat, Randy went to Dale's Bar, a small establishment just off the avenue. When he walked in, Simmy was cleaning up. Taking a seat at the bar, Simmy joined him.

"Randy, what can I do for you?" he asked.

"Simmy, I'm hearing the new sergeant is shaking the tree to see what comes down. Has he visited you?"

"Confidentially, he's been in here twice. He grabbed some guy that I always thought was legal age. When he checked his ID, he was only 19, you know these reformed junkies, they don't age well. He threatened to shut down the bar and notify the Liquor Control Board. I didn't have a choice but to cough it up."

"How much?" Randy asked.

"It cost me $20 dollars, and he told me I was lucky, that prick."

"You mean he came in here specifically to catch you serving minors?"

"I don't think so. I think he wanted to find Black Harry, but Harry didn't come in that day. I'm not sure what his game is, but if he hits up every bar in the lower end, even once a month, you're talking a hefty sum. I just as soon pay it and forgo the aggravation."

"Na! that shit ain't gonna fly with me. We'll have to find a way to get rid of that guy."

"It sounds like he's treading on a lot of toes. Why is he such a hard ass?" Simmy asked.

"I think I know the reason, but just keep it under your hat about our discussion."

"You be the man Randy. If you need more information from any of the other bars," glancing up at the clock he continued, "My daytime bar tender should be here in an hour. After he comes in, I'll personally go around to The Knotty and the other bars and ask if he visited them."

"Thanks Simmy."

Just as Randy was about to leave, a radio call was broadcast of a holdup in progress at the State Liquor Store on Oxford Avenue, one block off the beat. Running out the door and across Frankford Avenue, he was at the Liquor Store in several minutes. A bystander gave him a description of the getaway car, and the direction it went. After relaying that to police radio, he went inside the store. Other than being shaken by the event, no one was injured. In a few minutes, he heard another broadcast of an auto accident several blocks away near the high school. It was a hit and run by the same description as the suspect car from the holdup. Flagging a police car heading in that direction, he jumped in.

Arriving at the scene he saw, Champ wrestling with one of

the students from the school. After assisting with the arrest, she said, "Thanks Randy, this mother fucker and his buddies are probably the ones that did it. I heard the description of the car and knew who it was. I came outside and sure as shit they were just parking the car. That's fresh damage to that fender."

"Did you look inside the car?"

"No, I didn't have a chance."

"Was this one armed? The people in the State Store said they had guns."

"He doesn't have one on him. Maybe they're in the car."

Just then, a few police cars and a police wagon arrived. After putting the prisoner in, they followed Champ into the school to look for the others. She knew them to be trouble makers, and didn't have a problem locating their classrooms. After making the arrests, Randy followed her to the security room. Looking around, he upsettingly asked, "Where the fuck is Jimmy? He should have been out there with you?"

"I don't know. He must be around somewhere. He had to have heard the call." Looking around, he was still nowhere in sight.

Turning to Champ, Randy said, "I was in Alma's this morning. She said you were there yesterday and wasn't feeling well. Should you be out here dealing with this shit?"

"It's just a little morning sickness, nothing to worry about."

"How long do you think you can hide it?"

"I was hoping I could make it till May, this way, I only have to be detailed in June, and the summer vacation will take care of the rest."

"Have you spoken to Jimmy about it yet?"

"I think I already mentioned it to you that I did, but nothing since then."

"Are you going to press the subject?" he asked.

Turning to look at him she replied with a shrug of her shoulders, "Do you think it would make any difference?"

"I guess you're right. It probably wouldn't. I just got a handle on something today. It probably has something to do with you."

She looked at Randy, and he could tell she was wondering whether it had anything to do with her relationship with Jimmy, and asked, "What is it?"

"It doesn't have anything to do with Jimmy, if that's what you're thinking. How much support was Sergeant Howard giving you?"

Embarrassed at his statement, she turned away and said, "Do we really have to get into this kind of discussion?"

"I think it's better if we talk about it now. I heard from Alma that he was shaking down Teddy's newsstand for taking numbers. After I confirmed it with Teddy, he turned me on to Black Harry being shaken down for taking numbers at Simmy's Bar. When I asked Simmy, he told me Howard was in there but Black Harry wasn't. There was an underage drinker and it cost Simmy $20 dollars for Howard not to break his balls."

"What does that have to do with me and Sergeant Howard?" she asked.

"Nothing, but you did tell me he wanted to stop paying for Lea. Has he gone back on his word and agreed to continue to pay?"

Looking troubled that Sergeant Howard would resort to doing that, she asked, "He didn't directly say it, but he handed me $100 on Monday as I was going off duty. Do you think that's where it came from?"

"If he all of a sudden hands you money, I would imagine so. I know things must be tough financially, but it could get tougher for you if it gets out."

"There's no way I can ask him where he's getting the money. What am I going to do?"

"There's nothing you can do at this point, but ask why all of a sudden he changed his mind."

"I will, Randy. Thanks."

Just then, Jimmy entered the room. "Where the hell have you been? Champ was wrestling with a holdup man outside. You had to have heard it," Randy said.

"I did, but I was confronted with dealing with Eric, your husband."

She surprisingly asked, "Eric! What the fuck are you talking about Jimmy?"

"When I was checking the back of the school, he confronted me about us going together. I took the precaution of him possibly being armed so I sucker punched him in the mouth, and threw him against a car. I was right. He had this," taking a small pistol from his pocket, showing it to them.

Startled, Champ said, "He's losing it. Now he's really got me scared. Where did he go after you took it?"

"He shoved me, and ran down the back-alley of Allengrove Street. He exited the other end and turned the corner, but I lost him in the next block. I was looking for him when I heard the auto accident broadcast. That's when I hurried back."

Randy said, "Well Champ, we better head to the detective division to handle this arrest. My vehicle is in the parking lot at the bank. Wait here you can ride with me."

In 15 minutes Randy returned. Driving to the detective

division she said, "That takes a lot of balls for Eric to confront Jimmy like that. He must be crazy."

"Hopefully, he'll leave him alone, but what about you? Did he own a gun when you were together?"

"No, he must have bought it recently. Maybe Jimmy should run the serial number and see if anything comes up. When I became a cop, he never let me carry my gun home. He always wanted me to keep it in the locker. He was even against me carrying an off duty piece."

"Just make sure you carry one from now on. With me confronting him at your apartment, I can't believe he still had the balls to confront Jimmy, I wonder how he knew you two were seeing each other?" pausing for a moment she said, "Wait a minute. He had to be the one that called the captain. Did you ever see him when you and Jimmy were going anyplace together?"

"I don't think so. We were pretty careful. If he thought we were secretly seeing each other, why would he be hawking you? It doesn't make sense. You were the one he saw me with at your apartment. Some other mother fucker must have told him."

"You told me Sergeant Howard used to go to your house for domestic disturbance calls. Does Eric still live there?"

"Yes. What are you getting at?"

Suddenly, it struck him. Looking at each other they thought, *"The only other person that could connect her with Jimmy was Sergeant Howard. But how did he know they were seeing each other, and what was his motive for telling Eric?"*

"Did Sergeant Howard know you and Jimmy were seeing each other?"

"Not unless someone at the school told him, or maybe he

just might have guessed. Why?"

"That's what I'm trying to figure out. When you get to the district, make your presence known to the captain. Maybe he'll ask you about the anonymous phone call. If he does, you can ask whether it was a male or female and whatever else he can tell you about the caller."

"Suppose he asks me whether or not it's true? What should I say?"

"That's up to you. But I wouldn't say anymore than you have to. You're allowed to have a private life."

Pulling into the district parking lot, they saw the captain getting out of his vehicle.

"Good morning boss," Randy said.

He replied, "I was in traffic on route 95 and heard the job at the liquor store. Good job. Champ, when you're through with the paperwork, I'd like to see you in my office."

"Ok captain."

Walking into the building Randy said, "That was convenient."

When they were through at detective division, they went downstairs. Champ knocked at the captain's door, and Randy proceeded into the operations room. Corporal Tyler from two squad was on duty, and asked, "Randy do you need a ride back to the beat?"

"No, thanks Corporal, I'm waiting for Champ. She's in the captain's office. We rode in together in my private vehicle."

In a few minutes, Champ came from the captain's office looking a little pissed. Randy asked, "What happened? What did he say?"

She remained silent, until they got in his vehicle. "Ok, what did he ask you?" Randy repeated.

"He asked me straight out whether Jimmy and I were secretly seeing each other."

"And what did you tell him?"

"I put it on my ex. I told him Eric was jealous I wouldn't give him a second chance. Then I asked if he could tell whether the caller was black. He said whoever it was sounded like they were, but he thinks it was someone trying to fake it. Eric has a really base voice. When you spoke to him when you were cleaning up my apartment, you should have noticed. When he was a kid, he had a problem that left his voice-box that way."

"Yeah, I did notice it. Why?"

"The captain said the caller didn't have that kind of voice. That leaves him out, and Jimmy wouldn't have ratted on himself. He would never want to give up a steady day work job. That only leaves one other person, Sergeant Howard. That mother fucker."

"I wonder why he did it?" Randy asked.

Thinking for a moment she replied, "I wonder? Maybe he's trying to knock me off the detail and thinks he'll get me in his squad. They are short a few people."

"Could that bastard be that vindictive?" Randy asked.

"Obviously, he is."

After dropping Champ off at school, he returned to the beat. It was already 2 o'clock so he made a quick pass of the avenue, and got to Alma's just in time for dismissal. Seeing Champ and Jimmy walking down with the first rush of students, it usually signaled trouble. Most of the time, it would indicate there was going to be a fight between students from different neighborhoods. Before joining them, he told Alma to lock the door after he went out. The fight turned out to be more threat, than action, but he walked along with the students to the elevated stop where they dispersed.

Getting together with Champ and Jimmy, he asked, "Did you tell Jimmy what happened at the district?"

"I was about to, when one of the teachers told us about the fight. I didn't have a chance."

"Tell me about what?" Jimmy asked.

Looking at him, Champ said, "The captain wanted to speak to me when Randy and I were in the district. Somebody called him, and told him you and I were seeing each other."

"No shit! When did this happen?" he surprisingly asked.

"He said the call happened this morning. The captain said the call had to be made from around the El- he could hear it in the background. I don't think it was Eric." Champ said.

Jimmy replied, "We've been pretty discreet about our meetings, I wonder what the motive is?"

Randy could see in Jimmy's face. His concern wasn't for Champ as much as it was for his own benefit. Leaving the conversation there, he asked, "Champ, are you going back to the district with me, or Jimmy?" Hesitating, she looked at Jimmy, hoping he would answer the question. Randy waited for an answer but nothing was given, and after a few moments, Champ said, "I think I'll ride back with Jimmy."

Walking away, Randy replied, "Whatever floats your boat."

Before leaving the beat, he went back to Simmy's to find out if Sergeant Howard put the arm on Benny Tucker, the owner of The Knotty Bar. After walking in, Simmy waved for Randy to join him at the far end of the bar. Randy asked, "Simmy, what did you find out?"

In a quiet tone he said, "Yeah, he got to The Knotty too.

From what I hear, he's like a fuckin' vacuum cleaner. He's taking everything that ain't nailed down. Remember Randy, you didn't hear this shit from me."

"Don't worry about it." After thanking him, Randy headed for the front door. Before he could get out, Pauline came in. She had obviously been drinking and said in a loud voice, "Randy baby," looking around the bar she continued, "Is one of these fuckin' people causin' trouble? Tell me who it is, I'll straighten they ass out."

Smiling as he walked past her, Randy replied, "No Pauline, everything's cool. Try not to drink too much and wind up hurting yourself."

"I won't baby. Let me buy you a drink," she said.

"No thanks. I have to report off."

"Why don't you come on back down when you done? We could have a few."

"Maybe next time," he said.

Simmy called out from behind the bar, "Pauline, let the man alone or you'll get flagged."

"Sorry Simmy, I'll be good," she said as she quietly pulled up a bar stool and sat down.

Looking back, Randy said, "Thanks Simmy. See you later Pauline."

Arriving at the district parking lot, he saw Jimmy, Champ and Jimmy's wife Donna. Exiting his vehicle, he heard Donna screaming at Jimmy, and apparently picked up on half a conversation.

"What the hell do you call it then?" Donna shouted.

Champ was standing with her arms folded looking at Donna screaming at Jimmy.

"What's going on Champ?" Randy asked.

Looking at Randy, she replied, "Ask her! She's the one that's doing all the fuckin' screaming."

In a rage Donna angrily replied, "I caught this asshole kissing this bitch! He's got the balls to tell me it was nothing. Does he think I'm stupid or something?" screaming again, as she fought back tears of anger.

Champ quickly replied going at her, "Who you calling a bitch? Bitch! He's your husband. Don't put that shit on me."

Grabbing Champ, Randy forcefully led her to the gas shack and down the stairs toward the locker room. Donna followed, still running off a triad of profanity at Champ from the top of the stairs, "You haven't heard the last of this shit yet__ bitch!" she screamed once again before returning to the parking lot where Jimmy was standing.

In 10 minutes, Randy had changed clothes and was heading to his vehicle, when he saw Donna driving away without Jimmy. He asked, "What the fuck's happening Jimmy?"

"Nothing that concerns you," he said, then turned to walk into the building. Before he got in, Donna came back to the parking lot and exited the car. Still yelling at Jimmy, she said, "Asshole, me and the kids will be at my mother's. If you prefer that bitch over your family? Go for it." With that, she got back in her car and sped out of the parking lot onto Harbison Avenue.

Randy returned to the building to see if Champ was okay, and going toward the locker room, he saw Champ step from a small bathroom designated for female cops.

"What's that shit about?" he asked.

"Jimmy and I were in the parking lot and kissed. We didn't realize his wife was sitting in her car waiting for him. When she saw us, that's when she started yelling and screaming."

"It must have been some kiss," he replied.

"Yeah, well you know, if she leaves him, that's better for me."

"What makes you think he's going to change his relationship with you? You're assuming a lot," Randy said.

"Well, at least my chances will be a little better," she said, unbuckling her gun belt slinging it over her shoulder.

"It's up to you, but you seem to have too many irons in the fire already."

Just then, Jimmy came down the stairs and joined the conversation. Randy commented, "Do either of you remember the motto on the wall at the Police Academy?"

"What was that?" Jimmy replied,

"The one that read, 'The three things that can wreck your career as a cop are, money, booze and coos.' I guess you realize that now. Hopefully she won't pursue it through the police department. If she does, you'll at the very least, be shit canned from your detail, if not transferred to separate districts," Randy said.

"I'll try to straighten it out when I get home. She's just pissed at the moment," Jimmy replied.

"She looks like she's more than just a little pissed," Randy said.

Looking at Champ, he could tell immediately, her reaction to Jimmy's statement was disappointing. Turning, she kicked the door of the women's locker room open, and angrily said, "Thanks a lot you mother fucker. I know where I really stand now. I guess you don't want anything to do with the baby I'm going to have either," pausing for a moment she continued, "Well maybe it's time I say something official too."

Jimmy was stunned at her remark.

Randy asked, "Jimmy, when you came to my apartment and told me you suspected your wife of seeing someone else, do you think it was because she was suspecting you of doing the same?"

"I don't know. Maybe that's why she was here. I wonder if someone told her."

"That sounds logical. If someone called the captain and told him about your relationship, it's probably the same person that told your wife."

Leaving the locker room, Randy looked back at him hanging up his jacket and said, "Jimmy, for your sake, I hope you get it straightened out."

Chapter 8

On the way home, Randy thought about Champ's options. She was obviously still in love with Jimmy, but it was a situation she couldn't change. It was something Jimmy had total control over. Her situation with Eric wasn't going to change either. She definitely wasn't going back that way, if not for herself, for Lea who's afraid of him. Sergeant Howard was another matter. Randy was almost 100% positive he was the one making the phone calls, but why? It would seem that if Champ and Jimmy were heading for a relationship together, it would be to Sergeant Howard's benefit. It was becoming clear he was on the right track. Logically, Howard would be the one that called Donna to tell her about her husband's infidelity. Another thought in mind was his tactics for extorting money from the bars and gamblers. The sums of what he's been getting were well above what he would have been contributing toward raising Lea. Randy never thought to ask Champ what that sum was, so he put the thought in back of his mind until the next time they met.

Arriving at his apartment, there was a note pinned to his front door. "Dinner's at 5:30 in my apartment. Nothing formal- come comfortable."

Laughing to himself he wondered, *'what would she say, if I came the way I sometimes lounged around, in my underwear.'*

After a shower, he dressed and proceeded to her apartment. After knocking, she answered and he stepped in. He could smell the aroma of a roast as she took it from the crock pot. It smelled terrific. The table was already set, a stark difference from his place and usual TV dinner in a tin foil tray.

"Are you trying to spoil me with this set up?" he asked.

"No, I just thought it might be a pleasant change. I put the roast on low this morning, so it would be done when I came home from work. I wouldn't want you to think I was slaving over a hot stove all day. Speaking of the day, how was yours?"

He replied, "You know, boring as usual. I did handle a job today that Champ made the arrest on."

Opening the refrigerator door, she looked over the top and asked, "Before you get into the story, can I get you a beer or something to go along with your dinner?"

"I'd like one, thanks."

After pouring the beer she asked, "What kind of job?"

"A holdup of a state liquor store just off my beat. They made their getaway toward the school, and crashed into a parked car. Champ heard the description of the car, and knew one of the trouble making students who owned one like that. When I got to the scene, she was battling with the driver who was stunned by the crash. It was a pretty good arrest."

Handing him the glass of beer, she replied, "Oh, boring as usual huh? How do you speak so calmly about things like that?"

"Part of the job, you get use to it."

She said, "For a woman, Champ seems to have the same attitude. Frankly, what happened to her apartment would be enough to scare me out of town."

After taking a sip of beer he replied, "With all the other shit Champ has going on in her life, that event seems mild."

Surprised at his statement, she paused from laying out the diner and looked at him, "What do you mean?"

Hesitating for a moment, not knowing whether he should divulge Champ's private life, he thought, *maybe a woman's input might be a different perspective.*

After the food was on the table, she invited him to sit down and repeated her question, "What did you mean? Is her life in shambles because of her husband?"

"Not exactly, that's the least of her emotional problems. She's in love with a married man."

"Well, that's easy enough to remedy if she just finds the courage to walk away."

"I wish it was that easy for her," pausing for a moment he said, "She's pregnant by him. He led her on, thinking they would have a life together, and it just ain't happening. He's happily married, at least for now. After what happened today, I wouldn't think his marriage is rock solid."

"Now you really got me interested. What happened today?"

Relating the story for the exception of Sergeant Howard's part in it, or what he assumed was his part in it, she said, "You're right, it doesn't sound promising for his marriage or Champ's future."

She began to continue, when he suggested, "Why don't we drop this conversation? I refuse to let someone else's problems ruin this great dinner. Now, how was your day?"

"If you want to talk about boring, everyday at my job is boring, compared to yours. We're the kind of bank that doesn't even see robbers. We're more like a business office, no cash, everything's done by draft."

Looking up from his dinner, he replied, "Well, I guess you'll never have to worry about my name crossing your desk."

Changing the subject, he asked, "When do you think you'll

plan your next trip home?"

"I can't say for sure. I think it'll have to wait until the Christmas holiday. What are your plans?"

"I don't have any really. I'll probably just pop by and see my family, you know- sisters and brothers with their kids," he said pausing, "I'll tell you what I will do. On my list to Santa, I'm asking for a crockpot. This roast beef is outstanding."

"Do you really like the roast beef?" she asked.

"I sure do. I guess it's the way you've added the vegetables. The juices all seem to blend together with the beef."

Putting down her fork, she looked across the table, "The meat isn't beef, it's venison. My mother gave me the roast to bring back."

"I've never tasted it before, but if this is the result, I'll become a hunter. I'll have to get you to show me how."

"Well, it won't be this year. The reason is, opening day for deer was Monday after Thanksgiving, and only lasts two weeks. My dad got this deer during archery season in October. My family keeps a freezer pretty well stocked with deer meat."

After a pleasant dinner and dessert, they small talked until 8. Looking at the time, he said, "Here, let me help you clear away the dishes."

"No, I'll do it. I wanted to pay you back for taking me out for Thanksgiving dinner."

He replied jokingly, "I'll have to tell the cook at the Hofbrau House to add venison to the menu. It'll be a big hit."

Laughing, she commented, "Just as long as he doesn't tell them it's deer meat. That turns some people off before they try it, you know, killing Bambi's father."

"I have to express, if you would have told me what it was

before I tried it, my expectations may have been hampered by knowing what it was too. I have to be going. Are you sure you don't want me to help clean up?"

"No, I'll be fine," hesitating for a moment, she added, "I thought you might want to stay for awhile."

Wondering whether it was an invite, to continue the kiss from when they last met, he replied, "Only if you'll let me help with the cleanup."

Tossing a dish towel to him she said, "Ok, you can dry."

After clearing everything away, they sat on the sofa. She asked, "Randy, you don't seem like your usual self this evening. You're usually talkative. Is there something on your mind?"

Brushing off her question with a smile, he replied, "No, just thinking about the job. You know, cop stuff."

"Well, try not to let it worry you."

Leaning forward, he kissed her replying, "I won't." After a few more kisses and words of conversation, they parted for the evening.

When Randy opened the door to his apartment, the phone began ringing. Hurrying to pick it up, he quickly said, "Hello, who's calling?"

There was still someone on the line, but they didn't speak. He repeated, "Hello, who is this?" without an answer, whoever was calling didn't speak, but hung up. Looking at the phone for a few minutes, he decided it may have been someone who dialed the wrong number. Not recognizing his voice, they opted to hang up.

***

The following morning, he met Charlotte in the parking lot getting ready to leave for work. She rolled down her window and said, "Randy be careful today."

"Thanks, Charlotte. You be careful driving too."

"I will," she replied, giving him a wave as she pulled away.

After getting in the car, he noticed an envelope under the windshield wiper. Thinking *it may have been a note from Charlotte,* he smiled then got out to retrieve it. Opening it, he was shocked. It wasn't from Charlotte. The note read, "Keep the hell out of things that aren't your business," it was unsigned.

He thought, *I wonder who would have balls enough to threaten me. Could it be Eric?* He'd have to wait until he got to the district and ask if Champ can possibly recognize the hand writing. Arriving late, he saw Champ as she was exiting the building. Rolling down the window, he yelled out, "Hey Champ, come here a second. I want to show you something."

"What is it Randy?" she said, coming in his direction.

Opening the passenger door he said, "Get in."

Taking the note from the envelope, he asked her to read it. After reading it she gave him a surprised look, "Damn, where did you get this?"

"I found it under my windshield wiper this morning."

"I wonder who the fuck would have the balls to confront you."

"I don't know. I wanted to ask if you could possibly recognize if the handwriting was Eric's."

After examining it for a few moments, she said, "It's not Eric's, that's for sure."

"Does it look like Jimmy's?"

"I can't say. He always prints his reports like most cops."

"Well, it's getting close to home. Do me a favor, try and find out if it's Jimmy's."

"Ok, I'll do that," getting out of the car she turned and said, "Randy, I'm sorry you got caught up in all this shit."

"It's not your fault. Nobody's going to dictate to me what I do."

Putting the note back in the glove box, he went into the building. Entering the operations room, he picked up a portable radio. Corporal Tyler said, "Randy, you know you have the New Year's parade, right?"

Looking over his shoulder, he replied, "What else is new? I only missed one of those damn parades in 18 years. What assignment does five-squad have?"

"You have the front steps of the Bellevue Stratton, you and the captain's clerk, Jimmy Raffer."

"Thanks, loads. Who gifted us with that?" he asked.

"The captain's clerk I guess. He must have figured you wouldn't mind."

"I guess he doesn't realize we have to keep people from entering the building through the front door. They set up a checkpoint on the side of the building, so people don't just come in off the street and crash parties going on in different suites. It's a pain in the ass."

"Well, the captain wanted me to notify everyone. Just think, you won't have to be there at 6 like the rest of us to set up barricades. Your detail doesn't start until 7."

Looking up from signing out the portable radio, Randy said, "It's still a long day. We can't leave until most of the crowd is gone and hotel security can take over again. That's always about 7 o'clock."

After leaving the operations room, he headed downstairs to his locker. Seeing Jimmy getting ready to leave, he asked, "Did you and Champ get your assignment for the parade?"

Jimmy replied as he reached in his locker for his jacket, "Yeah, Corporal Tyler just told us. He couldn't wait till after Christmas to deliver that news could he, the prick?"

Randy replied, "Since two-squad has the parade too, it really doesn't matter. I guess he figured misery loves company, as the saying goes. By the way, what are working conditions going to be like now, between you and Champ?"

Giving Randy a stern look he asked, "Are you the one that called my wife and told her about us?"

Randy couldn't believe he was accusing him. Looking at Jimmy, he replied bluntly, "Hey Jimmy, go fuck yourself__ asshole. Why the fuck would I do that?"

He seemed to back off at the hostile answer, but quickly recovered saying, "Well, it seems like you've been coaching her these last couple months."

Closing his locker, Randy got face to face with little room to spare between them. "I didn't volunteer. She came to me. It all started with that asshole husband of hers almost running me down on the parking lot. I was going to go after him, but Champ asked me not to pursue it. She wanted to talk to me privately so she followed me to my apartment to finish the conversation. While she was there, she asked me about you. I only told her, I knew you were married but didn't really know what your relationship was with your wife," he said, purposely holding back any statement about the note. As he was walking away, he said, "You know Jimmy, since I've been caught up in this shit, her husband's been hawking me even at my apartment. This morning I found a note under my windshield-wiper, telling me to mind my own business. Do you think he would put that shit there?"

Jimmy looked up from tying his shoe, "You mean he had the balls to do something like that?" Studying his face, Randy saw he showed no outward sign of embarrassment, and Randy could almost wager Jimmy wasn't the one who did it.

"I'm sorry you're caught up in it, but someone called my wife, and I'm sure as hell going to find out who it was," he said.

"Good luck with that," Randy said, as he left the locker room. Leaving the building, he went up the stairs leading to the gas shack. It began snowing when he walked into the district, and there was already a half inch accumulation on the ground. The guy assigned the gas shack duty, was a cop named David Turner. Opening the door, he said, "Hey Dave, how's everything going?"

Looking up from his paperwork stomping the snow from his feet Dave replied, "Pretty good. Got the parade though, that sucks."

Pulling up his coat collar, Randy replied as he headed for his vehicle, "Don't feel bad, I do too."

Before getting in his vehicle, Randy noticed Sergeant Howard swinging through the parking lot. Rolling down his window, he said in a half joking manner to Randy, "You're late!"

After the confrontation with Jimmy, he was in no mood for jokes and quickly replied, "Tough shit!"

Taken back by the comment, Sergeant Howard asked, "What's up your ass this morning?"

Half-way apologizing, Randy said, "Ah, nothing Sarge, just a rough start."

Realizing Randy was pissed at something, he commented as he rolled up his window, "Well, I hope your day gets better."

"Yeah, me too," Randy replied.

Arriving at the beat late, he made an immediate run of the avenue. The stores were beginning to come alive, and the shoppers were already out in force. Going into Alma's for his usual coffee, he noticed Champ sitting at the counter and asked, "Shouldn't you be at the school?"

Looking up at him, she said, "Randy, this place is kind of small. Can we go somewhere where we can have some privacy?"

"No sweat. Did you walk down from the school, or did you drive?"

"I was so pissed off at Jimmy I just wanted to get away from him. I walked."

"We could go into Kramer's. The store is big enough, and I know we could use their office."

Getting off the stool, she replied, "Let's go."

Anxious to know what she had to say, they hastened to Kramer's. Entering the store, he asked one of the brothers standing behind the counter. "Victor, can we use your office for a few minutes?"

Looking up from counting receipts, he replied, "Go ahead Randy."

After closing the door, he was about to ask what she wanted to say, when she took what looked like a picture from her inside jacket pocket. It was a small photograph of Jimmy and his wife.

Randy asked, "What's this for?"

She replied, "I was looking through a desk drawer at the security-room at school for a truancy notice, when I came across this."

"What's so secretive about that? I know___," he was cut short.

"No, Randy, where's the note you found under your windshield?"

"It's in the glove compartment of my car, why?"

Looking at the photo, then at him, he began to realize what she was getting at. Could the hand writing be the same? There was only one way he could tell. "Let me have the picture, I'll compare the writing with the note from my car," he said.

"I think it might be, I remember noticing the word *your* on your note. It had an upward flair at the end. Now look at the word here on this picture, 'From your loving wife,' the same flair at the end of the word *your.*"

"I wonder why she thinks I'm involved with you and Jimmy's business?"

"Maybe it's from when she saw you get involved when she was screaming at me on the parking lot. That's all I can figure."

"Well, before I go jumping to conclusions, let me have the picture. I'll walk back to my car and compare them."

"No, we'll walk to your car and compare them. Then you can drive me back to the school."

Getting to his car, he took the note from the glove box. Comparing them, he said, "The handwriting looks the same."

"Randy, they are the same. What are you going to do about it?"

"There's not much I can do without involving you. You're the one that showed me the picture. When I told Jimmy about the note this morning, I'm positive he didn't know anything about it. How can I tell him we compared signatures and it might possibly be his wife that left the note? I just wonder how she knew where I lived. There would be no reason for Jimmy to tell her."

Looking at him, she smiled and said, "Hey, you don't have to hide it from me. I was in the operations room when Corporal

Tyler asked you if you were running for mayor. All the calls he was getting from different women on your beat. Maybe one of them asked for your address for some sort of emergency, and some asshole in the operations room gave it to her."

"That's a possibility. I better get you back to the school."

On the way back, she said, "You haven't asked what I was going to do about my relationship with Jimmy."

He candidly replied, "I think I'm going to back away from your problem. Only you can settle things with Jimmy."

He could tell she didn't feel comfortable with his statement, and personally, he hated to say it. He felt like someone who desperately needed his shoulder to lean on, and he suddenly took it away. She was quiet the rest of the way to school, and when they arrived, she got out without comment. Returning to the bank parking lot, he continued patrolling his beat.

At 11:30, he went back to Dale's Bar. Seeing Simmy getting ready to open, he asked, "Any more problems with Sergeant Howard?"

"Not me, Randy, but I've been hearing a word here and a word there. Put them together and you begin to get a picture. That guy's making a tidy sum. What's going to happen is one of these bar owners are going to drop a dime. I hate to see that shit. It puts the heat on all of us."

Giving him a hint, he replied, "Well, maybe someone should just drop a dime to the captain first, before going downtown. He's a square shooter and won't put up with that shit."

Looking at him, Simmy stopped wiping the bar replying, "Thanks for the tip. I'll do it. When would be a good time to call?"

"First, get the other owners to go along with it, then start jotting down the time and date he comes in. You'll be better off with something the captain can verify, like what tour of duty he was on at the time."

"Thanks, I'll let the other bar owners know."

Randy replied with a chuckle, "Don't tell Black Harry to keep track. Numbers aren't legal yet."

Simmy laughed as Randy walked out the door.

***

The next couple weeks were just about normal. Other than a few shop lifters and some traffic problems, there weren't any major events. Champ must have taken his word literally about not wanting to get mixed up in her affairs; she never mentioned anything. It seemed like whatever problems she was having, she was taking care of herself, or they were solved. At any rate, they didn't involve Randy, and he was happy about it. He didn't dwell on the similarity of the hand writing on the photograph and the note, and it was never mentioned to him again by Champ or Jimmy.

***

The week before Christmas, Randy was standing at the corner watching traffic, when he noticed the captain's car pulling to the curb. He waved for Randy to join him.

Getting in, Randy asked with a smile, "Boss, what gives, you checking on me?"

"No. I got a phone call last week from a bar owner here in the lower end. In fact, I got a phone call from a second bar owner today too. That's why I'm down here. Has any of the bar owners approached you?"

Acting surprised Randy asked, "About what?"

Hesitating for a few moments he said, "Both callers refused

to identify themselves, but said they're being shaken down."

As if he was surprised, Randy asked, "They didn't leave their names?"

"No, but they did say the person that was doing it was a sergeant."

"That means it could be any one of the four that handle the different shifts. Did they tell you when and what day he came in?"

"I asked that question to the caller this morning. He said he was in last Wednesday about 7 p.m." the captain said.

Not wanting to give away what he knew, Randy said, "Let me think," pausing for a moment, "That would be two squad, Sergeant Howard."

"That's right. I don't want to accuse him without proof, but he's relatively new in the district. I never had these phone calls before he arrived, but I don't want the callers to think I'm sitting on this thing either. I don't need them calling downtown," the captain said.

"I see your point. What are you going to do?"

"You know almost everyone down here, I want you to feel your way around and see if you can come up with anything."

"If they're not telling you boss, what makes you think they'll tell me?"

Seeing a frustrated look on the captain's face, he said, "Ok boss, I get the message, but if I find out, don't ask me who it is."

"See what you can do. I don't want this thing to get out of hand."

Exiting the car, Randy said, "If I find out who the bar owners are, I'll have them call you."

After he pulled away, Randy went back to Simmy's. As he

walked in, Black Harry was just leaving. Grabbing him by the sleeve, he pulled Harry aside. "Harry, have you been approached by a Sergeant?"

"For what?" Harry nervously replied.

"Come on Harry, do you think I was born yesterday? I've been pretty fair with you haven't I? I need a strong favor."

"What do you want me to do?"

"I need you to make a phone call."

Taking him by the sleeve, he led him to the far end of the bar where Simmy was talking to someone on the phone. Waiting until he hung up, Randy said, "Simmy, the captain came down and spoke to me. He wants me to find out who made the anonymous phone calls about Sergeant Howard."

"Look, Randy, I never mentioned who it was. I don't want my name out there like that, I don't want no trouble."

"I figured out a way you wouldn't have to identify yourself."

Not sure of what Randy was about to say, he became quiet.

"It's simple. Harry here can call as if he was just a friend of yours and say he saw you passing Sergeant Howard money."

Looking at Randy unsure of the plan, Simmy reluctantly agreed.

Turning to Harry, Randy asked, "Do you think you can handle that Harry?"

"When do you want me to do it?" he replied.

"Today's Thursday. Call Monday. When you call the captain, I want you to say you were in Simmy's when a sergeant came in and picked up some money."

"Supposin' he asked me what day that was?"

Looking at Simmy, Randy asked, "Well Simmy, when was he here last?"

Simmy turned away, as if he no longer wanted to be a part of it, when Randy said, "That's the only way it's going to get done. If you don't go along with it and one of the other bar owners does, your place is going to get caught up in the investigation anyway."

Reluctantly agreeing, Simmy said, "He was in last Wednesday around 7.

Turning to Harry, Randy laughed and said, "Look Harry, when you call, don't tell him you're a numbers man. Just say you're a friend of the guy that owns the bar."

"Well what if he asks me what bar it is, should I tell him?"

"You'll have to. Tell him the owner was the one who called him, but he's afraid to identify himself. Do you got that?"

Looking at Simmy for reassurance he was doing the right thing, Harry replied, "Yes."

Black Harry was a unique kind of guy. Extremely dark skinned, he was around 50 years old, and about five foot two. He always wore a big apple hat, cocked to one side, and his disguise when he was taking numbers was wearing shabby clothes, and hanging out with a few derelicts just off the beat.

After leaving the bar, Randy returned to the beat. The rest of the tour was without incident, and he was able to report off on time. While he was in the operations room, the captain's clerk came in.

"Hey Randy, you and I have the front steps of the Bellevue Stratton on New Year's Day."

Turning to him, Randy replied, "Thanks. You say that like you were doing me a favor."

"I thought I was. At least we'll be in out of the weather and can step inside the lobby every once in awhile to catch a heat. It shouldn't be that bad."

As Randy walked out the door, he looked back saying, "I guess we'll know that when we're there."

Chapter 9

Arriving at the apartment complex, Randy saw Charlotte getting in her car. Pulling into a parking space next to hers, he quickly rolled down his window and asked, "Are you by any chance going to the supermarket?"

"Yes, do you need something?"

Getting out of the car he replied, "I could use a can of coffee. Here, let me give you the money."

"That's okay, you can pay me when I get back."

As she pulled away, he walked across the lot and entered the building. After looking in the mail box, he entered his apartment. Going through the mail, he took out the electric bill. The rest looked like greeting cards and advertisements. After tossing the junk mail, he quickly glanced at the return to sender on the Christmas Cards, one from Charlotte another from Champ, and several from other squad members. The addresses, no doubt, were from the printed sheets the district makes up for that purpose. All of a sudden, something struck him. Looking at the return address, he found one from Jimmy's address. Quickly opening it, he examined the hand writing. There it was; the same hook on the letter *Y* in, "Wishing *YOU* a Merry Christmas," the same as on the note he found under the windshield wiper. He thought, *"That's where she got his address from."* It all began to add up. She had to have been the one who wrote it. Taping the card against his chin, he wondered if he should confront Jimmy with it. Putting it aside, he decided to bring it to the district the next day to show him.

Leaving the door partially open for Charlotte's return, he went to the bedroom to change. While he was there, he heard a voice from the living room, "I'm back."

"I'll be right out," he replied.

"Ok, do you want me to make coffee? I can sure use a cup."

"That sounds great. I'll only be a minute," he replied.

Entering the living room, he noticed she looked a little shaken, and asked, "Is there something wrong?"

"Coming out of the supermarket parking lot, a guy went through the red light and almost creamed me. On top of that, he gave me the finger."

"Well, at least you didn't get hit."

After the coffee was brewed, they sat down to enjoy it.

"I'm off for the week during Christmas. I'm going home to spend it with my parents," she said.

"Christmas is this Tuesday. Will you be at your parents for the week?" he asked.

"I'll probably leave Sunday and be back on the following Saturday."

"Then you'll be here on New Year's Day?"

"Yes, since it's on Tuesday, I'll have Monday and Tuesday off."

"If you don't already have plans, would you care to spend New Year's Eve together?" he asked.

"That's a deal. Where are we going?"

"I thought we could go for dinner at the Hofbrau House, and listen to the German music. I have to be up by 5:30 a.m. for work. If you wanted to make other plans with someone else that last most of the night, I'll understand."

"No, I don't want to make other plans. Since I probably won't see you until then, I might just as well give you your present. Let me get it. I'll be right back."

Quickly returning, she had two gifts, one large box, and one smaller one beautifully gift wrapped.

"Ho! Ho! Ho, Merry Christmas!" she said.

"You shouldn't have done that. Should I open them now, or wait until Christmas day?" he asked.

"The big one is for you. The little one is for Champ's daughter Lea. If you want to open yours now, that's fine, but give the other gift to Champ."

"You know Charlotte, that's one of the things I really like about you. You're considerate."

Putting his gift on the table, he began to peel away the wrapping. To his surprise, it was an electric crock pot. "Thanks, that's just what I asked Santa to bring," she said, then gave her a light kiss on the lips.

She smiled, "The instructions along with some helpful recipes are in there too. Make sure you clean it out before using it."

"I will. This weekend will be a good test of my cooking skills. I have to work through it, right up to Christmas Eve."

"Don't you have off the weekend?" she asked.

"No, whatever day the holiday falls on, we have to work the avenue right up to Christmas Eve. That is, until the stores close. Even the school detail has to be out there. It won't be too bad though, most of the stores close by 3 p.m. We'll be able to get that time back after the holidays, so it's not really a big deal."

"That's still a real bummer for someone who has young children," she replied.

"Well, when I was in two-squad, the single guys always seem

to work it out, so people with kids get some time off. Since you're not leaving for your parents until Sunday, what are you doing tomorrow evening?"

"I still have some shopping to do for my mother and father."

"Did you already get gifts for your brothers?" he asked.

"Yes, I stopped on the way home from work the other day, and got them gift certificates at Cabella's. It's a gift I can't be wrong giving. Why do you ask?"

"I have to do a little gift buying myself, for a niece and two nephews. I thought maybe you could go with me and we can have dinner someplace afterward."

"That sounds good. Where are we going?"

"There's an Italian restaurant in South Philadelphia I thought you might like."

"That sounds good, what time should I be ready?"

"I'll try to get away early, say around 5," he replied.

"I'll be ready. I have to get back to my apartment, I brought some work home. If we're going out tomorrow evening, I should do my packing tonight."

Walking her to the door, they kissed. "Thanks for the gift. I'm sure Champ will appreciate what you got for Lea too. I'll give it to her tomorrow."

After she left, he put Lea's gift by the door so he wouldn't forget it, then returned to the kitchen for a second cup of coffee. While he was sitting there, he thumbed through the recipe book that came with the crock pot. He thought, *"It looks simple enough. It would probably save me a few dollars too, not to mention a change from the drab choices from Swanson."*

***

Friday morning, he headed for work. Pulling into the lot, he saw Champ getting out of her car and called to her, "Champ, I want you to look at something."

"What is it?" she replied.

"We were right about the note under my windshield," he said, taking the greeting card from his pocket, "Look at this; it's from Jimmy. No doubt, his wife wrote out the greeting cards," pointing at the similarity of the letter *Y*. "There it is, the same hook on the letter *Y*. Did you get one?" he asked.

Looking at him with a frown, she replied, "Come on man, do you think that bitch would send me one?"

Smiling, he replied, "I guess you're right. Oh, by the way," reaching back in the car, he handed her the gift Charlotte gave him for Lea. "This is from Charlotte for your daughter. She wanted me to wish you and your family a Merry Christmas."

"Thanks, Randy. Make sure you tell her thanks from Lea. I know she'll appreciate it. You know, she seems like a special kind of person. Are you two serious?" she asked.

"Not yet, but I'm leaning that way."

"Well, don't wait too long. Somebody might get there before you."

Walking away, he replied, "That's good advice."

After checking out a radio, the captain saw him walking toward his vehicle.

"Randy, have you been able to find out anything yet?"

"No, boss, I've made a few inquiries, but so far everyone seems mum on the subject. I'll ask around again today."

As he was getting in his vehicle, the captain replied, "Stay on it, will you? I don't want this thing getting out of hand."

"Sure thing, boss."

Getting to the beat, he made a pass of the avenue then stopped at Alma's for his usual coffee. She quietly asked, "Have you been able to do anything about that pain in the ass Sergeant?"

"Not really, but I'm working on it. This being Christmas week, we're pretty busy making sure the shoppers won't have a problem."

"I guess you're right. Is school letting out early today?" she asked.

"I think they're getting out at noon. I'll be here, and I think the school detail will be walking down with the students too."

"Good!" she replied.

Finishing the coffee, he returned to the beat. Walking south on the avenue, he heard a radio broadcast of a purse snatch, at Frankford and Sellers Street, two blocks away. Hurrying down the avenue, the captain pulled up in his unmarked car.

"Randy, get in!"

Pulling up to the location, there were several people assisting an elderly woman, who appeared to have a head injury. Getting out of the vehicle, one of the people assisting the woman told Randy she was pushed to the ground after a youth snatched her purse. Getting a description, he relayed it to police radio then asked, "Did anyone see which way he ran?"

"I did," a woman standing close to him said, pointing to an alley just off the beat. From the years he worked the district, he knew the alley was a dead end. There was no exit to another street.

After radioing for a patrol car to take the woman to the hospital, he walked in the direction of the alley, with the captain following slowly in his car. As Randy approached the alley, a youth fitting the description bolted, running west on Sellers Street. The captain sped up and came to a stop at the end of the block, cutting off the youths escape. Trying to run back in Randy's direction, Randy grabbed him by the coat, and flung him head-first against the captain's car. He was dazed but didn't resist, and after handcuffing him, Randy sat him in the rear seat of the captain's car. Returning to the alley, one of the neighbors opened their backyard gate, and handed Randy a purse with some of the cards belonging to the woman who had it snatched.

After radioing for a wagon, he returned to where the captain was parked. After he put the kid in the patrol wagon, the captain noticed an indentation on the rear door of his vehicle, where Randy threw the kid headlong into it. The car was a new unmarked vehicle issued to the captain only a few days before, and after seeing the dent he said, "What the fuck Randy! Why didn't you throw him against the wall or something else?" he asked, running his hand over the obvious dent.

"Sorry, Boss, I didn't realize I did it that hard."

Frustrated, they got back in his vehicle and drove to headquarters for the paperwork.

Driving to the district, the captain said, "That arrest deserves another commendation."

"You know how I feel about that boss. I get my commendation every two weeks in the pay box."

"Yes, but I'm in on it too, so you'll have to change your philosophy again."

He looked at Randy waiting for a comment, but Randy remained silent. When they arrived at the district, Randy got out of the vehicle and asked, "Who's going to fix your door boss? I know a garage on Paul Street that will handle it for no charge."

"Hey, go fuck yourself Randy," the captain replied with a grin.

Randy knew that for several years, the captain had a running battle with the owner of that garage for parking cars being worked on all over the sidewalk. That's one of the things everyone liked about "Mean Gene," he never held a grudge. He could chew your ass out one minute, and it would be forgotten an hour later.

Going inside for the paperwork, the captain said, "Don't forget to keep digging for an answer with the bar owners."

"I won't boss."

After finishing the paperwork for the arrest, Randy got a ride back to the beat. It was already 2:30, so he made another pass on the avenue then called it a day. Going into the locker room, he saw Jimmy.

"Hey, Randy, nice arrest," he said.

"Yeah, it worked out alright. I want to show you something."

"What?" Jimmy asked.

Taking the greeting card from his pocket and the note that was under the windshield wiper from his locker, Randy said, "This! I got this greeting card in the mail yesterday. I take it your wife writes them?"

Before Randy could finish his statement, Jimmy replied, "I'm glad you like it."

"No, that's not what I'm referring too. Look at this note. It's the one I showed you that was placed under my windshield wiper. Remember?"

"Yes, I remember. Have you found out who did it?"

"I think so. Look at the handwriting on the note, especially the letter Y. Now look at the letter Y on the greeting card I got from you. They're identical."

Looking up from the note and the card, Randy could tell

Jimmy saw the similarity immediately.

"You're right, Randy. They are the same. There's no denying it. That's Donna's handwriting."

Randy asked, "Why does she think I'm somehow involved in you and Champ's relationship?" pausing to open his locker Randy added, "You better straighten this shit out with her."

"I don't know why, but I'll sure as hell find out when I get home," Jimmy replied.

"After you do, call me tonight. I'll be home about 10."

Slowly closing his locker, Jimmy seemed to be engrossed in deep thought. Looking at Randy he said, "I will Randy, I will," then slowly walked away.

Driving home, Randy thought, *"If he could so readily identify her handwriting comparing the two now, how is it he didn't recognize the hand writing when he first saw the note? Was it because Randy had the card from her to compare it with, something he definitely couldn't dispute? He wondered how Jimmy would approach her with it, and what the phone conversation would be like tonight when he calls."*

After arriving at his apartment, he immediately began getting ready for his dinner engagement. After getting dressed, he called Charlotte. She picked up the phone on the second ring and before he could speak, she said, "I'll be ready in about 15 minutes. Why don't you come over? I'll leave the door unlocked."

"Suppose I was the insurance-man or someone else you weren't expecting to call? Those words would be pretty encouraging."

She laughed, "I'll leave the door unlocked. I'm trying not to mess up my fingernail polish, it isn't dry yet."

Making sure he had everything he needed, wallet, keys and

the Christmas present for Charlotte, he put on his coat and locked the door. Walking into her apartment, he was somewhat surprised. She had a small Christmas tree in one corner completely decorated. The table lamps were off. But the glow of the multi-colored tree lights made the room look festive.

"I like the Christmas tree. When did you get a chance to decorate it?" he said aloud.

In a raised voice from another room, she said, "I have to confess, I lied to you last night when I told you I had to pack. I said that so I could decorate the tree."

"You should have mentioned it to me. I would have been more than happy to help. When you come out, look under the tree, Santa was here already."

Poking her head around the corner from the hall, she replied, "I'll only be a few more minutes. Should I open it before we go out?"

"That's up to you."

Sitting on the sofa, he couldn't help staring at the tree. It brought him back a few years, when such things would have been foremost in his mind.

Coming out to the living room, she saw him staring at the tree. As she reached under it for her gift, she said, "Penny for your thoughts?"

Looking at her, he replied, "I was just thinking about the time when decorating for the holiday meant a lot to me. It sort of got lost a few years back. I think I needed someone like you to remind me of that. The first few years on the department, it seemed like right before Christmas every year, there was some kind of job that would screw up my holiday cheer."

Giving him an inquisitive look, she asked, "What do you

mean?"

"There always seemed to be an assignment that would kill any holiday spirit I had."

"For example?" she asked.

"I got an assignment one year, two days before Christmas when a guy with five small kids blew his brains out."

Shocked, she asked, "Why did he do that?"

"He was working at a manufacturing company in Frankford that folded. He was only a working stiff, and wasn't able to find any work. His wife became a waitress to pick up the bills that were piling up, and I guess it was too much for him to handle."

"That would be pretty tough on a family. What other assignments did you get that soured you about the holiday?"

"Another time, I was called to a house on Christmas Eve, day work, to meet a complainant. Going in the house, there was a guy in a wheelchair. The living room had a linoleum floor covering with children's clothes strewn around. There was an old sofa and living room chair with worn arms where stuffing was visible, and it wouldn't take a genius to figure out they were dirt poor. There were three small children between the ages of 1 and 6. The 1-year-old had a dirty diaper hanging around his knees that probably hadn't been changed since the day before. The other two looked like they hadn't been washed, and looked like they were wearing dirty clothes for a few days. They seemed to be afraid of me, and hid behind their father's wheelchair. The place was a mess, and from the inside, you couldn't tell what time of year it was. He looked to be in his mid 30's and told me he was in the early stages of Parkinson's disease. He said his wife told him two days before she couldn't handle the home life with him or the kids and left."

"What did you do with that kind of situation?" she asked.

"There's nothing you can do, but call child welfare, and let them handle it. That's why I started taking one of my vacation weeks at Christmas. One day working the police wagon, Jesse and I got a call to a catering hall of a hospital case. In those days, the police wagons carried stretchers for that purpose. A local company was having a Christmas Party, when a young girl about 25 collapsed on the dance floor. She was taking a drug of some sort as I can remember, but she had a few drinks. By the time we got there, she was dead. Another instance was a guy that went to midnight mass and dropped dead of a heart attack in the isle before the services. Now you know why cops are a little hard nose at times."

"I wouldn't call it hard nose. I think the better word is callous," she said, as she picked up the gift he gave her.

He watched as she bent down and examined the present. The box was small, and she rattled it for a clue of its contents. It didn't make noise, so she sniffed it thinking it might be perfume.

"Well you tried everything else. Why not open it and end the curiosity?" he said.

Gently untying the ribbon, she carefully peeled back the wrap, and saw the name engraved on the outside of the box, *Grace Jewelers*. Opening the lid, she unfastened the bracelet. It was a bracelet with different festive miniature charms attached: a wreath, Christmas tree, Santa Stocking, Sleigh, Reindeer, and Santa Claus.

"It's beautiful! I'll wear it tonight," she said, kissing him gently on the lips.

After helping her with her coat, she pulled up the sleeve continuing to admire the bracelet, "You shouldn't have done that."

Embracing her from behind he replied, "No, it's my pleasure. I think being in your company is making me a changed man."

Looking over her shoulder she smiled, "I'm glad."

After arriving at the restaurant, they were escorted to a table. After helping her off with her coat, she commented, "The place really looks nice, adorned with holiday decorations. It's a perfect way to forget about work and enjoy the evening."

He replied, "After the encouragement of possibly having a serious relationship with you, that already erased my mind of any problems I was thinking about."

Scanning the room, he said, "I think I spoke to soon."

"Why, did you forget to do something?" she asked.

"No. Do you see that guy and woman sitting at the table in the corner?"

Looking in that direction she replied, "Yes, are they friends of yours?"

"No, not exactly, the guy is someone that works with Champ. That's Jimmy, he's the one that didn't show up to help straighten her apartment."

"Do you think he's the one that wrecked it?"

"I don't know for sure. That's his wife he's sitting with. They had a hell of an argument at the district. He must be trying to get it resolved. I hope he doesn't notice us."

"That's easy enough to remedy. Why don't we change seats so you have your back toward him?"

"It's too late. He already caught a glimpse of me. He's heading in our direction."

"That's Donna you're sitting with isn't it?" Randy asked Jimmy

"Yes, we're just getting ready to leave. Who's this gorgeous young lady?"

"I'm sorry, this is my neighbor Charlotte. We're celebrating Christmas dinner early. She's going home for the holiday. Charlotte, this is Jimmy, Champ's partner."

Extending her hand, she was cordial and said, "Pleased to meet you."

"Did you straighten things out with your wife?" Randy asked.

"I'm working on it. She's staying with her mother presently, so it's a little difficult. That's why we're here. I'll call you tonight around 10 as we planned."

"I'll be waiting for your call."

Randy watched as he returned to his table and helped Donna with her coat. She glanced in Randy's direction but didn't make any overt gesture to acknowledge his presence. It immediately caught the attention of Charlotte, and after they left, she said, "It seems like she's pissed at you about something. Is she?"

"Let's just say she did something she shouldn't have, and leave it there."

She was about to say something when the food order came to the table, and Randy was happy he didn't have to pursue the conversation any further.

Half way through the meal, the band took the stage. After their warm up, they began playing music. She watched as the other couples vacated their tables heading for the dance floor, and asked. "Do you want to try it after we finish?"

"I'll give it a whirl, but I have to warn you. I'm all thumbs when it comes to my feet."

She smiled, "Well, the people out there don't exactly look like Fred Astaire's either."

"Ok. I think the waitress is coming to our table, do you want another drink?"

Tapping her finger on her chin trying to make up her mind, she said, "Yes, I think I'll be brave and have a highball."

After the waitress left the table, they headed for the dance floor. It was a little crowded, but they found a spot with a little room to maneuver. She out did him with her dancing skills by miles, and it was obviously something she enjoyed.

Getting back to the table, she looked at her watch, "Shouldn't we be going if you want to get a few things for your niece and nephews?"

"I guess you're right. There's a mall not very far from here. Hopefully, they'll have everything I need."

Helping her with her coat, she twirled the bracelet on her wrist again. "I think you're pretty good at picking out gifts. You just don't want to admit it," she said.

While shopping, he glanced at his watch. It was almost 9, and a few stores that weren't busy began turning out lights.

"I think we better be heading back to the apartment. I don't want to miss the call from Jimmy."

Suddenly she went quiet, and didn't comment until they were in the car.

"This must be an important call. Is there something wrong? The look his wife gave you tells me there is."

"It's something I have to get straightened out. He's supposed to call me at 10. If you care to wait in my apartment, I don't think the call will take that long."

"We'll see," she replied.

Opening his apartment door was a completely different atmosphere compared to Charlotte's. If a person had to guess what season it was from inside, they'd be hard pressed to do it. There was no indication Christmas was two days away, other than a few Christmas cards displayed on the end table. After taking off their coats, he asked, "Can I get you something, a glass of wine perhaps?"

"I don't want to mix drinks. I think I'd like a cup of coffee. I'll make it," she said.

"Fine, the coffee filters are in the cabinet over the stove. If you'll excuse me, I have to visit the bathroom."

"No problem," opening the refrigerator she asked, "Where's the coffee?"

He replied in a loud voice from the bathroom, "It's in the cabinet to the right of the sink."

After returning, she said, "Did you know, if you keep the coffee in the refrigerator it stays fresher longer?"

Taking a seat at the table he replied, "I didn't know that."

When it was finished she poured two cups. Occasionally he glanced at the wall clock, 10:10- 10:15- 10:20 "I wonder what's keeping him?" he said.

Just then, the phone rang. "Hello, Jimmy?"

Charlotte made a motion as to whether she should leave, but holding up his finger to indicate wait, she paused. He returned to the conversation with Jimmy and said, "Look Jim, it's already 10:30, I do have company. Is it necessary to come here and talk?"

After giving Randy his answer, he replied, "Ok, I'll wait." Cradling the phone, he said, "Charlotte, I'm sorry for this. He wants to come here and talk. I'll make it up to you. Tell your family I wish them a Merry Christmas."

Opening the door, she replied, "I will. I'll have to get up early anyway. It's a three and a half hour drive to my parents."

Wishing him a Merry Christmas, she kissed him on the lips.

In 20 minutes, Jimmy knocked at the door, and as soon as he stepped in, Randy said, "This better be as serious as it sounded on the phone. You just screwed up my whole evening."

"I'm sorry, Randy, but I think you'll agree after I tell you what I've learned. Remember, I mentioned to you I thought Donna was fooling around?"

"Yes, I remember. Why?"

Hesitating, Randy realized he was examining his face for a reaction to his next statement. He continued, "I was suspicious because over the last two months, she would always find an excuse to get away for several hours. Like, she'd say watch the kids while she went to the mall or something like that."

"How long would she be gone?" Randy asked.

"That's it. That's what I couldn't figure out. It wasn't long enough to have what you would call a serious relationship. Tonight when I went to the house to pick her up to take her out to dinner, she was speaking to someone on the phone as I walked in, then quickly hung up. I asked her if I interrupted something, and she said she was speaking to her mother."

"So, what's wrong with that?"

"When she went upstairs, I picked up the phone and dialed *Star*-11, guess whose answering machine picked up?"

Randy was becoming annoyed at the prolonged conversation. Shrugging his shoulders, he replied, "Whose?"

"Sergeant Howard. I wonder if he's behind Donna being at the district when she caught Champ and me kissing? Maybe he's the one that gave her the idea it might be you pushing Champ and me together too? Why would he be concerned? He's not in five-squad. Maybe that's why she put the note on your windshield?"

He was right, it was a statement that was worthy of cutting the evening short. Thinking for a moment, Randy replied, "I hate to say it Jimmy, but it's time you came clean to Donna about Champ. I know she isn't going to appreciate your infidelity, especially if Champ tells her she's pregnant. I know it's not going to be easy, but I can't see any way out of a divorce for you."

Looking at his face, Randy knew the answer he gave was something Jimmy already realized. There's no doubt Donna was going to file for a divorce, and maybe screw up Jimmy's future in the police department too. The immediate concern was Randy's involvement, and he made it plain to Jimmy he wanted it to end. He offered Jimmy a drink, but he declined. Walking toward the door, Jimmy suddenly turned, "Do you think I should confront Sergeant Howard?"

Realizing he was still grasping for straws trying to figure a way out, Randy said, "Jimmy, did Champ ever tell you about her home life before coming on the department?"

"Only that she had an abusive husband. Why?"

"She never mentioned anything else?"

"No."

"Well maybe it's time you two sat down and had a discussion."

Curiously looking at Randy, he asked, "Is it something you can tell me?"

"Not really. Let's just say you should both come clean with each other."

Randy left it there as he closed the door behind him.

Getting ready for bed, he mulled Jimmy's question over in his mind, *"If it was Sergeant Howard leading her to believe it was him pushing them together, for what purpose? Is he on to him knowing about the shake down of the bar owners?"* Randy wondered.

.

Chapter 10

In the morning, Randy met Charlotte carrying her hanging garment bag and suitcase to her car. She asked, "How did your meeting go, or shouldn't I ask?"

"There were a few thoughts thrown my way, but I think the conversation was more for Jimmy's sake than mine. Here, let me help you with your luggage."

"If you can carry these, I can go back for the gifts I'm taking," she said.

Carrying them to the car, he put them in the trunk. After she came back, he wished her a Merry Christmas, and she did likewise. After kissing, she got in her car. Rolling down her window, she said, "I'll see you when I return on Thursday or Friday," holding up her coat sleeve, to show him the bracelet.

Getting in his car, he replied, "That will be great. Remember, drive safely." He watched as she made her exit from the parking lot.

Arriving at the district, he saw Champ leaving the building, and asked, "Did you see Jimmy?"

"Not yet. Since there's no school, we're assigned beats. He has the lower end and I have the upper end, Cottman Avenue. I'll probably see him after work. He called before I left the house this morning and said he had something important to ask me."

Thinking Jimmy took his advice about asking her what the relationship with Sergeant Howard was, he asked, "Did he say what it was about?"

"No, that's what I'm curious about."

"Well, I hope you get things straight between you two."

"Me too!" she replied.

Getting in his car, he wondered if he should ask Champ later, what Jimmy had to say. Shaking it off, he headed for the beat.

After parking on the bank lot, he made a quick pass of the avenue. Being two days before Christmas, the shoppers were already out in force. Kramer's was opening a little late, and Joe Kramer waved to Randy as he opened the metal security gates. Barry, the salesman, was standing there, and waved in return shouting from across the street, "Hey Randy, Merry Christmas," he said, as he held out his hand letting the flakes build up on his glove. It reminded Randy of what he said when it snowed around Thanksgiving, 'A little dusting, just a little dusting, to make my Christmas sales a little brighter.' Randy laughed as he watched traffic slowly creeping along.

After making his regular appearance at Alma's, he headed for the bar.

Walking in, he was greeted by Simmy at the far end of the bar, "Hey Randy, I have something to ask you."

"What's that Sim?"

Lowering his voice as Randy approached he said, "There was a guy in here last night, a black guy. He was asking me about that sergeant who's been causing the problems. Is he somebody from the police department?"

"I don't know. Did he show you his badge?"

"He showed me some kind of badge that said detective, but I couldn't tell whether it was real or not. I don't know what they look like. I thought maybe one of the other bar owners called downtown about that shit. I just wanted you to know it wasn't me."

"What did he ask?"

"He asked if he could set up a surveillance, that's why I thought he might have been sent from downtown."

"What did you tell him?"

"I told him I didn't want a bunch of undercover cops in here; it's bad for business."

"What did he look like?"

"He was a little shorter than you. Average build, and had a small fro. He was dark complected, really dark."

"What else did he ask?"

"He asked if that police woman from the high school ever came in. I can tell you one thing though."

"What's that?"

"When he left, I went to the front door and watched him get in his car and drive away."

"Did it look like an unmarked city car?"

"No, it was a dark colored Buick 225, that's why I was glad I didn't say too much, it just didn't seem right."

"Thanks Simmy, I'll let you know if anything comes from downtown."

Driving into the district, he thought about Simmy's description of the 225 he saw driving away. It had to be Champ's ex, but why did he ask if she ever drank in the bar? Could he be fishing to see whether she was in there with anyone else? Randy made up his mind to let Champ know what he discovered, and after changing clothes, he got in his car and waited for her to report off.

As she walked to her car, he called to her, "Champ, come here, I have something to tell you."

After getting in, she asked, "What is it Randy?"

"I think your ex tried to pass himself off as a detective in Simmy's bar. He showed Simmy a badge that read detective, then asked him some questions."

Staring at him for a moment she replied, "What kind of questions?"

"First, he asked about Howard coming in to shake him down. Then asked if the police department could set up a surveillance in the bar."

"Surveillance! Surveillance for what?"

"I thought it might have been someone from downtown trying to catch Howard collecting the money. When he asked Simmy whether you ever came in the bar, that's when I asked Simmy what he looked like. He described Eric to a T. Simmy also said when he looked out the door to see where the guy went, he saw him drive away in a dark Buick 225."

"He must be really losing it. I wonder how he knew about Simmy being shaken down?" Champ asked.

"I don't know. It sure as hell wouldn't be from Howard. That only leaves one option, Jimmy. Did you say something to him? I know I never did."

"No, it was only between you and me. Remember when you asked about the support money I received? You told me then, not to say anything."

Looking out the passenger window in deep thought for a few moments, she turned, "Come to mention it, I did say something to Jimmy."

"You mean you told him Howard was paying you support money?"

"No, just that he was suspected of doing the bar thing. I

don't think he would tell Eric about it though. Why would he? It doesn't make sense. I'll ask him when he reports off."

"Do me a favor. If you find out anything, call me at home."

"I sure will. This shit is definitely getting out of hand."

Driving home, Randy realized the earnestness of her words, and wondered what the outcome of her meeting would reveal.

Before opening his apartment door, he could smell the aroma of the stew concoction he hastily put together in his new crock-pot that morning. He had completely forgotten about it until this very moment. By the odor, anyone passing his door would think he was a connoisseur, a real chef. The aroma alerted his taste buds, making him realize he was hungry, and as he lifted the lid, the phone rang. Assuming it was Champ, he was surprised to hear Jimmy's voice.

"Randy, this is Jimmy. I spoke to Champ this afternoon, and she told me about your conversation. She asked if I thought Donna told Eric about Champ and me. I didn't know how Donna would have gotten Eric's address until I got home. I looked in my desk and found a Christmas card list with Champ's address before she split with Eric. Maybe she contacted him about me and Champ, and the conversation somehow drifted to what Howard was like. When he went to the bar, maybe he used the shake down excuse, to find out whether Champ was there with anyone. She did say Eric asked Simmy that question. That's the only thing I can think of."

"Do you think Donna is capable of doing that?"

"The way she is now, probably. I still can't get her to come around to forgive me. In fact she asked me to move out after the holidays. I don't think it's going to be resolved amicably."

"That bad, huh?" Randy replied. Keeping it to himself about

knowing Champ was pregnant with his child, he asked, "Did Champ ever tell you anything about her life before she became a cop?"

There were a few moments of silence before Jimmy answered his question, "She confessed she knew Howard when he worked the district where she lived, and told me they had a relationship."

"Did she say anything else?"

"I asked her why she felt she couldn't tell me about Howard before. I do realize one thing," he said, pausing for a few moments.

"What's that?" Randy asked.

"Eric has really dark skin and Champ is really light. Her daughter is a lot lighter than her. Do you think there could be a connection?"

"Did you ask?"

"Yes, but she never gave me a straight answer. Maybe he's shaking down the bar owners to pay support for Lea."

He hit the nail on the head, but Randy didn't reveal his knowledge, asking, "What do you intend to do with what you discovered?"

"Is there anything you can help me with in that respect?"

"There is something I can do. I just have to wait until tomorrow to set it up."

"Can you let me in on it?"

"I might be able to convince Simmy to call the captain's office again. I mentioned it to him before, and he did call, but he was anonymous. If he calls tomorrow morning and asks the captain about Eric, the captain might take action by getting the detective division to investigate Eric. By posing as a detective, Eric can be charged with impersonating. It might get the investigation going about Howard's bullshit, but I don't see any way out of it for you and Champ."

"Well, I'd appreciate it if you could put it in a way that only takes down Howard."

"I'll try."

After hanging up, he took a bowl from the cabinet. Filling it with a generous portion of his culinary concoction, he got his eating utensils. He was about to put in the first mouthful, when there was a knock at the door. He thought, *"Damn, another interruption. I wonder who the hell it could be."*

Opening the door, he was surprised to see Champ. Rolling his eyes at her, he said, "Come in. I just got off the phone with Jimmy. What is it with you two? You're consuming most of my life."

Hesitating to answer, she said, "Smells good. What are we having?"

"Stew, if I ever get a chance to eat it."

"I thought that's what it is. I could smell it before you opened the door. Go ahead and eat. I'll get my own plate and silverware."

As she reached for the plate, he said, "I guess that means you're staying for dinner."

She paused looking over her shoulder, "Why, don't you want me to stay?"

Feeling embarrassed his words came as a surprise, he recovered by replying, "Yes, but let's not get into heavy conversation until I'm finished my dinner."

"That's a deal." After dishing out her stew, she asked, "What did Jimmy have to say?"

"He said it was probably his wife that contacted Eric. What they discussed is up in the air, but you can be sure, it has something to do with you. I've decided to ask Simmy if he'd call the captain, and ask if a detective was sent to the bar to question him. The captain's bound to want to investigate it. That might crack this thing wide open."

"I hope so. That might just scare Eric away from bothering me too," she said, looking up from her plate. She continued, "You know, you're a pretty good cook."

"Don't kid yourself, the crock pot is a good cook. Charlotte gave it to me as a Christmas present."

"She seems like a nice person, any chance for a serious relationship?"

"You asked me that before. I'm still working on it."

Randy was happy she decided to leave right after dinner. It was taking a toll on him at home, something he never liked to do, and always made it a policy to leave work in the locker-room. In fact, he made it a point at social functions, not to discuss the job. He developed that attitude when he dated a nurse. It seemed as though if there were a few at a party, they always wound up in a group, discussing the hospital, and different cases they treated. The men, if they were cops, usually wound up in another group talking about the job. Putting things aside, he settled in for the rest of the evening.

***

Going into the operations room the following morning, he was greeted by a boisterous, 'Merry Christmas, Randy' from some of the crew. Checking out a portable radio, he looked over his shoulder replying, "Baa! Hum bug. I hope Santa's fat ass gets stuck in the damn chimney."

Corporal Taylor replied, "I hope you don't telegraph your Christmas spirit to John Q Public today."

"No, I just have something on my mind."

Leaving the operations room, he saw the captain coming in the building. "Hi boss, anymore phone calls about the bars?"

"No. Have you been able to find out anything?"

"Not yet, I'm working on it."

"Stay on it, will you. I don't want it to go downtown."

"Ok, boss."

Before leaving the district, Randy had an idea. *"What if he called Simmy now? The captain's in his office. It's perfect timing."* He opened the door of a small office used by Accident Investigation Unit, which was empty. Closing the door for privacy, he looked up the phone number of Simmy's place. By luck, Simmy answered.

"Simmy, this is Randy. The captain's in his office alone right now. Call him and tell him about the detective that spoke to you."

"Are you sure it's alright?" he asked.

"Yes, the timing's perfect."

Randy detected some hesitancy in his voice, and wondered whether he would do it, and after a few minutes, he left the building.

Driving south on the avenue, he thought about the long day ahead. Being Christmas Eve, he couldn't leave the beat until all the stores were closed. If it followed tradition, the owners would begin closing around 3 and the rest between 3 and 6. Around noon, he received a radio call to meet the captain at Frankford and Margaret Street. Realizing Simmy must have called, he was anxious to hear what the captain had to say.

After getting in the car, the captain said, "Randy, I got a call this morning from a bar owner. He said a detective was in his place asking about setting up some sort of surveillance. Do you know anything about it?"

"Did he say who he was?"

"He said he owns Dales Bar. Do you know him?"

"Yeah, boss. That's Simmy's place. There it is," he said, pointing in the direction of the bar.

"I figured you must know him. I'd like you to go in with me."

Exiting the car, they went in. Simmy was hanging a few Christmas decorations, and stepped down from the chair he was standing on. He appeared to be nervous as they approached and asked, "What can I do for you Randy?"

"Sim, this is Captain DeGregorio. He wants to ask you a few questions."

Realizing he was acting as though Randy knew nothing about what was going on, Simmy played along.

"Well captain," __he was cut short.

"Call me Gene," the captain said.

It seemed to put Simmy at ease. "Gene, like I said when I called, there was a guy in here the other night who said he was a detective. He asked if he could set up some sort of surveillance to try and catch a Sergeant hitting on me."

"Hitting on you? What does that mean?" Gene asked.

Simmy looked to Randy for help, and he answered, "He means shaking him down boss."

Gene asked, "Did he show you a badge?"

"Yes, he had a badge with the word detective on it, but I never saw a real one, so I couldn't say whether it was real or not."

"Did you ever see him in here before?"

"No, he just came in the other night about 7. When he left, I watched him drive away in a dark colored Buick 225."

Randy asked, still concealing his knowledge about Eric, "Boss could it have been someone from downtown?"

"I don't know, but I'll find out. If it wasn't, it looks like a job for the detectives. Impersonating is a criminal offense."

Simmy asked, "What do you want me to do if he comes back?"

Gene replied, "Try stalling him and call the police. They'll take over from there. If he leaves, try to get his license number."

"I'll do that," Simmy replied.

As they were leaving the bar, Randy turned, "Thanks Sim, I'll keep you posted."

Walking to the car, the captain said, "It's always good to have someone that's worked a section for a long time. They gain the trust of the people and make it easier for this kind of thing."

"Thanks, boss. I guess you're going home now?"

"No, I just want to ride the district for awhile. Hop in, you can go with me."

"If you don't mind boss, I'd like to stay on the beat until the stores close."

"Whatever you say. If I don't see you, have a Merry Christmas."

As he pulled away from the curb, Randy waved, wondering whether his scheme would work.

By 3, the traffic on the avenue was beginning to wane as shoppers completed their last minute buying. Stores were beginning to close and Randy made a last run of the beat, checking security gates on store fronts.

Pulling on the lock of one of the jewelry store security gates, he thought, *"It's funny, when I first came to this police district there were no gates on any of the store fronts, not even the jewelry stores. I could recall when people exited the two theatres that were once here, and window shopped."*

Times sure have changed, and not for the better. He knew what made a great difference in 20 years. The change of economics was one factor, and the influx of drugs was another. Industrial jobs that once occupied most of the lower half of the district were gone. That, and with the drug culture invasion, seemed to be a recipe for disaster. He felt sorry for the people trapped here as the neighborhood changed. It was the same scenario in the neighborhood he grew up in.

Making a stop at Kramer's, the last store closing for the night, he was offered a nightcap. Getting ready to report off, he saw no harm in it, and as he left, Barry said, "Merry Christmas Randy," waiving a fist-full of cash he received for his commission. After they closed the store, Randy escorted one of the brothers to the bank across the street, to deposit today's cash in the night deposit box.

Getting in his vehicle, he waited till it warmed, then slowly drove up the avenue. Other than a few people still out, everything was quiet. The silence was a stark contrast from the hustle and bustle of a few hours ago, and the lighted decorations adorning the El pillars seemed to add to the tranquility.

Returning to the district, he made his way between the police cars lined up waiting to be fueled. Several Christmas salutations came from cops he knew as they serviced their vehicles. The short cut to the locker room was through the gas shack and down the back stairs. As he entered the hall leading to the locker room, he heard voices coming from an area designated for Juvenile Aid Division. It wasn't a closed room per se, only an open area with a few desks. It wasn't manned on a full time basis, only when there was a person under the age of 18 being processed for one offense or another.

The basement floor made of concrete block as the rest of the building, wasn't acoustically designed for loud conversation. He recognized the voices immediately to be Champ and Jimmy. Passing the small bathroom designated for police women, he rounded the corner. Jimmy was sitting on the edge of a desk with his arms folded, and Champ was pacing the floor in front of him, steadily increasing the volume of her voice, while flailing her arms in anger. Her eyes were tearing and when they noticed Randy they became silent.

"Whoa, whoa- you two, if your conversation is supposed to be private, you're picking a hell of a place to do it. Why not find an empty room or use one of your vehicles? I could hear your conversation from the gas shack."

"How much did you hear?" Jimmy asked.

"I wasn't paying attention, but I looked up the stairs to the gas shack as I passed, and Dave the gas man was looking down. He obviously heard you."

Realizing the situation was addressed, Randy headed for the locker room. As he entered, he looked back. They were coming in his direction still in conversation, but were becoming louder again. As they passed the women's bathroom, Champ grabbed Jimmy by the arm, pulling him in. Randy heard the lock engage on the metal door, and the conversation continued. The sound was muffled, but anyone passing the door could easily make out what they were saying. Jimmy must have mentioned to her about trying to make amends with his wife, and Champ must have told him about being pregnant with his child, something she obviously hadn't told him until now. It sounded as though he was rejecting the idea of being the father, and Champ was assuring him she had no qualms about telling his wife. Randy knocked at the door to let them know they were still audible then returned to his locker. While he was changing, Jimmy walked in and asked, "Randy, how much did you hear?"

"I heard enough to know Champ said she was pregnant by you, and threatened to tell your wife," Randy lied. He only knew it by Champ telling him, but wanted to see what Jimmy's reaction would be. His face became red with embarrassment, and Randy could see he believed him, probably wondering what else Randy might have heard.

"Well, Jimmy, it seems like you have a bigger problem than you thought when you called me. What do you intend to do?"

Turning, walking toward his locker Jimmy replied, "I don't know. If she tells Donna as she threatened, I'm finished. She might possibly go downtown with it too. At the very least I'll be transferred, or possibly lose my job. I'll have to think of something."

As Randy left the locker room he turned and said, "Remember, I told you before about the golden rule at the academy. Three things will fuck you up on this job, 'money, booze and coos.'

Closing his locker, Jimmy replied, "Yeah, I should have had it tattooed on my fuckin' forehead."

As Randy was leaving the building, he saw Champ sitting in her car. She was holding the steering wheel with her arms folded and her head resting on them. Tapping on her window, she looked up. Obviously still upset with what had taken place, her bloodshot eyes told him she had been crying for awhile. Rolling down her window, he asked if she was alright.

"Yes, Randy, I'll be fine. It's just that he pissed me off with denying our relationship. Eric, Sergeant Howard, now Jimmy. It seems like everyone's rejecting me. I can't seem to get a relationship right."

"Champ, I would have thought you were aware of what men want by now. Only you can control their desires. My father, rest his soul, had a saying that's very true. Women are on top when it comes to control of any relationship, married or single."

"What's that?" she asked.

'Women own half of everything in the world, and all the pussy.' You still have your mother and Lea to lean on if you're that troubled. I mentioned it to you before, Jimmy's commitment was only to get what he wanted- a little on the side."

"You're right, Randy, I wasn't using my brain. It's just that Jimmy painted a pretty nice picture, something I was looking forward to."

"Well, try to pull yourself together. It's Christmas Eve and I'm sure your mother and Lea are patiently awaiting your arrival. Go home and try to forget about it."

"Thanks, Randy, that's good advice- Merry Christmas!"

"You, too."

Rolling up her window, she drove away.

Getting in his car, he saw Jimmy leaving the district and thought, '*What a contrast. Champ seems devastated over their lost relationship, but he didn't seem upset or even concerned that he was ruining someone's life.*' Laying it aside, he left for home, determining not to allow their problems infect his days off. Getting to his apartment, he settled in for the night.

***

The following morning, he awoke to church bells clanging from a belfry near the apartment complex. The sun was shining through the window, and pulling back the drape, revealed a clear blue sky. The light snow that had fallen the previous day was still on the trees and grass, but had melted on the concrete and other surfaces. Stretching, feeling pretty good about going to his sisters for the day, he was looking forward to seeing his niece and nephew. Being 7 and 9, they were always fun to watch.

Showering, he thought about Charlotte and what her day might be like. After lathering his face to shave, the phone rang. Going to the bedroom, he picked it up, and put it to close to his face getting some lather on the receiver, "Damn!" he said aloud.

A familiar voice replied, "Who can you be damning this early in the morning?"

"Myself. I'm sorry Charlotte. I just got shaving cream on the receiver."

"Should I call back?" she asked.

"No, bare with me for just a minute while I wipe it off," after doing so, he continued, "Now, Merry Christmas. How are you enjoying your visit?"

"Just fine, we're all at my mother's, the whole family."

"They must have a pretty big house."

"Yes, they do. My brothers asked why I didn't invite you to come along. I told them you had to work late, and the drive would have been too much. I told them you'd be able to come up sometime after New Years; they're anxious to meet you. What did you do last night?"

"Nothing, I got home around 7:30 and just settled in. I'm heading to my sister Eleanor's around noon. I'll have dinner there and will probably be home around 9. When are you returning to the city?"

"I'm leaving Thursday around noon, and will probably be

there by 4. I thought we might be able to go out for dinner."

"That sounds good. I'll see you when you get here."

Returning to the bathroom to finish shaving, he thought about Charlotte's phone call. *"Being with her family and still having the thought of phoning him was more encouraging.* He realized she had all the qualities he sought in a woman, and was definitely looking forward to a serious relationship."

He arrived at his sister's early afternoon in the midst of a throng of relatives already in high spirits. The kids were running around, busily chattering about what they received from Santa, and his entry was barely noticed. When a brother saw him, he came over to give a Christmas greeting. His first words of conversation after that, were, "How's the job treating you Randy?"

Raising his eyes, he let him know, bringing up a question about the job on a day off, was offensive. Realizing his mistake, the brother commented, "Just thought I'd ask."

His sister seeing him, gave him a hug then asked, "Are you by yourself?" Her voice and facial expression told Randy she was disappointed. After pausing for a moment, he replied, "No, my date's up in Scranton with her parents. She's not returning till the day after tomorrow."

Eleanor seemed elated there was finally someone in his life he thought enough to tell her about, and it was like opening up a flood gate to questions.

"Do I know her? Is she someone from the police department? Is she divorced too? When are you going to bring her around?"

"Whoa! Why don't you give it a rest? All in good time sister, all in good time."

Mixing in with the family, he caught up on current events.

Being on his own seemed to be taboo with some family members, but he passed it off as personal preference. He couldn't see living a lifestyle he wasn't happy with, regardless of what they thought. Maybe they'll view things a little differently when they meet Charlotte.

It was enjoyable watching the kids tearing open their gifts and the conversation with family. The delicious food was an added treat, and around 7, everyone began to call it a night. He said goodbye to family members as they left, and was about to leave when Eleanor captured his arm. She was the shortest in the family, but had a way of demonstrating her strength through intimidation, and the uncertainty of consequences if you didn't listen.

"Not so fast brother," she said, forcing him to sit down on the sofa, "We're not finished talking about this girlfriend of yours. When do we meet her?"

Not wanting to have her curiosity bug her until their next meeting, he replied, "How about if I ask if she wants to come over one night this week?"

Shocked at his suggestion, she realized he had someone he thought enough of, who might want to meet family.

"Great, what night should I have dinner?" she asked.

"I didn't say for dinner. I won't know until I ask."

"Fine, just give me some advance notice."

Replying as he headed for the door, "I will."

***

Arriving at the district the following morning, he met Champ going into the building.

"Hello Champ. How was your Christmas?"

"Fine Randy, until I received a phone call."

Stopping to listen he asked, "What kind of phone call?"

"From that bitch Donna, she told me to go fuck myself for ruining her marriage with Jimmy. Do you believe that shit?"

"Forget it. You didn't think she was going to blame Jimmy, do you?"

"I guess not. I was going to tell him about it today, but I think I'll give it a pass. I know she told him he had to move out after the holiday, but I don't know whether she meant Christmas or New Years. How was your Christmas?" she asked.

"Not as bad as yours, obviously, I spent it with relatives. You know, same old- same old. Good seeing everyone though. How did Lea like her gift?"

"She really liked it. Tell Charlotte I said thanks."

"I will. We're supposed to go out to dinner tomorrow night."

"That's good."

Holding the door open for her, they went in. Jimmy was already checking out a radio when they entered the operations room, but didn't acknowledge either of them.

"What's up with your attitude Jimmy?" Randy asked.

Looking at them together, he replied, "You know what I'm thinking."

Randy fired back, "No, damn it- I don't."

Brushing by them, he mumbled words in a low tone Randy couldn't quite make out.

"If you got a beef with me Jimmy, get it off your chest."

Champ looked at Randy to let him know the inside crew was listening. His words got everyone's attention in the operations room, and Jimmy's response was to leave without replying. Randy wasn't about to let it go by without confronting him later, and he knew Champ realized it. After checking out their radios, they left the building. Randy was surprised to see Jimmy exiting his car walking in their direction. Before he could speak, Randy raised his voice, "What the hell's with you?"

"Nothing that you and Champ can't answer," he replied, with a suspicious look as if Champ and Randy had a relationship.

Champ getting between them said, "Jimmy, you're an asshole. You're the only one I've been with. If you're trying to paint a picture to justify not being with me, don't lay that shit on Randy. You know damn well it's your baby."

Without saying another word, he got in his car and headed for his assignment in the upper end. Seeing Champ pissed at his reaction, before getting in the car Randy remarked, "Forget it. His attitude isn't going to change. He's looking for a way out."

"I think you're right. I'm going back inside and ask for the day off. I don't feel good."

"Is it what he said?"

"Partly, but morning sickness more than anything."

"See you later. I'll tell Charlotte Lea said thanks for the gift."

Randy wasn't on the beat an hour when he received a radio call summoning him to Northeast Detective Division. Arriving at the district, he went upstairs. Detective Salvatore Curchino met him as he entered.

"Hello, Randy, I interviewed the bar owner at Dales," he said, looking at his paperwork he continued, "His name's Simmy. Do you know him?"

"Yes, I do, why?"

"What kind of place does he run?"

"Sim's a pretty decent guy. I never had any problem with him. He runs a clean set up."

Re-assured he wasn't being played for a fool, Curchino

replied, "He said he would call if he had any more information on the guy impersonating. Do you have anything to add?"

"Yes, I do. Whether it's the same person, I can't say. Do you know the woman cop at Frankford High School?"

"The one they call Champ?" Curchino asked.

"Yes. I know her ex drives a dark colored Buick 225. When whoever it was went into the bar passing himself off as a detective, he asked Simmy whether she ever came in there with anyone. I believe that's who it was. His name's Eric Johnson."

"Do you know whether he has a record?" Curchino asked.

"I don't know. Champ can give you his date of birth."

"Is she working today, school's closed?"

"She was supposed to, but went off sick. You can probably get her at home. I have her number in my wallet." Taking it out, Randy handed it to him.

After a brief conversation with her, Detective Curchino hung up. Redialing records downtown he relayed Eric's name and date of birth. After a few moments, he replied with a thank you, and hung up the phone. He sat staring at it for a few seconds before Randy asked, "Well, does he or doesn't he have a record?"

"He had two arrests, one for theft, and one for being an accessory to a homicide."

"Homicide, I wonder if Champ knew that," Randy asked.

"I'll call her back and ask."

Redialing, Randy listened to their conversation. It didn't sound as though she was aware of it, and after Curchino hung up, Randy asked, "Sal, how old was he when he got locked up for that?"

"Seventeen, he was found not guilty. It looks like it might have been a teenage gang thing."

"Are you going to pick him up?" Randy asked.

"Definitely, if for no other reason, I want the threat of him being arrested to get information."

"What kind of information?"

"Confidentially, Gene, your captain, wants me to get to the bottom of a Sergeant shaking down bar owners in the lower end. I have an idea who it might be, but I have to have proof."

"Isn't it proof enough that one of them called?"

"Not really. It would be better if we had a few get involved. Up until now, I don't think there's anyone else that's giving their name; any suggestions?"

"You could try The Knotty on Orthodox Street. Benny Tucker owns the place. He's a pretty good guy too."

"Thanks, I will."

Going downstairs, Randy met Gene coming from his office. "Hi boss, I just got finished talking to Sal upstairs. He filled me in on what's happening. I gave him another name of a bar owner. I think he's going to interview him today."

"Thanks Randy, I appreciate anything you can do to keep this from getting out of hand."

Leaving the building, he returned to the beat. There were a lot of people shopping for after Christmas sales, and the avenue was almost as busy as Christmas Eve. In about an hour, he received a call to meet the detectives outside The Knotty Bar. Detectives Curchino and another by the name of Thomassi exited their car when they saw Randy approach.

"Randy, we'd like you to go in with us," Curchino said.

"Sure thing," he replied.

When they walked in, Black Harry looked at them and was startled. He was jotting down numbers from some of the patrons, and began to head for the door when Randy grabbed him by the arm.

"Not so fast, Harry!" he said, pulling him to the side.

"Aw, come on Randy. You ain't gonna bust my balls are you?"

"That depends on you. These guys are detectives. Tell them what you told the captain when you called."

Nervously, he said, "What do ya'll wanna know?"

"We want you to describe the sergeant that shook down Simmy."

Benny, the bar owner, joined the group, "What's goin' on Randy? What's this all about?"

"Benny, these guys are detectives. They want to know from Harry, what the sergeant looked like that shook down Simmy."

Not sure of how to reply, he looked at Harry to give the answer, "Well, come on Harry, tell them what they want to know."

Reluctantly, Harry described Sergeant Howard to a T. Benny verified his description, adding, "I hope ya'll take care of that mother fucker. I run a decent place here. I don't need his bullshit."

After leaving, Randy got in their vehicle and asked, "Sal, how are you going to handle it without going downtown?"

"That's impossible; we have to let internal security handle it."

Randy replied, "The captain isn't going to like it. He was trying to avoid that."

"They're the only people that can set it up. It's fortunate we're turning them on to it by this report, rather than have the bar owners complain to the commissioner's office."

"I guess you're right."

Getting out of the vehicle, Sal said, "Hey, thanks for going in with us."

"No problem."

Returning to the beat, he couldn't help but wonder how this would all play out. The rest of the day was uneventful, and he was looking forward to Charlotte's return.

Chapter 11

Pulling into the parking lot, he saw Charlotte's car. He entered the building and decided to knock at her door first before going to his apartment. She answered it and he asked, "How was your trip?"

"Fine, what time are we going out?"

"I want to take a quick shower," he said, looking at his watch, "How about in an hour?"

"That will be fine. I only arrived a half hour ago. Where are we going, should I dress casual?"

"I want to take you to a special place since we'll miss what I planned for New Year's Eve. It's an old sailing ship converted into a restaurant. I'm wearing a sport jacket, no neck tie."

"Is it the one on the Delaware River at Penn's Landing?"

"Yes."

"I've seen it, but never had the chance to eat there. It looks so nice the way they have the entire ship decked out in lights, especially the rigging. I'll put on something nice. Thanks for the warning."

At 5:30 they left for dinner.

The ship is always outfitted in lights, but with the holiday decorations, it seemed more festive, and being with Charlotte probably added something to the mood. After being ushered to a table in a quiet corner by the maitre' d, a waiter came to the table. After ordering drinks, Randy asked, "How was your trip home?"

"A little hectic, but it was fun being together. My parents are looking forward to meeting you."

Looking up from the menu, he replied, "It flatters me that you've been speaking with your family about me. It brings up another subject."

Putting down her menu, she asked, "What's that?"

"I was doing likewise at my sister's on Christmas day. She, in her pushy way, asked if I would bring you to dinner one night. I was afraid to say *NO*."

Looking down at her wine glass, she slowly raised her eyes replying, "And what did you tell her?"

"I said I would have to ask you, before giving her a date. Would you mind going?"

"I'd love to. When's it a good time for you?" she asked.

"My sister's really a great cook. If you wanted to make it this week, I'm fine with that. Let me know what day you're free."

"How does Saturday sound?" she replied.

"That will be great- I know she doesn't expect me to come without being comfortably dressed so dress casual."

The dinner engagement went well, and they were both sorry to see the evening come to an end. Although they only passionately kissed, it was obvious, that they both wanted it to go further. Instead, they chose to show restraint for the present, ending it with another midnight kiss.

***

Thursday and Friday on the beat was uneventful, but Friday evening, Randy was able to speak to Charlotte. He told her he was looking forward to Saturday's dinner engagement, and in turn, she expressed some concern about being nervous. He assured her it wasn't going to be an inquisition, and put her mind at ease, saying, "Don't worry, you'll be fine."

***

Knocking at her door at 5 p.m. on Saturday, she was ready to go. She had a gorgeous red satin silk blouse with gray slacks. He asked, "I thought we agreed to go casual? You look stunning, but you have me out dressed. I'll have to go back to my apartment and change. Come in and sit down, I'll only be a few minutes."

While he was in the bedroom changing, she said, "You know something, I'm feeling a little nervous about meeting your family."

"I thought we went over this last night?"

"We did. But, I don't know, I just feel nervous."

"Well, my sister was adamant about meeting you. I didn't really have a choice. I guess she figured if I thought enough to speak about you, it was a relationship that may be serious."

There was a few moments of silence, and he asked, "Did you hear me?"

"Yes, I heard you, and what do you think?"

"Coming into the room he replied, "I'd like it to be."

Looking at him she said, "I think I like the idea too. Likewise, my parents hearing I want to bring you up to meet them, feel the same way."

Feeling good about it being a long term commitment, they left.

The visit to Eleanor and family went as well as could be expected. Somehow, when there's a divorce in a family, some family members seem to have a hidden resentment towards a new relationship. Although the new person had nothing to do with a failed marriage, the new relationship has to carry a hidden burden to prove themselves before being accepted. With a sort of inquiry rather than interest, Eleanor asked questions that bordered on being personal between Charlotte and Randy, and he believe Charlotte held her ground quite well in that respect. The evening came to a close, and for a first encounter, Randy thought she did well.

On the way home, she commented on whether Eleanor was normally that inquisitive, and he told her no. He related his experiences with friends that went through the same ordeal. After hearing what he had to say, she seemed to feel better, realizing it was nothing personal.

***

Sunday, he was invited to dinner at her apartment, and brought a bottle of red wine to go along with the roast and potatoes. Although it was a great way to relax, his mind was still on Champ's problems, and the pain in the ass New Year's parade detail.

"What's troubling you?" she asked.

"I'm sorry. I didn't realize I was so distant. I was just thinking about how I have to give up so much being a cop. Maybe it's time I pull the plug and retire."

Looking surprised, she asked, "What do you mean 'give up so much?' You seem to be good at your job."

He replied, "Working holidays, listing to complaints, putting up dealing with lowlifes sometimes, the real under belly of society most people aren't aware of, and much more, refuse to acknowledge their existence."

"Wow! That's surprising. What brought this on?"

"I'm just frustrated with my lifestyle. It's something you don't even realize is changing. For example, what you've seen in our short relationship as strange, I've grown to accept as normal.

Don't get me wrong, there are good aspects of the job. I'll miss the people I work with, but even that's changing. Somehow, our society in general has changed, and it's carried right into the police department. There definitely seems to be a lack of respect between people, especially toward authority."

"Then maybe, as you said, it is time to retire."

Looking at her, he said, "You know, it's funny, tomorrow is New Year's Eve, and I can't plan a night out that doesn't have to come to an end before midnight, unless I want to spend the next day on the parade detail with a hangover."

"Well, we'll just have to ring in the New Year a day late," she said.

He smiled at what seemed to be aggressiveness on her part, replying, "Let's change the subject."

"I agree."

After clearing away the dishes, they retired to the living room to watch football. Propping himself against a throw pillow on the floor, he made himself comfortable leaning against the sofa. She joined him and it took the strain off his mind about the job. It felt good having her close, and after a few passionate kisses, she led him to the bedroom.

"What's this?" he asked.

"Why wait to ring the New Year in late, when we can do it early?"

"No complaint here," he replied.

After a fulfilling night, he realized that's exactly what he needed to pull him out of the doldrums he worked his way into.

***

The next morning after showering, he headed for the district. New Year's Eve on the beat wasn't much different from

Christmas Eve, other than the lack of shoppers. The holiday spirit was still there, but celebrating was geared more toward adult entertainment, and the line of people at the State Liquor Store was testimony to that. After passing by the store, he stopped in at Alma's to wish her a Happy New Year.

"Did anyone do anything about that Sergeant yet?" she asked.

"No, Alma. Why?"

"Benny Tucker from The Knotty was in this morning picking up a tray of sandwiches for the bar tonight. He was telling me about being hassled by him again."

"It's being worked on. I think they're giving him enough rope to hang himself."

As he was about to have his coffee, a radio call came out of a disturbance at the liquor store. Going in, he saw a pair of local alcoholics named Billy James, and a drinking partner named Wilber.

"Billy, what's up?" he asked.

"Randy, this mother fucker's putting less money up, but wants me to buy that shit, Thunder Bird Wine. It's cheaper, but that shit gives me a headache."

Reaching in his pocket, Randy pulled out the few dollars difference and handed it to them.

"Here, Happy New Year."

"Thanks Randy." Putting his hand out, he gave Randy the street hand shake, a slap back and forth on the open palm then a clenched fist, tapping each others, top and bottom.

Leaving the state store, Randy went into Simmy's. He asked, "Has anyone been in touch with you from the police department?"

"They were in this morning. They want me to hand Sergeant

Howard some marked money if he comes in. One of the detectives said they're setting up surveillance in the newspaper office across the street, but I don't know when."

"Well, at least you know the captain isn't full of shit, he wants to do something about it."

"Yeah, he seems like a pretty good guy. Care for a sandwich? I picked the tray up at Alma's this morning. Benny from The Knotty was picking up his too."

"Yeah, she told me Bennie was in. She didn't mention you though. A sandwich sounds good. Can I have a soda to go along with it?"

"How about a beer instead, it goes better with roast beef?"

"Soda will be fine."

He watched as Simmy busied himself preparing for the evening. Half way through his lunch, the door swung open, admitting sun light to the dimly lit room.

"Hey, my man Randy! You drinkin'?"

"No Pauline, just having lunch."

Putting her arm around his shoulder, He could smell she had already been drinking. Sitting on a bar stool next to Randy, she said, "Come on baby, buy me a drink."

Simmy, hanging a *Happy New Year* sign, said from across the room, "Damn Pauline, let the man eat his lunch in peace."

"Ok Sim, I was just askin'," she said, removing her arm from Randy's shoulder. She continued, "Anyway, Happy New Year Randy."

Finishing the sandwich, he thanked Simmy then left. The rest of the day was uneventful and after reporting off, he retired to his apartment.

Before he could take off his coat the phone rang, "Hello,

who's calling?"

"It's me, Champ."

The temporary relief from last night was beginning to fade as he asked, "What is it?"

"I was just confronted by Jimmy's wife. She was at the district when I reported off, firing a bunch of nonsense about me taking Jimmy away from her. She had her two kids with her and kept yelling, 'You've broken up my family!' Jimmy was coming out of the district and had to physically restrain her."

"That's surprising. Did she threaten you?"

"Not directly, but she called me a whore and screamed at me about knowing Lea is Sergeant Howard's daughter."

"How would she know that?"

"The only way I can think of is, it has to be from Sergeant Howard. She accused me of trying to break up his family too. I don't know where this shit's coming from, but I'm beginning to get a little nervous about it," Champ confessed.

"That's for Jimmy and Sergeant Howard to straighten out, there's not really much you can do about it," he replied.

"I know, but Jimmy found his off duty gun in her handbag. He begged me not to lock her up for threatening me, so I let it slide. Do you think I did the right thing?"

"That's strictly up to you. I would at least have made a report of the confrontation."

"If it wasn't for Jimmy begging me, I would have. He's afraid if I did, he might get fired."

"Well, it's too late now, but I would certainly put it to Jimmy, if he can't control his wife, you'll take the issue downtown. It sounds like it's really getting out of hand."

"Maybe I will. I hate to go that route. Maybe I'll wait and see what Jimmy can solve before doing it."

Just then, there was a knock at the door, "Look Champ, I have to hang up now. Someone's at the door."

"Ok, Randy, I'll see you at the parade tomorrow."

"Yeah, I'll see you then."

Opening the door, he let Charlotte in. After a peck on the lips she said, "Happy New Year's Eve. How was your day?"

"Not bad, until I got home."

"Why, what happened?"

"I just got off the phone with Champ, she's still having problems."

Charlotte replied, "It must have been urgent, you're still in uniform."

"Yes, and if you'll excuse me I'll change."

"That's ok, I just wanted to stop and tell you I decided to go to my parents to spend the day tomorrow. I took off Wednesday so I won't be back until Wednesday evening."

"Is that why we celebrated last night?" he asked.

"Not really, I was speaking with an older woman that I work with, she gave me some advice."

Turning to look at her, he asked, "What kind of advice?"

"She said when you're dealing with a middle-age man; you have to make the first move."

With a smile he asked, "Why's that?"

"She said, 'They tend to be less aggressive and sometimes need that little extra encouragement.' I think she was right."

"Well, you didn't see me fight the issue. I thoroughly enjoyed it, how about you?"

"If I didn't, I wouldn't have knocked at the door."

Smiling, he replied, "Thanks, but you better start for your

parent's. I don't particularly like the idea of you driving all the way up there on New Year's Eve."

"I'll be fine."

After kissing again, he carried her overnight bag to the car. "Remember, be careful driving, and call me when you get to your parent's, just to let me know you made it OK."

Waving from the open window, she replied, "I will. I'll see you Wednesday evening."

Standing for a few minutes, he watched as she exited the parking lot. Being without a jacket, he shivered, then looked up at the cloud cover. There was dampness in the air, and without seeing the weather forecast for tomorrow, he hoped snow wasn't forecast for the detail. After returning to the apartment, he got comfortable for the evening.

He tried keeping awake for the big event, watching the pre New Year's celebration on TV, but before midnight, he fell asleep. He was awoken by the revelry of the apartment complex occupants in the parking lot. They were yelling, *Happy New Year,*' and activating various noise makers to go along with their jubilation. Opening the shade of the front window, several party goers looked at him and waved for him to join the celebration. Passing off the invitation, he shook his head and gave a wave, before pulling down the shade. After showering, he organized his uniform and set the alarm for 5 a.m. Just as he slid between the sheets, the phone rang. It could have only been one person. Picking up the phone, he heard Charlotte's voice. "Happy New Year," she yelled with a throng of voices in the background saying the same.

"Thanks Charlotte, same to you."

"I hope I didn't wake you. I just wanted to wish you a Happy

New Year."

"No, I was already awake from the people celebrating out on the parking lot. I'm glad you called, I was beginning to worry. I don't have your parent's phone number to call and find out whether you made it there safely."

"I'm sorry I didn't call sooner, but if you have a pencil and paper handy, I'll give it to you now."

Opening a bedside dresser, he retrieved a pad and pencil, "Ok shoot."

"The number is 570-673-4641, got it?"

"Yes, I have it. I'll see you on Wednesday."

After making a kissing sound, she hung up.

***

The alarm sounded, and it took all he could muster to drag himself out of bed.

After putting on the coffee, he went into the bathroom. Although he showered last night, a quick return would be a sure way to wake up. After putting on his uniform, he poured a cup of coffee into a travel mug and headed for the car.

There was hardly any traffic, and within 25 minutes, he was in center city. Arriving, he joined the other members of the squad that had already been there. They were in the process of setting up the last of the barricades, and he joined in to help. After it was completed, they were called together by the captain. His instructions were brief, "You've been on this detail enough times to know what your responsibilities are," pointing at Jimmy Raffer, his clerk, he continued, "You and Randy have the front steps of the Stratton Hotel, don't let anyone enter or exit from the front door. The hotel wants everyone to go through a security check at the side entrance, just to make sure they're either registered guests or people the guests invited."

Going in separate directions, Randy said, "Raff, I was hoping to skate out of this detail, but since you got us this assignment, I guess it won't be too bad, Thanks!"

Looking at Randy he replied, "I didn't think you would mind. He was going to put me with Jimmy from the high school detail, but when I knew you were a definite, I changed it."

A curious thought passed Randy's mind, and he asked, "I thought you two were pretty chummy, what brought on this change of attitude?"

He was quiet for a few seconds, as they positioned themselves behind the barricade they placed in front of the steps. Looking at Randy he said, "I don't know whether you know it, or whether I should even tell you, but his wife Donna was in the district blasting on Champ and Jimmy about having a relationship."

For a moment Randy didn't reply. Curious, he asked, "When was she there?"

"Last week. Why, did you already know it?"

"No, I wasn't aware of it, but I did see her blasting Jimmy and Champ on the back parking lot at the district last month. She apparently caught them two kissing. It was pretty heated."

Raffer replied, "If it was as heated as the exchange of words between her and the captain, it must have been pretty bad. I could hear the captain constantly reminding her to keep her voice down. From my office, even with the door closed, I could almost hear everything that was said."

He was about to continue the conversation, but was interrupted directing people who wanted to move the barricade and use the front steps to see over the crowd, "I'm sorry, you can't come behind the barricade," Randy said, a repetitive phrase that would become annoying after the first two hours.

"Raffer, I'm going to get a piece of rope from the hotel. We can tie each end of the barricade to the hand rail so it can't be moved."

"Sounds good," he replied.

After returning, he secured it in place and it seemed to work. The day was wearing on, but it was a relief to be able to go inside once in awhile to catch a heat and use the bathroom. For the most part, he avoided the conversation about Donna's visit with the captain, until he formulated in his mind what to ask. He didn't want to give away the fact Champ was pregnant by her partner, and her 9-year-old was a product of Sergeant Howard. He knew, that would have completely blew Raffer's mind.

Periodically, looking out at the crowded sidewalk, people were packed in like sardines, a perfect place for a pick pocket to operate. Randy did see a familiar face from a run in from the past, but as soon as he recognized Randy, he chose to move on. A few minutes later, a guy attempted to move the barricade by untying the rope. Pulling his hand away, Randy said, "Sir, if you want to get into the hotel, you'll have to use the side entrance."

In his inebriated state, he mumbled some offensive words at Randy, but over the crowd noise, Randy let it pass. He began to climb over the barricade again disregarding Randy's warning, and after a few more words Randy decided he had enough of this guy. Raffer came over to assist in getting him on the other side of the barricade, but by this time his words were distinguishable, and he spit at Randy. Normally, Randy let people's words slide off his back when they were intoxicated, but since he spit at him and brought Randy's mother into the conversation, he crossed the line. Reaching over the barricade,

Randy pulled him over, and as a bonus, gave him a few shots to the body with his fist, "There mother fucker, that's from my mom," he angrily said.

Raffer pulled Randy upright quietly saying, "Hey, Randy, there's a guy at the top step with a motion picture camera. He's taking pictures of you."

After handcuffing the drunk, Randy got him to his feet, "Here Raffer, call for a wagon and watch this asshole."

Going up the steps, Randy confronted the guy with the motion picture camera, "Do you want to get a good picture of my badge?" Randy said in a loud voice.

"Oh, no officer!" the man pleaded, "I'm a pilot for TWA. I had a midnight flight and had a 12- hour layover. I'm from Los Angeles, and have a few friends on the police department there. I wanted them to see how real police work."

Randy smiled, "Well, I don't know how long you were watching, but I hope long enough to see the whole story."

Putting out his hand to shake Randy's he replied, "Yes, I did, I particularly liked the words, 'That's from my mom,' he said, laughing, then went back inside. As Randy turned to look, Raffer was still holding the cuffed prisoner, laughing at the exchange of words.

Raffer's laugh is almost comical, the way he puts his tongue against the back of his teeth, as if he was trying to stifle his laugh, was contagiously funny. He was the kind of person that found humor in most things he had to deal with, and being the captain's clerk, that kind of demeanor was necessary.

The parade was winding down, and the crowd in front of the hotel began to dissipate with the end of the parade passing. After breaking down the barricade, they went inside, and let hotel security know they were leaving. Walking back to the staging area, Raffer asked, "Do you know anything about the relationship between Champ and Jimmy? Something I can enlighten the captain on?"

"Only what I told you about the confrontation on the parking lot."

Going quiet for a moment, he looked at Randy and said, "Did you ever see her husband?"

He caught Randy off guard with his question, and wasn't sure whether he was asking as a matter of fact, or from personally meeting him. Randy took a chance replying, "I saw him once-why?"

"He came into the captain's office the day after Jimmy's wife was there. I don't know what they discussed, but whatever it was, as he was leaving the captain's office, I heard the captain say, 'I'll see what I can find out.'"

Randy thought for a moment, *"That must have been the day the captain called Champ into his office."*

Raffer continued, "Her husband is as dark as my shoe. Did you ever see Champ's daughter?" he asked.

"Yes, she's a great little kid," Randy replied.

"Yes, and she's as light as me when I get a summer tan. Champ's light skin, but her daughter looks like she might have been fathered by someone white."

He looked at Randy for a response, but Randy gave him none as they joined the group. The captain said, "You're dismissed. No traffic posts, the 2nd District is handling it."

Those words were magic to everyone's ears. Waiting for the car to warm, Randy thought, *"Another New Year Parade in the history book, I wonder if it will be my last?"* Buried in his own personal thoughts, he never noticed Champ standing next to the car. Rolling down the window he asked, "What gives, didn't you come down with Jimmy?"

"Yes, but his wife showed up at the parade and I don't have a way back. He picked me up at the school instead of the district, so we wouldn't be seen together."

Reaching across to unlock the door, she got in. Giving her a frustrated look, he said, "You still trying to chase that dream?"

"I can't help it Randy; I love him," she said, breaking down crying.

"Well Champ, as the saying goes. You can lead a horse to water, but you can't make him drink."

"I know that, but he thinks somehow you may be responsible."

"Me! Wait a minute. Hold that shit right there. I told his sorry ass he wants to believe that to justify rejecting you. He had no intention of marrying you, or even living with you for that matter. He never did. I think it's time to confront him again."

Taking her hands away from her face, she said, "I should have never involved you in this damn thing. Please don't hurt him Randy."

After a few moments of silence, still coming down from his anger, he replied, "I think it's a little too late for that. He stuck his foot in it, and he wants me to wipe it clean."

The rest of the ride to the district was silent. It was obvious she didn't know what to say, and Randy was at the end of his rope with that asshole.

Chapter 12

Getting to the locker room the following morning, Randy saw Jimmy changing, and without hesitation confronted him. Jimmy stood up as he approached, and probably didn't expect it, but Randy grabbed him by the shirt and shoved him against the locker. The surprised look on Jimmy's face told Randy he wasn't about to dismiss his anger.

"Jimmy, you're a jerk-off. I never expected this kind of shit from you. I'll tell you what, if you don't straighten it out, I'll take this shit to the captain myself and let him handle it. Now, how's that?" He angrily said.

Regaining his composure, Jimmy replied, "I'm sorry you feel that way, but what am I supposed to do?"

Walking to his locker, Randy looked back, "You can start by owning up to your fuck up, and get me out of the middle. You got till Friday to do it. I hate to be a rat, but you leave me no alternative."

Going up the back steps to the gas shack, Randy met Dave the gasman. In his western drawl Dave said, "Hey Randy, how you doin', you look a little pissed about something."

"Na, just dealing with people sometimes sucks."

"Well, that's what we get paid for, to deal with John Q Public."

"I know, but I never expected to have to deal with it from other cops."

Looking up from his small writing shelf, he replied as he turned off the gas pump, "If you're talking about Sergeant

Howard, I know what you mean."

Pausing for a moment before leaving Randy asked, "You're not under his control, why should he affect you?"

"I wasn't referring to me, I was referring to Champ. I heard them two arguing downstairs."

Thinking for a moment about the argument between Champ and Jimmy, Randy asked, "Are you sure it was him?"

"Yes, the argument came out to the hall and he saw me looking down the stairs at him."

"Did you hear what the argument was about?"

Looking up from his desk again, he leaned toward Randy. In a hushed voice he replied, "It was about paying her money for something. Do you think they're into something illegal?" Dave asked.

Before stepping out the door Randy replied, "What made you ask that?"

"I had to refuel two unmarked cars over the last several days that were registered to internal security."

"Well, if it has anything to do with him getting shit canned from here, it makes me happy."

Taking a receipt from the gas pump, Dave replied, "You, and about 50 more cops I know."

"I'll see you later Dave, I have to get to the beat."

"Yeah, take it easy Randy."

Driving to the beat, he wondered what Howard's conversation with Champ was about. *"Could it have been the shakedown money? Did she tell him anything about knowing he was doing it to pay her?"* It would have to wait until he asked Champ. Today was the last day of two squad's day work, and they would be off until Friday night midnight to 8 shift.

***

Randy didn't get a chance to see Champ for a few days, due to her having a few court cases, and was just as glad. He didn't want anything spoiling his attitude, because today was Wednesday, and he was looking forward to Charlotte's return.

After work, he went straight to the supermarket for a pre-cooked chicken with some sides then headed home. Pulling into the parking lot, he saw her car which was a welcome relief. Opening the door to his apartment, he heard a voice from down the hall, "Hey, dinner's here tonight."

Holding up the bag, he replied, "Well, we have two choices. I have cooked chicken with sides, what do you have?"

With a disappointing voice she replied, "Chicken with a few sides."

They both laughed. "I'll be right down after I change," he said "Ok, I'll leave the door unlocked."

It was good conversation over dinner, something he strongly needed. It was relaxing to listen intently as Charlotte chatted on, telling him about her New Year's celebration at her parents. When she finished she asked, "How was the parade detail?"

"About the same, nothing really changes from year to year. I had to straighten out a guy that wouldn't listen. It got out of hand when he brought my mother into the conversation, but I think he learned his lesson."

"Anything else happen that's interesting?"

"Nothing, other than Champ still having problems; she just can't seem to get her act together."

Replying with a concerned look, "I'm sure she'll be fine."

"Well, I hope so, it's starting to involve me, and I have enough to worry about."

"What kind of worries can you possibly have?" she asked.

Looking up from his coffee cup, he replied, "I'd like to have a permanent relationship with you. You don't have to answer right now, but I hope you'll consider it."

"This is somewhat of a surprise. I thought we already made that commitment. What brought this on so sudden?"

"It's not so sudden, as you say. I've been thinking about it for awhile, and you casually approved, but it was no real commitment."

"Well, since you asked so sincerely, let me reassure you, I like the idea too."

Getting up from the table, she did likewise, and they kissed.

It seemed like some of the burden of the job and all the other crap, faded from his mind, and for the first time in several days, he felt relieved.

***

After spending the night together, it felt good getting up next to someone he cared for. She headed for the shower to get ready for work, and he returned to his apartment to do likewise. After showering and dressing, they met in the hallway and kissed lightly before exiting the building. Walking to their cars she said, "We'll have to make some other arrangement in the near future."

"What's that?" he asked.

"Maybe we should save rent by only having one apartment."

"That sounds good. We'll talk about it over dinner."

Arriving at the district, he was met by the captain getting out of his vehicle. The captain said, "Randy, come into my office."

"Ok, boss, let me get my uniform on, I'll be right up."

Entering his office, he motioned for Randy to close the door,

"What's this about captain?"

"Internal Security set up to try and catch Sergeant Howard shaking down the bar owners. I want you to let Simmy know they'll be in touch with him."

"Ok, boss, I'll make it a point to see him when he opens this afternoon. Do you want me to talk to Benny at The Knotty Bar too?"

"You might as well- he's part of the payoff."

Getting to the beat, his first stop was Alma's. "Good morning girls," he said as he walked in the door, "How's the coffee?"

"Good morning yourself," Alma replied, pointing at the sign over the coffee urns. "Did you have the parade detail?" she asked.

"You know, Alma, I was having a good day until you reminded me of that."

"Sorry! You look pretty chipper this morning. What's going on?" she asked.

Leaning forward, he replied, "Keep this under your hat, but I think the problem child is almost out of here."

"That's good news, but that can't be all you're happy about."

"No, Alma, I just began a serious relationship with someone."

That statement even drew the attention of Elsie, Alma's partner.

She asked, "Is it someone from the beat?"

"No, she's a neighbor at my apartment complex."

Turning to look at him she said, "She must be trusting."

Elsie looked around from turning the bacon on the grill, and with a wave of the spatula she added, "Ain't that the damn truth."

"What do you mean by that, Elsie?"

"If I was someone you were steady with, I'd quit my job and follow you around all day, just to keep you honest."

He laughed, and after finishing breakfast, made a run of the beat.

At 11, he saw Simmy opening the bar. Walking across the street, he entered with him. Turning on the lights, Simmy asked, "What's goin' on Randy?"

"Sim, the captain wanted me to tell you there will be two plain-clothed detectives in here later today or tomorrow morning. They're the real deal, so you don't have to wonder. They're going to set up something to try and relieve your problem. I already told Benny at The Knotty."

Looking up from checking the beer cooler, he replied, "Thanks. Are they going to ask me to do anything?"

"I don't know, but whatever they ask, try and go along with it. Sergeant Howard's shift comes back tomorrow night 12 to 8. He may not even attempt it tomorrow, but I'm sure somewhere along that shift he'll be in."

Shaking his head, Simmy replied, "I hope you're right. I hate having cops in the bar. It takes away business."

After doing what the captain asked, Randy phoned the office informing him.

Standing on the corner at the El stop, there was a radio call of a disturbance on the El platform above. Hurrying up the steps, he saw Champ in a scuffle with a youth. Assisting her, he asked, "What gives Champ?"

"I just got back from juvenile court. This asshole was the court case, he never showed up. The judge issued a bench warrant for him."

"Wasn't he represented by a parent or guardian?"

"No, I don't think he has one. He keeps running the streets at night and hanging out at the school during the day. I think he knows the judge was about to put him away."

After assisting with putting him in a police wagon, Randy asked, "You get anything straightened out with Jimmy? I told him he has until Monday to get it settled."

Looking surprised, she replied, "I didn't know you gave him an ultimatum. What was it for?"

"To get me out of the accusation, that I have something to do with your pregnancy."

Thinking for a moment, she replied, "Maybe that's why he's been cold to me the last few days."

"I don't know, but a friendly reminder from you wouldn't hurt."

She replied, "I have to get to the district to handle the paperwork on this kid. I left my car parked at the school, if I see Jimmy, I'll let him know."

Walking away without an acknowledgment, Randy knew it added urgency to his demand.

The rest of the day was uneventful and after a last pass on the avenue, he headed for the district. Going down the back stairs, he was surprised to see Donna coming up, and asked, "What are you doing down here? This is restricted to police personnel."

Surprised to see him, she stuttered for an answer, but finally replied, "I was looking for my husband. Did he report off duty yet?"

"I don't know, I haven't reported off myself. If you wanted to know that, you should ask in the operations-room and not wander through the building."

She turned to go back down, and Randy suddenly realized

she must have been familiar with the building or she would have continued up the stairs.

"Where are you going?" he asked.

Stopping briefly, she replied, "Oh! Which way should I go, I'm confused?"

"The same way you came down."

Continuing up the stairs, he watched until she left the building. Curious as to whether she was really looking for Jimmy, he went back up the steps. From the gas shack window, he saw her get into a Green Chevy. He thought, *"That car looks familiar. It was. It was Sergeant Howard's car. What the fuck's going on here?"*

Seeing Sergeant Howard in the vehicle, he watched until they drove out of the lot. He thought, *"Could she have been looking for Champ?"* He couldn't imagine she would have the guts to confront her on her own if that was her intention.

Entering the locker room, he noticed the trash can piled-high. Another cop that walks the same beat on the 4-12 was getting ready for duty, and asked, "Randy, what's with the trash cans not being emptied?"

Randy said as he opened his locker, "Bruce, the cleanup-man is on vacation this week. He won't be back till Monday."

"Yeah, but you would think someone else would do it."

Laughing, he replied, "It goes to show you how valuable he is. On another note, take it easy out there."

With that, Randy reported off and headed for home, anxious to see Charlotte.

Pulling into the lot, he noticed her car wasn't there. Entering her apartment, he realized he must have made it home before her. Quickly writing a note for her to come to his apartment, he pinned it to her front door. Popping the extra dinner they hadn't used the evening before into the stove, he hurried to the bedroom to change. Within 5 minutes, he heard a voice in the living room, "Randy, the dinner smells familiar. I'll bet it's what we didn't use last night."

Humorously replying, "No, I was in the kitchen all day preparing it. Set the table will you, I'll be right out."

"Ok, what would you like to drink?"

"Coffee would be great."

Entering the living room, he stopped to stare at her. She turned from making the coffee and asked, "What are you staring at?"

"You; and how glad I am you're part of my life. That doesn't make you feel uncomfortable does it?"

"No, but what brought all this on? It must have been a bad day at work."

"Not really. Well in a way yes, but I'm glad to be home with you."

After another enjoyable evening, it was time to return to her apartment, something she didn't really want to do, but didn't force the issue to stay.

***

Friday morning, the operations room seemed to be buzzing with more activity than normal. Accident Investigation Unit was there, and Randy suspected it had something to do with one of the police vehicles being involved in a traffic accident.

"Corporal Silverman, what's this all about, police vehicle involved in an accident?" he asked.

Looking up from his paperwork, Silverman replied, "No, I wish it were that simple. A car ran into a school bus in the upper end. No serious injuries. But I have to notify the parents. The bus was full of kids and that's about 50 phone calls. Some of the parents are at work so it's hard contacting someone to notify them."

As Randy was checking out a radio, he heard one of the operations crew say to a caller, "No, Delores Johnson isn't in yet. Is there a message?"

Randy stopped for a moment to listen. That was Champ's given name. After the officer receiving the call hung up, Randy asked, "Phil, who was that?"

Looking up at him, Phil replied, "It sounded like an older woman asking for Champ. She didn't leave a message, why?"

"No particular reason, just asking."

Late in the day, Randy received a radio call to meet the captain. He thought, *If it was important enough to see him personally, he assumed it was about Sergeant Howard. His squad was coming in for their first night of their tour, 12 to 8 shift.* Getting in the car, his suspicions were confirmed.

"Randy, I want you to notify the bar owners about Internal Security. They're going to be here at some point today and give them bait money. The surveillance will be set up across the street at the newspaper office."

"Is that all boss?"

"That's it for now. Oh, wait! What do you know about Jimmy Bryan and Champ?"

"Only that they have the school detail boss, why?"

"I keep getting phone calls every day from Jimmy's wife that Champ's ruining her marriage."

"Have you confronted them?" Randy asked.

"That's where I'm going now," he replied.

After getting out of the car, Randy watched as he headed in the direction of the school. He wondered how far he would get talking to them, and felt uneasy about Jimmy possibly mentioning him in their conversation. If he did, he wondered what his reaction would be. Giving up on something he had no control over, he headed for the bar, as the captain requested. After filling Simmy in on what he could expect, he headed to The Knotty to relay the same message to Ben Tucker.

After finishing his shift, he was in route to the district when he noticed a green Chevy in front of him. Giving it a closer look, he realized the occupants were Jimmy and Sergeant Howard.

Randy thought, *"What the hell is he doing with Jimmy in the car? He's on duty at midnight. What could they have in common other than their association with Champ? Could he have possibly told Jimmy about Lea being his child? If he did, what could either one of them gain by such knowledge?"* Randy didn't like it, and wondered if he should hang around after reporting off to mention it to her.

Getting to the locker room, he saw Jimmy changing clothes. "Hey Jimmy, the captain stopped by the beat and asked me a few questions about you and Champ. I didn't tell him anything he didn't already know from your wife, but I hope you and Champ didn't drag me into your conversation."

Turning to Randy he replied, "I didn't see Champ today. She never showed up at the school. Maybe she had a court case and forgot to tell me."

Randy didn't mention seeing him with Sergeant Howard, but all of a sudden, it seemed like he was no longer interested in Champ's whereabouts, or what Donna might have said to the captain. Randy didn't like the way things were shaping up, and thought about calling Champ at her mother's. Looking in his wallet for the phone number, he took it out and looked at it, but for some unknown reason, decided not to call.

Before leaving the operations room, he asked Corporal Silverman, "Mark, did Champ have a court notice today?"

Looking it up on the court notice clip-board Silverman replied, "I don't see anything here. Did you ask her partner?"

"I just spoke to Jimmy in the locker room but he didn't know."

"Well, maybe someone forgot to log it in. Why are you asking?"

"I just wanted to speak to her about something."

Reaching in his desk for the phone directory of police personnel, he asked, "Do you want her phone number?"

"No, that's ok, I'll see her Monday."

"Have a good weekend," Silverman said.

"You too." Randy replied.

Driving home, he thought about the phone call he overheard in the operations room this morning, The person who answered said it was an older woman's voice, and Randy wondered whether it was Champ's mother- Angelique? and decided to make the call as soon as he got home.

Entering the building he was about to open his apartment door, when Charlotte came in the front door of the lobby.

"Randy, are you busy this weekend?"

"No. Why?"

"I thought you would want to take a trip to meet my parents."

"That sounds great. I just want to make a quick phone call and I'll pack some things. I'll only be a few minutes. Have you had dinner?"

"No. I thought we might get a bite on the way," she replied.

"That was my plan," he said as he closed the door.

Taking the phone number from his wallet, he dialed. It was picked up on the second ring by Angelique, and his instincts told him she was anxious for the call to be Champ.

"Delores where have you been?" she frantically asked.

Randy's instincts were correct. "Hello Angelique, this is Randy. I'm the guy that helped Champ move, do you remember?"

"Yes, I remember. Did you see her today at work?"

"No. I was calling to ask her something. Hasn't she returned from work yet?"

In her frail voice she replied, "I don't know whether she went to work. She never came home last night. I'm kind of worried."

Hesitating for a moment, not wanting to upset her more than necessary, he said, "I'll make a few phone calls to see what I can find out. I'll get back to you."

"Thank you, very much. Even if it's late tonight, please, don't hesitate to call."

"I won't, and try not to worry."

Hanging up the phone, he wondered who else he might be able to call that would possibly know her whereabouts. The only person would be Jimmy, but didn't think he would know any more than he did, since he didn't know whether she had a court notice for today.

Randy recalled a conversation with Champ about one of the gym teachers at the school, and wondered if she started a relationship with him. Even if she had, he didn't think she would let Angelique worry without saying something. Tapping his fingers on the counter top, he was searching his mind about who might know his name. He came up with the same answer, Jimmy. He works at the school. He would know the gym teacher's name. I'll give him a call. Dialing the number, he got a busy signal.

Just then, there was a knock at the door, "Come in Charlotte, I'm on the phone," he said.

Coming in the room, she saw he was upset and asked, "Is everything alright? You seem to be annoyed at something. It isn't about going to my parents is it?"

"No, it's not," motioning for her to be quiet.

A female voice picked up the phone, and he assumed it was Donna. Not wanting to give away who he was, he said, "Hello, who am I speaking to?"

"I'm Donna Bryan, who are you?"

"This is the district calling. I wanted Jimmy to know he has a court case scheduled for Monday. If he comes in tell him to call Corporal Silverstein."

Pausing for a moment, she said, "Wait one minute, I think he's coming in now. I'll tell him to come to the phone."

Randy could hear her put down the phone and say aloud, "Jimmy, it's the district calling."

In a few minutes, he answered, "Jimmy Bryan. Who's calling?"

"It's Randy. I didn't want your wife to know it was me. Can you talk, or should I just tell you flat out?"

"What is it?" he replied.

"Champ never made work today, and never got home last night. I called her mother and she's worried sick. I remember her telling me about a gym teacher she talked about, so I thought you might know his name. If you don't know where she could be, maybe he does."

"I believe his name is Ronald Rawls. He's the assistant

football coach. I don't know whether he's single or married so if you happen to find his number, be careful what you ask."

"I will. Thanks!"

Hanging up the phone, Randy thought, *"He didn't even ask if he could help."* Randy realized he was home with his wife, but he could have made some excuse to get out of the house and come here. He's come here for lesser reasons.

"Are you saying Champ's missing?" Charlotte asked.

"I don't know. All I know is she didn't show up for work today, and when I called her mother, she said she didn't come home from work last night."

"Is there anything I can do to help?" she asked.

Taking the phone directory from a drawer he replied, "You can help by looking up the name Ronald Rawls. That's the name of the gym teacher she mentioned once. Jimmy just gave it to me."

Handing her a pen and paper, he said, "I'm going in to change clothes, I'll be right back."

Returning to the living room, she said, "Here's the list of names with the spelling *Rawles*. I don't see anything close to the spelling that would sound different. There is one *R. Rawles*, and at least 12 more listed, with varying first names."

"Well, I might just as well start with *R. Rawles*."

Dialing the number, a female picked up the phone. He asked, "Is this the residence of *Ronald Rawles*, I see it listed under the initial *R. Rawles*?"

"No, I'm sorry, may I ask who's calling?"

"I'm a cop in the neighborhood where a high school is located. He's a gym teacher there."

She replied, "The initial is for my first name, Rita."

"Would you happen to know him by chance?" Randy asked.

"No, I'm new in the city, I just moved here from Virginia. I hope it's not an emergency, I wish you luck with finding him."

After thanking her, he made a few more calls, but without success. Charlotte asked, "Could he still be living at home with his parents?"

"I don't know. I'll just have to keep on calling people on the list."

After a few more calls, he got lucky. The person who answered the phone identified herself as Ronald's mother. Randy asked, "Is your son home? I'd like to speak with him."

"He's upstairs, wait one moment." She must have had the phone to her chest; Randy could hear the muffled sound of her calling his name.

"Ronald, there's a call for you."

"Who is it?" he asked.

"He says he's a policeman that works near Frankford High School."

In a few minutes, Ronald answered, "Who am I speaking to? Is this Jimmy the school cop?" he inquired.

"No, Ronald. I'm the beat cop from the avenue. I'd like to ask if you saw Champ today, I mean Delores Johnson. She has the police detail with Jimmy."

"We were supposed to meet at the Riviera Restaurant for lunch at noon, but she never showed. I asked Jimmy, and he said she might be tied up with a court case. Why?"

"When's the last time you saw her?" Randy asked.

Becoming quickly alarmed, he replied, "I saw her Thursday afternoon, when we made the arrangement for lunch today. Is there something wrong?"

Avoid alarming him any further, Randy asked, "How long have you and Delores been seeing each other?"

"Other than speaking to each other at the school, we haven't. Today was the first time we were supposed to see each other. Did you call her partner?"

"Yes, he couldn't throw any light on the subject either. If you should hear from her, could you give me a call? My number is BA-3-3729."

After agreeing, Ronald hung up the phone.

Randy stared at the phone for a few moments, wondering if there was someone else he could call. Snapping him back to reality, Charlotte asked, "From what I gather, he didn't know where she could be either."

Slowly cradling the phone he replied, "No, he couldn't."

"Where do we go from here?" she asked.

"Did you make definite plans to go to your parents this weekend?"

"Not really, in fact, I never told them I was coming. It was going to be a surprise."

"Then, if you don't mind, I'd like to stick close in case anything comes up with Champ."

"I don't mind. I know you're worried."

"Yes, I am. But we still have to eat. Let's go to the diner around the corner."

"Sounds good, let me get my coat."

In a few minutes, they met in the hall then left the building.

Being Friday night, the parking lot was full, and through the diner window they could see patrons waiting to be seated. He asked, "Shall we wait or go elsewhere?"

"I think we're going to run into the same problem wherever

we go. We might as well stay here; maybe it won't be too long of a wait."

At dinner, he was quiet and knew Charlotte sensed it. She asked, "Is there something you're not telling me about her being missing?"

Leaning forward in the booth, he quietly mentioned his concerns, "It isn't normal for Champ not to at least check in with her mother regarding her daughter Lea. I don't like what's happening. I told Angelique I would call if I found out anything. I know she's going to call if she doesn't hear from me tonight. I just don't know what to tell her."

"Well, let's just hope Champ returns home soon, and you won't have too."

Raising his water glass as a gesture he replied, "Me too!"

After dinner they retired to his apartment to enjoy the rest of the evening. At 9:30 the phone rang. Jumping to his feet, he quickly picked up the phone. "Hello, who's calling?"

"Randy, this is Jimmy. Have you heard from Champ?"

"No, but I did get a hold of *Ronald Rawles* the gym teacher. He said they were supposed to meet for lunch at noon at the Riviera Restaurant, but she never showed. If she made that arrangement, she couldn't have had a court notice. You said she never got to the school, and didn't seem concerned when I told you. Is there something I should know? Her mother's at her wits end. Champ never made it home last night either."

He replied, "Ok, I lied. I knew she was going to meet Ronald for lunch. I was there when he asked. I just didn't think it would make a difference whether you knew."

"Well, you're a cop. You know perfectly well with a missing person, you back track until you find the last person that saw them. If you said you were there when he asked Champ, you were possibly the last person that saw her."

When Jimmy didn't respond for a few moments, Randy asked, "Are you still there?"

"Yes, Randy, I'm still here. I was just thinking. Could it have been her ex that's somehow involved?"

"That's a possibility, but I don't think she would voluntarily be in his company. If you know where he lives, why don't you pick me up? We can both go over."

He quickly replied, "I can't do that, Donna is home. She wouldn't like the idea of me chasing after Champ who appears to be missing. She hates her."

"Then, why concern yourself now, when you obviously don't give a shit?"

With that, he replied, "Randy, Donna is coming down stairs. I gotta go."

When the phone went dead on his end, Randy slammed down the receiver. Disgusted with dealing with people he thought he once knew, he was sorry for allowing it to enter his home life. Suddenly he thought, *"When I asked Jimmy to go with me to Eric's, he didn't hesitate. He must know where he lives and the only way he would have known that, was from Champ. Wait a minute. Sergeant Howard knows where Eric lives too. Champ said that's how they first met."*

With everything running together, it was becoming confusing. Turning to Charlotte, he began to tell her his disappointment in Jimmy, when she grabbed his forearm, "Look, Randy, there's nothing we can, or rather, you can do. Maybe the drive up to my parents is what you need. Step back; get away from it for awhile."

216

"I think you might be right, I'll go pack an overnight bag."

"I have my bag already packed. I just have to get my coat, I'll be right back," she said.

Before hitting the turnpike north, they stopped for a cup of much needed coffee to go. With her driving, he looked over at her and realized she was right. The farther away from the city they went, it was like a veil being lifted. Between being pissed off at Jimmy and Sergeant Howard shaking people down, it all began taking a back seat. He was looking forward to meeting Charlotte's family. Two hours of sporadic conversation went by quickly, and before he knew it, they were at the exit exchange off-ramp. He got out the proper amount of money with the ticket, and handed it to her when they came to a stop. "I think this is correct," he said.

Looking at it, she replied, "Yes, it is. I've paid it enough times."

He remarked, "Even with the snow on the ground it's beautiful country. I can imagine it in the fall. The leaves changing must be magnificent."

"It is. That's my favorite time of year," she said.

Within 15 minutes, they were on a secondary road, and he asked, "How far off the turnpike is your parent's home?"

"Another 15 minutes."

Pulling into a driveway leading to a farm, he could see a bright red barn 50 yards behind the house. He asked, "Is this a working farm?"

Looking at him she replied, "Semi-working farm. My father and grandfather were dairy farmers. You just can't make a living being a dairy farmer these days without a huge investment in equipment and several hundred cows."

"Several hundred! Where would you keep several hundred

cows?"

"These large dairies don't have cows that roam free. They only go outside while the barn's being cleaned. That's one of the reasons my dad got out of the business. It's just not natural."

"So, what does he do now?"

"He's semi-retired and my brother's got jobs in road construction for the state."

Coming to a halt in the driveway, the porch light went on and a woman stepped out of the house. Thin, she appeared to be in her late 60's with gray hair. She had a shawl draped over her shoulders holding it tight to her neck. Stepping from the porch she excitedly said, "Hello dear, I take it this is Randy?"

"Yes, mother."

"You should have called, or at least gave me a warning. I could have baked a pie or something."

Randy said, "That's quite alright, I'm sure it would have been delicious, Mrs. Yard."

In a few moments her father stepped from the house. Putting his arms around his wife's shoulders, he said, "You better step inside dear; it's pretty cold tonight."

After shaking hands, Charlotte introduced him, "Mother, father, this is Randy. Randy I'm named after my mom and my father's name is William."

Looking around, Randy said, "Pleased to meet you both, you sure have a beautiful place here."

William replied, "It use to be a working dairy farm, but that's all in the past. I just try to keep the place looking good."

"I know. Charlotte told me all about it."

Inside, the fireplace was aglow, and sitting on the sofa with Charlotte was relaxing. At 9:30, two men entered the house.

Getting to his feet, Charlotte introduced Randy. "Randy, these are my brothers Eugene and Herm."

They were just as the picture Charlotte showed him in her apartment, big men.

Coffee was served, and the conversation was light. Eugene asked, "What's it like being on the police force in the city?"

Charlotte quickly responded, "Gene, he came up here to get away from that. Let's talk about something else."

Surprised at her bluntness, he did as she asked, and began talking about hunting, describing in detail Charlotte's ability.

"Yes, she showed me a picture of the three of you. She'll have to teach me some day. I really enjoyed the deer roast."

William replied humorously, "Charlotte can out shoot the three of us. She'll be a good teacher."

Leaning back in his chair, Randy replied, "When she told me she hunted and fished, I could hardly believe it. With what you're saying, I guess I will have to let her teach me." Everyone laughed.

The rest of the weekend went well, but occasionally Randy's mind drifted back to the city. Having to fight the idea of it invading his weekend, he shut it out of his mind completely. Whatever was going to happen, was going to happen, or rather did happen, and he resolved himself to the fact he couldn't do a damn thing about it. Sunday morning after breakfast they said goodbye and were in route to the city by 11.

Chapter 13

Arriving at his apartment, Randy unlocked the door and stepped in. Just as he anticipated, the light on his answering machine was blinking several times, indicating more than one call. After winding it back, he pushed play. The first message was a call from his sister Eleanor, wanting him to come over with Charlotte for dinner Sunday. The second call was from Angelique, asking him to call her. The third and forth calls were also from Angelique with added panic in her voice. While trying to decide whether to return her call, the phone rang. Looking at the answering machine waiting to hear the message, he heard Angelique's voice. It was almost a plea for him to return her call and his conscience wouldn't allow him to ignore it. Before her message ended, he picked up.

"Hello, who's calling?"

He could tell in her voice by him merely answering the phone, it was as though he threw her a life line, which told him she hadn't heard from Champ.

"Randy, this is Angelique. I've been calling you all weekend. I haven't heard from Champ, and Lea here is in tears. I just don't know what to do."

Stalling for words, he asked, "Did you call all her friends and relatives?"

"We don't have many relatives, and I don't know the phone numbers of her friends."

She began to cry hysterically, and he could hear Lea pleading for her grandmother to stop. He recalled seeing Champ's phone book the day Charlotte and him helped her move, and said, "Angelique, I know you're upset, but it sounds like you're upsetting Lea. When I helped Champ move, I recall seeing a blue telephone book. See if you can find it."

It was a grasp at straws, but the only thing he could think of.

"If you find it, call me. Maybe we can get in touch with someone that knows where she might be."

"I'll look for it. If I do find it, I'll call you back."

Hanging up the phone, he headed for the bathroom. Within minutes the phone rang again. Expecting it to be Angelique, he asked. "Did you find it?"

The familiar voice on the other end replied, "Find, what? Big boy," it was a favorite cliché of the captain. Randy wasn't sure, but thought it might be about Champ being missing. If it was, it was probably because Angelique called the district several times arousing suspicions of Champs whereabouts.

"Hello, boss, I was expecting someone else returning a call. What can I do for you?"

"I'm in my office. Would it be a problem for you to come down?"

"What's it about boss, something I did or didn't do?"

"No, nothing like that, it seems we're missing a police woman. Delores Johnson hasn't been seen since Thursday afternoon. I was wondering whether you knew anything about it."

Pausing for a few moments, Randy asked, "Did someone report her missing?"

"Her mother's been calling the district on every shift since Friday, 4 to 12, asking about her. This afternoon, Corporal Atkins thought he should notify me. I'm glad he did. I called

Delores' mother, Angelique. She said she hasn't seen her since Thursday morning."

"I know boss. That's who I thought it was when I answered the phone. I was just speaking to her. I told her to look for a phone book or something we could use to check with friends of Champ's. Angelique said they didn't have many relatives."

"Do me a favor, come on in. Maybe we can get a handle on this thing."

"Ok, boss, I'll be right there. Just let me get changed and call Angelique."

"Randy, don't come in through the side door to the district. Come in through my private entrance."

"Okay Boss, I will."

Pushing down the button on the telephone, Randy cleared the line and dialed Angelique. The phone was picked up on the second ring and an anxious voice asked, "Randy, is this you?"

"Yes, Angelique. I was just speaking with the captain. I'm going into the district. We'll work on this thing together. Did you by chance find the blue telephone book?"

"Yes, do you want to pick it up?"

Pausing for a moment he said, "That's a good idea. I'll drop by on the way to headquarters."

Arriving, at the district Randy knocked lightly on the captain's door.

"Come in, Randy. Look, I know your philosophy when it comes down to talking about other cops. You keep quite a bit to yourself, but this thing is different. We have a missing cop since Thursday. No one has seen or heard from her. You have to help on this. What can you tell me?"

Taking Champ's private phone book from his pocket, he

placed it on the captain's desk.

"Boss, we can start with this. It's Champ's phone book. I went by her mother's on the way here and picked it up. It might give us a starting point."

Looking up from the book, the captain replied, "Ok, cut the crap. This will only give me phone numbers. Don't tell me what's in the book. I want to know what's in your head. I know you know almost everything that goes on in the district, don't hold back on me, okay?"

There was a look of desperation on his face, and Randy knew although he had a standard of keeping things to himself, he would have to violate that principle. He asked, "Boss, you mentioned before, you received a few phone calls from Jimmy Ryan's wife. What did she have to say?"

"She accused Delores of breaking up her marriage," he replied.

"That's all?"

"Pretty much, I just took it as her being a jealous woman. She ranted most of the time about changing his assignment, something I was going to do anyway at the end of the school year. I explained to her that it wouldn't really change things if there was a relationship between them."

Randy realized he knew more than he suspected, and assumed all his information came from Donna. "Are you telling me about the phone call you received from a male caller just before Thanksgiving? You said whoever it was, was in the area of the El, because you could hear it in the background. How many times did that person call?"

"I only remember him calling once, why?" the captain asked.

"Just asking, I know Champ had an abusive husband, so it

might have been him at the time. I know he was trying to get back with her."

Opening the phone book, there were red pen marks beside each name. "I wonder what these marks mean?" the captain asked.

"They might have been made by Angelique. That's Champ's mother. She probably checked off each name after she made the call. Her, and Champ's daughter Lea, are worried to death about this."

Thumbing through the book, the captain looked up replying, "I guess so."

As the captain thumbed through the last few blank pages, he saw one with writing. When he turned back to it, it wasn't a name and phone number, but a written note; something that read more like a diary. Turning back the pages, he read it. With a surprised look on his face he looked up at Randy and asked, "Do you know anything about this?"

Leaning toward the desk, focusing on the page the captain held open, Randy replied, "About what boss?"

Handing Randy the open book, he said, "Read this!"

Trying to hide the fact he already knew about Sergeant Howard's involvement with Champ, he couldn't fake it. Not with the way it read. It was obviously written while she was in conversation with Sergeant Howard years ago. There were doodle marks and a four digit number 7105, as well as a full characterization of her feelings at the time. What disturbed Randy, and surely the captain, was a remark made in pen on the following page. The ink was a different shade, as well as a different ink width, and they wondered if it was more recent. At the bottom there were three numbers 416.

Randy asked, "Boss, do you have a list of personnel?"

"Yes, why?"

Not divulging the reason, Randy replied, "I just want to look at it."

Puzzled at Randy's request, he opened his desk drawer and handed it to him. Looking up the name Sergeant Howard, Randy ran his finger across the page to his badge number. It was the same, badge 416. A patrolman has a four digit number. Sergeants and Lieutenant's have a 3 digit number. Just for accuracy, with identifying it, Randy asked, "Boss, do you have Sergeant Howard's personnel folder?"

Going to his file cabinet, he removed a manila folder, and handed it to Randy. Opening it to the first page, there it was, as a patrolman his badge number was 7105. Coming around the desk he pointed out the obvious. It was a more recent entry. He had only been in the district since September, less than four months. Looking at Randy, he said, "You thought enough about showing me this for a reason; what is it?"

Under the circumstances, Randy couldn't hide it any longer, "Boss, according to Champ, her 9-year-old daughter Lea, is by Sergeant Howard."

Stunned by the revelation, he looked at his watch and said, "I think I'll have both of them in early tomorrow and start the investigation there. Did Jimmy know about Champ's involvement with Howard when he was a cop in the 37th?"

"I don't think so. I think he put two and two together and knew Lea was from a white person, but I assume she never told him."

Thinking for a moment, Randy continued, "I might just as well tell you. Champ told me she was pregnant by Jimmy."

Throwing his pencil across the room; then slamming his open hand down on his desk, the captain pushed his chair away replying, "I can't believe this shit. This sounds like a regular *Payton Place!* Thanks for coming in and shedding some light on this. Maybe a little pressure on these guys might open something up."

Randy asked, "Has anything happened with the surveillance by Internal Security?"

"No, and I was told there was a fight at Simmy's bar on Friday night, and Sergeant Howard didn't go to the scene, something he should have done."

"Do you think he's purposely avoiding it?"

"I don't know. Anyway, it's too soon to tell."

"What are you going to tell Angelique when you call?" Randy asked.

"All I can tell her is we're working on it."

"If you don't need me any longer boss, I'll leave."

"Thanks for coming in. I'll see you tomorrow."

Driving home, Randy couldn't help but wonder where all this would lead. For Champ's sake, he hoped it wouldn't be difficult.

Arriving home, it was a blessing the answering machine wasn't blinking and he attributed that to the captain possibly giving Angelique a call after he left. He was in the apartment only a few minutes when there was a knock at the door. Opening it, Charlotte stepped in, "Were they able to contact Champ?"

"Not yet. I went by the house and Angelique gave me her private phone book. The captain and I went through it, and it shed a little more light on Champ's life. Where it's going to lead, is anybody's guess. He wants me to come in early tomorrow."

She replied, "I guess I shouldn't keep you up then." Looking at the wall clock he said, "It's almost 11:30. You have to work in the morning too, so maybe it's better to say goodnight now. How about dinner tomorrow evening? I'm dying to try my crock pot again."

"I'll see you after work tomorrow," she said, giving him a peck on the lips before closing the door.

Getting up a few times, he thought he experienced the worst sleepless night in years. Something in the back of his mind kept telling him this thing wasn't going to turn out well. Rolling over in bed, he looked at the alarm clock- 5:30, and thought, *"I might as well get up and brew a cup of coffee. It's too late to get back to sleep."*

After putting it on, he headed for the shower. He got dressed and sat at the kitchen table, sipping coffee. It was just what he needed. He thought about the latest entry in Champ's phone book, and wondered just how recent the entry was. Realizing the captain was probably in his office already, he knew he wasn't doing any good sitting here, and decided to head to the district early. At least he'd be there in case something did break.

Pulling onto the lot, he noticed the captain's car still there. His office lights were still burning and Randy assumed he never left last night. Hoping there was something new to tell him, Randy rushed inside. Jimmy Raffer, the captain's clerk, was in his office too, and Randy asked, "Is there anything new?" Raffer shrugged his shoulders replying, "If it's about Champ, no. He called me at home and wanted me to come in early," pausing briefly after closing his file cabinet drawer he continued, "He wants these personnel files for some reason."

"Who's?"

Holding them up he replied, "Jimmy Ryan, Champ, and

Sergeant Howard's, why?"

"Just curious."

Putting them down on his desk, he replied, "You're full of shit! There isn't a damn thing that gets by you in this district."

Smiling, Randy said, "Let the boss know I'm here, will you?"

"He already knows. He saw you drive in. He told me to tell you to go right in."

"Thanks, Raffer."

Before entering the captain's office, there was a loud knock at Raffer's door. Answering in a loud voice Raffer said, "Whoever it is, don't bust my balls this early on a Monday morning. Come in."

Turning to look, the district clean up man Bruce, entered the room and sat down. Leaning his chair against the wall, he said, "What's pissing you off this early in the morning Raffer?"

Breaking Bruce's balls he replied, "I was fine while you were on vacation last week. Now, what do you want this morning?" adding the captain's favorite cliché, "Big Boy!"

"I need the key for the small women's bathroom outside the locker room. One of those assholes pulled it shut and locked it."

Raffer replied, "You were on vacation last week, skated the parade detail, now you want to come in and break balls?"

Randy laughed as Raffer opened the small key cabinet. Searching for the right tag with the key attached and finding it, he tossed it to Bruce. "Here! Why don't you have a sign made up and put it on the door, 'Do Not Lock After Leaving!'

Smiling, Bruce replied, "I should. They do that shit at least twice a week." turning his attention towards Randy, Bruce asked, "Hey Randy, what's new in Frankford?"

"Same old, same old. How was your vacation?"

"I had the kid's home from school for the week, so I didn't really get to do much. Why are you guys and the captain here so early?" he asked.

Raffer replied, "We're working on something important."

Looking inquisitive Bruce asked, "What is it?"

"Champ's been missing since Thursday. No one seems to know where she is," Raffer replied.

Looking puzzled, Bruce left the room.

After he went out, Raffer knocked lightly at the captain's door and they stepped in.

"Good morning boss. Are you early, or didn't you go home last night?" Randy asked.

"I never left. I've been making calls to command most of the night. I think they're going to handle it like a missing person. Sit down, Randy. You're going to help with this investigation."

Looking surprised, Randy replied, "Why me?"

"I called her ex husband last night and he told me about the incident at Champ's apartment." Looking at Randy shaking his head, he asked, "Did you shove your gun in his face?"

Surprised he told the captain, Randy replied, "Yes, boss. He was hawking me and tried to get into my apartment."

"Why would he do that?"

Realizing Eric must have told him about Champ visiting his apartment, he said, "Champ visited me one day wanting to know about Jimmy Ryan's home life. Other than that, I had no involvement with her. The day I shoved my gun in Eric's face, was the day my girlfriend and I were helping Champ move. Someone got into her apartment and really fucked it up. There wasn't anything taken according to Champ; she thought it was a revenge thing."

"What makes you draw that conclusion?"

"Several large framed pictures of her in the living room, and one in the bedroom, were purposely stomped on. It couldn't have been by accident."

After listening to the story, the captain replied, "Do you think Eric knows more about her whereabouts?"

"I don't know boss, but I don't think he wants too much involvement with the police on an official level. He looks brave when it came to harassing Champ, but when he's confronted, he's actually a coward."

Raffer was standing there taking it all in, when there was a knock at the door. Opening it, Sergeant Howard and Jimmy stepped in.

Sergeant Howard asked, "You wanted to see us boss?"

"Yes, I know or suspect you realize Delores Johnson has been missing since Thursday. Do either one of you know anything about it?"

Sergeant Howard replied, "She's not in my squad captain, why should I know her whereabouts?"

Looking up from Sergeant Howard's folder, he replied, "Because you probably know her better than we do. We have her personal phone book with your name in it, and it goes way back to when you were in the 37th as a patrolman."

His face turned red with embarrassment, and he replied, "I wouldn't know why."

Looking at him knowing it was a lie, the captain replied, "Let's cut the crap. Your name is in here with the badge number you had when you were a patrolman."

Looking at the captain, his face became redder. His only response was to confess. "Yes, boss, I did know her then. I had been at her house on domestic disturbances on several occasions, but that has nothing to do with her being missing. Am I being accused of something?"

"No. I'm exploring all the angles of her past. You just happen to be in it."

Jimmy said, "Boss, Randy called me Friday and asked me about her. I told him I hadn't seen her since Thursday. I just assumed she had a court notice Friday and forgot to tell me."

"Your wife has been calling me almost daily ever since the week after Thanksgiving. She's been complaining about a relationship with you and Delores. What do you have to say about that?" the captain asked.

Now it was Jimmy's turn to become embarrassed, "I didn't know she was calling you, Captain. We've been having problems, but I never thought she would do anything like that."

The captain replied, "She wouldn't call me, unless it was police related. Why did she do it?"

"I really can't say."

Looking at both of them, their body motion shifting from one side to the other, told Randy they were both uncomfortable with the meeting.

Suddenly, there was a knock at the door. Raffer opened it to Bruce standing there. He was about to tell Bruce it was a private meeting, when he realized Bruce was pale as a sheet. Bruce stood staring at them for a few moments without speaking, but whatever was affecting him, had to be something very wrong.

Raffer asked, "What the fuck is wrong with you?"

Continuing to look, speechless for a few moments, he finally replied, "The small women's bathroom downstairs by the locker room. I found Champ in it, she's dead."

The captain sprang to his feet, heading for the door, "Are you sure?"

"Yes, boss. By the looks of it, she's probably been there a few days."

Randy was shocked at his revelation, but glancing at Sergeant Howard and Jimmy, they didn't seem surprised.

Everyone quickly left the office following Bruce downstairs. In route, the captain annoyingly asked, "Bruce, a few days, why hasn't someone found her before now?"

Bruce replied, "I was on vacation last week boss. I don't think anyone else cleans that bathroom. With the door being locked from the inside, most likely if someone wanted to use it, they would just assume it was accidently locked. That's why I got the key from Raffer this morning, that's what I thought."

Opening the door, Bruce was right, it was obvious she had been there a few days, the blood on the floor was coagulated and the outer edges of the blood pool were dry. She was face up still in uniform, with what appeared to be a bullet wound entrance near the heart.

The captain said, "I don't see her revolver."

From the doorway they couldn't, and they all stepped into the room, closing the door. Bending down, Randy saw it under the first stall and said, "There it is boss, under that partition."

Before the captain could respond, Sergeant Howard reached under picking it up.

"Why the fuck did you do that?" the captain annoyingly shouted.

Replying as if he didn't understand the statement, Sergeant Howard said, "What boss?"

"Pick up the damn weapon before Crime Lab looked at it?"

"I just assume it was suicide."

By all appearances, it looked like it. But still, with the experience he had on the job, it shouldn't have been done.

Turning to Raffer the captain said, "Call the Chief Inspector at home, and the Crime Lab. Tell them what we have. Bruce, lock the door and post yourself outside until they arrive. Sergeant Howard, Jimmy, come to my office. I want you to write statements as to what you know about her and her personal life. Don't be shy with what you know either, it's for the record. I don't think I have to tell you there will be disciplinary actions against both of you."

"No, Sir," they both replied.

"Raffer, get the master key to her locker; I want to check it out. Tell the Lieutenant to detail another two people to the high school for today. Better yet, tell him to select two new people permanently."

Jimmy heard him as he walked away, and Randy could hear Jimmy grumbling something in a low voice, but couldn't make it out. The captain hearing it, turned to look at him saying, "Don't get pissed off at me. You're the one that fucked up. You had an easy detail and didn't have the sense to see it. Until the decision comes up from downtown as to whether you get transferred or not, you're assigned to three squad, they're on the midnight to 8 shift. When you finish your statement, you can go home."

Randy didn't think Jimmy expected that, and now Sergeant Howard was wondering what was going to be his fate. Randy wasn't sure, but had a suspicion they knew more about this than met the eye. When they were in the captain's office and Bruce came in to tell them, their reaction to hearing it wasn't as it should have been, shocked.

When Raffer returned with the key, the captain opened her locker. The first thing that stood out was a photograph of Jimmy in uniform taped to the inside, and a few with both of them at a neighborhood gym. Taking out the contents on the shelf, the captain laid it on the bench. Sorting through the papers, he found a letter from an Obstetrician. It was a positive report that she was pregnant. Turning to Randy, he asked, "How far into her personal life can you tell me?"

"What do you mean boss?"

"Here, look at this."

Looking at the report, which was dated just after she told Randy she suspected she was pregnant back in November, he asked himself, *"Could that be why when Donna showed up at the Thanksgiving Parade with the kids, it made Champ realize his home life wasn't as bad as he told her?"* Another letter was a restraining order for her estranged husband Eric. The captain asked, "Did you know about this?"

"Yes, boss. I'm the one that advised her to get it. He was locked up for threatening her."

Reaching as far as he could in the rear of the locker, he took out a small notebook, the kind someone would use for a personal diary. Opening it, there were a few notations where Sergeant Howard made support payments. On one page in October, there was a notation of Sergeant Howard hitting her in the face. Randy thought, *"That must be when Smitty saw her in the Green Chevy?"*

Turning to Randy, the captain said, "I hope they put all this in their statements. It's all questionable."

Searching the pockets of her uniform, he found $200 dollars. Taking it out, he asked, "I wonder why she has this in her pocket?"

"I don't know boss. It's been almost two weeks since we were paid. I wonder if it was something given to her recently?"

Turning to Randy, he asked, "What made you say that?"

"I know she mentioned her mother didn't have much, and Champ moving in with her would help out financially. If that's the case, with us getting paid every two weeks and not getting paid until tomorrow, I think she would have brought it home."

"That sounds logical."

With nothing else to search through, he had Raffer secure the locker. Leaving the room, he said, "Come upstairs and write out your report."

"I will boss, but what are you going to do about telling her mother?"

He didn't reply, obviously pondering the question. Entering his office, he frustratingly shuffled the papers on his desk and said, "Randy, I'd like to go to her house and tell her personally. You know her, and where she lives. I want you to go with me."

"Ok, boss, but it would be better if we go after 9. By then, her daughter will be at school."

"That's a good idea. Even at that, it still isn't going to be easy."

"Amen to that, she's a sweet old lady and I know it's going to hit her hard."

Retreating to the outer office with Raffer, Randy began typing out his report. He hadn't been typing very long, before there was a knock at the door. Before Raffer could open it, the Chief Inspector Anthony Pasquale entered the room. Getting to his feet, the chief said, "Remain seated. Is the captain in his office?"

"Yes, Sir, I'll get him," Raffer replied.

"Don't bother, I'll go in myself."

After hearing the captain and chief inspector greet each other, Raffer and Randy strained their ears at the door, trying to hear their conversation. The chief asked, "Have you begun your interviews with people that may have last seen her?"

The captain replied, "Yes sir. I have the two people that are close to this investigation making out reports now."

"That's good. Now let me ask you another question. Are the people writing the reports personally involved?"

There were a few moments of silence before the captain responded, "How did you know?"

"There's been an older woman calling my office and the commissioner for the last two days. She's the mother of the deceased."

"You're right, there is a personal attachment between her and the two people making out their reports, but I don't think it will affect anything other than a suicide. I already took the liberty of moving the person detailed with Delores back to a squad. The Sergeant on the other hand, I was hoping downtown would get involved."

"You mean a demotion or something stronger?"

The captain replied, "I don't think we can go that far. As I said, there's nothing visible to warrant that sort of discipline. If their report reflects anything other than what I know, they can be disciplined for filing a false report."

"Then that's what we'll have to wait for. Where are they?" he asked.

"They're in the small office down the hall, the accident investigation room. Did you want to talk to them?"

"Not until they finish their statements. I saw the crime lab van outside the gas shack. Let's go down to the bathroom and see what they have."

Entering the hall outside the bathroom, the crime lab was almost finished with the scene, and a police wagon was standing by to transport Champ's body to the medical examiner's office.

The Chief asked the crime lab lieutenant, "What do you make of it, Gus?"

"Chief, there's no indication other than suicide until the coroner report comes back and say's otherwise," turning to Gene the chief asked, "Was the weapon in the position that's chalked out on the floor?"

"Not exactly, we didn't see it at first. It was picked up by Sergeant Howard after he saw it under the stall."

The chief replied, "Picked it up! He knows better than that."

"I know chief. I broke his balls about it."

"Well, let's go upstairs and see what their report looks like."

Returning to the office, Raffer said, "Captain, here are the reports from Sergeant Howard and Jimmy. How do you want me to file them?"

The chief took them replying, "I want to read them. Captain, let's use your office and compare what you have."

After closing the door, Raffer and Randy put their ears to it once again. They assumed the silence was the chief reading what was written, and in a few minutes, heard him say, "Something's missing here. Officer Ryan makes no mention of a personal relationship with her. Why?"

The captain replied, "I found a report from an obstetrician in her locker, she must be pregnant. The cop she's on the assignment with may be the father, but we couldn't prove it."

"Why would you think he would deny it?"

"He's already married, and I'm sure at this point, he's not going to say he was."

"Did you know anything about this prior to today?"

"No chief. There was no indication other than a few phone calls about her having an affair by Officer Ryan's wife. I just took her to be a jealous woman."

Listening, Randy could tell some of the blame was being shifted on the captain. With his concern of the district, he couldn't hold his silence any longer. Knocking at the door, their conversation came to a halt. "Who is it?" the captain asked.

"It's me Captain, Randy Bishop."

"Come in Randy, close the door."

After introducing Randy to the chief, he asked, "What can I do for you?"

"I couldn't help hearing your conversation. I do know a little about their relationship."

The chief looking at Randy asked, "What is it?"

"According to Champ, and that's before Thanksgiving, she asked me what I knew about Jimmy's home life. After I told her what I knew, she said she was pregnant with his child."

The chief picked up a paper weight from the captain's desk examining it. After putting it down, he turned to the captain, "I want his report and what you discovered scrutinized as much as possible. I'm going to banish him to west division. I'd really like to see him out of the department."

The captain asked, "What do you want me to do with Sergeant Howard?"

"How much time does he have on the job?"

The captain asked, "Randy, tell Raffer to bring in his file."

Opening the door, Randy relayed his message. A few

minutes later, Raffer entered the room handing it to the chief. After reading it, he turned to the captain and said, "He was disciplined for having a complaint filed by an Eric Johnson. Did you know about this?"

Taking the folder the captain replied, "No, I didn't chief. Let me see."

After reading it, he said, "It looks like a disciplinary action for hitting a complainant. I can't imagine it has anything to do with this, what are you getting at?"

"I'm trying to find a way to get rid of him too. I got word from the commissioner's office he may be shaking down bar owners."

The captain replied, "I didn't know you knew about that."

Randy interjected, "Captain, I might be able to shed some light on the subject. Eric Johnson, is Champ's, I mean Delores' husband. She told me Sergeant Howard was the father of her daughter. That's probably what it was. After I found out what he was doing with the bar owners, I asked Champ if she thought he was doing that to pay her child support. She said she didn't know for sure, but knew he wanted to stop making support payments, then suddenly backed off. Maybe it's because she threatened to tell his wife?"

The chief looked at Randy, "You seem to know an awful lot about her personal life."

"Chief, I guess she wanted someone to confide in. According to her, she just couldn't get a relationship right, and needed someone to tell her what she already knew."

"Thanks for the information. Now, if you'll excuse us, I'd like to speak with the captain privately."

"Sure thing chief," Randy said, exiting the room. He wondered what kind of damage he had done to Jimmy, but felt he did the right thing defending the captain. Sitting in the outside office with Raffer, he was finishing his report when the chief left the captain's office. Looking at Randy, he said, "Thanks officer for your input. Make sure you add it in your report. It's going to the commissioner's office."

"Chief, will this report be confidential?" Randy asked.

Looking over his shoulder as he left the room, he replied, "Strictly confidential."

In a few minutes, the captain emerged from his office, "Randy, are you ready to go with me to see Delores' mother?"

"Yes, boss, I'm almost finished this report."

Closing the door to his office again he replied, "Knock when you're ready."

Dreading the trip, they were pretty much silent for most of the way. Finally, he asked, "Randy, you've been there, what kind of person is Angelique?"

Looking at him he replied, "One of the sweetest old ladies you'll ever meet."

Glancing at Randy, Randy could read the look of despair on the captain's face having to do this, and his frustration was verified with his next statement,

"I wonder if there was anything I could have done to prevent this?" the captain asked.

Randy realized the captain was looking at him, as if in some way, could ease the burden of what he had to do, but Randy could only sit silent until they arrived. Pulling up in front of the house, they hesitated for a few moments; then the captain took a deep breath before getting out of the car. It reminded Randy of an assignment he once had when he worked a police car. He had the unpleasant duty of telling parents, their 14-year-old son was killed trying to hop a slow moving freight train.

Getting to the front door, Randy rang the door bell. After entering, he introduced the captain, and went into the living room with Angelique. She was sitting impatiently wringing her hands together, waiting for the captain to speak, and after the captain told her Champ was dead, she broke down crying. Randy went to the kitchen to get her a glass of water then returned. He asked, "Angelique, should I call a relative to stay with you?"

"If you would, I'd appreciate it," she replied.

They stayed for a half hour until her son joined them, and after telling him what they knew, they left.

Driving back to the district the captain asked, "Randy, you seem to know more about Champ's personal life. She obviously confided in you for that reason. Let me ask you a question. Do you think she would take her own life?"

Pausing to look at him, Randy replied, "I don't really know boss. On one hand, her love for that little girl would make me think she would never do it. On the other hand, with all the bad relationships, and being faced with a pregnancy from a failed love affair, it may have been enough to push her to do something like that."

The captain replied, "I wish she would have said something to me. Maybe I could have helped."

Randy saw how it was affecting him replied, "There's nothing either of us can do now."

Arriving at the district, the captain said, "The crime lab and the medical examiner's vehicles are gone. I guess they're finished. I see the chief inspector's car is still here. I'm not looking forward to this conversation."

"I know. I already made out my report. Unless you feel you need me boss, I'll head for the beat."

"I don't think I'll need you. If I do, I'll call you in."

The beat was uneventful and more than usual Randy looked forward to getting back to the apartment. After the events this morning he needed the solitude. He wondered, *"Should I tell Charlotte, or would she be pissed if I didn't? I think I'll go with not telling her right now."*

It was a pretty quiet evening and she sensed it. Although she asked on several occasions through dinner what was wrong, he never divulged the truth.

***

Going into the locker room the following morning, he saw Jimmy coming off the midnight shift. Jimmy asked, "What did the captain say after I left?"

"It's not for me to say, but I don't think I have to tell you this isn't the end of what he's going to do with you, or Sergeant Howard. I think whatever it is, will be coming from higher up, the chief inspector's car was still here after we came back from notifying Champ's mother yesterday. That doesn't bode well for your situation."

Looking nervous, he asked, "Do you think I'll be fired?"

Randy knew he was looking for more reassurance that he wasn't, but that was the best Randy could do. Closing his locker, Jimmy left.

As Randy walked past the small bathroom where it happened, the door was propped open. Bruce was still cleaning up.

Randy said, "I guess you wish you were still on vacation Bruce. That's a nasty job."

Looking pissed at Randy, he replied, "Thanks Randy, I really need you to break balls reminding me."

"Sorry, Bruce, I wasn't breaking your balls, just stating fact."

"I know, I just don't like doing this shit," he replied.

As Randy headed up the stairs to the gas shack, he turned around and said, "I don't blame you."

Arriving home, he went directly to Charlotte's apartment to tell her Champ had died.

Shocked, she asked, "Of what?"

"It was an accidental shooting. I think the viewing will be day after tomorrow. The family wants it as soon as possible to spare Angelique the prolonged grief. Did you want to attend?"

"Most definitely; I guess there will be a lot of police there?"

"Yes, there always is at an active policeman's funeral, regardless of the circumstance."

"How did it happen?"

Sparing any further questions, he replied, "I don't know. It's a shame for the family though. I know Lea is going to be affected. I hope it won't be too bad."

***

The next several days went by quickly, and Randy checked in with Simmy and Bennie Tucker to see if there were any more complaints of shakedowns. Nothing new was reported, and Randy wondered why all of a sudden Howard wasn't bothering. Was it because he knew he didn't have to pay support money?

***

The following evening, the viewing was solemn. As Randy and Charlotte signed the register of mourners, Randy noticed Jimmy's name was conspicuously absent, as was Sergeant Howard's. Randy stayed till the end of the viewing to see if they'd appear. At 9 p.m. the funeral parlor was closing, and Randy wasn't disappointed; neither one of them showed their faces. He could probably understand why Sergeant Howard wasn't there, but couldn't understand the absence of Jimmy. All of his seemingly concern, certainly wasn't shown by his actions. Randy wondered, *"Did his wife have something to say about it?"*

***

The following day, there was only a private viewing by the family and a graveside ceremony for everyone else. Again, they were both absent.

Laying his personal feelings about them aside, he chose not to make a comment to Charlotte. Before leaving the cemetery, they paid their respects to Angelique and Lea. On the drive back to the apartment, Charlotte's eyes began to tear. Randy looking at her asked if she was alright.

"It's kind of tough when it's someone you know, I guess your emotions run a little different than most people," she said.

Looking at her he asked, "In what way?"

"It seems like you're not emotional at all. It must be the callousness you spoke about from being a cop."

"Not really, that emotion is like elastic, it stretches when you need it," he replied.

After stopping at Smitty's for lunch, they headed home.

***

The following morning, he arrived at the district and took the short cut to the locker room through the gas shack. Dave was on duty filling the awaiting patrol cars and when he saw Randy he said, "Good morning Randy. Did they find out anything more about what might have happened to Champ?"

Randy wasn't paying much attention, and blew off his

question with a no, before realizing what he asked. Getting dressed in the locker-room, Dave's question finally struck him. Randy thought, *"I wonder if he knew something that hadn't been brought out."*

After getting dressed, he went back to the gas shack and asked, "Dave, you asked me if they found out anything more about Champ. What do you mean?"

Looking up from his gas receipts, he replied, "Frankly, I don't believe it was suicide. There's no way she would have done it. Not with the way she carried on about her little girl."

"What do you know about her and her little girl?" Randy asked.

"I lived down the street from her and her husband before we moved to the Northeast. I also know she was seeing Sergeant Howard when he was a cop in our neighborhood. I saw them together a few times in his private car when he was off duty."

Looking surprised, Randy asked, "Did you say anything to the captain about this?"

"No, I didn't think it would matter what happened years ago in another district. I do have one thing to say," pausing for a moment.

"What's that?" Randy asked.

"Last week, on the 4 to 12 shift, I was in here counting out the receipts, and heard what sounded like a backfire from a truck on Harbison Avenue. I was getting ready to go downstairs to the bathroom, when I saw a woman in the hallway at the bottom of the stairs. I asked who she was, and she said she was looking for her husband. I asked if he was a cop then told her she shouldn't be wandering through the building, it was off limits. If she wanted to speak with her husband, she'd have to go to the front desk and ask, like everyone else."

"Did she say who her husband was?"

"Yes; she said she was Jimmy Ryan's wife. She was supposed to meet him after work. Funny though, when she came up the steps, I watched her cross the parking lot and get into her car and drive away. She never went to the front desk."

"What day was that?" Randy asked.

"Let me think, we just started the 4 to 12 shift so it had to be__ last Thursday. Yes, I'm sure it was; it was last Thursday."

"Did you mention any of this to the captain?"

Looking up at Randy he replied, "No, is it important?"

Giving it a second thought, Randy said, "No, I guess not."

During the day, Randy couldn't take his mind off the fact Champ was last seen on Thursday. Coincidental to that, Dave heard what he thought was a backfire from a truck. Seeing Donna in the hallway outside the women's bathroom and hearing the backfire, he wondered if Dave hadn't mistaken it for being a muffled gun shot from the woman's bathroom. Giving it serious thought, he returned to the district and knocked at the captain's door.

"What is it Randy?"

"Captain, did the report from the crime lab on Champ come back?"

Looking up from his paperwork he replied, "Yes, it's officially classified as a suicide by a self inflicted gunshot wound. Why?"

Thinking for a moment, he realized the captain read his mind. Randy had something he wanted to say.

He thought, "*Should I mention what Dave said about Donna being in the basement and the backfire? Should he mention the coincidence of Sergeant Howard picking up the gun destroying any evidence to the contrary?'* Instead he chose to remain silent. To comment on hypothesis would only open up accusations and reveal very little of what was already uncovered. Instead, he diverted his question, "Is there anything I can tell Simmy and the other bar owners about Sergeant Howard?"

Going to his file cabinet, he looked over his shoulder replying, "Yes, you can tell them he's being transferred. Confidentially, between you and me, he's also under investigation for being involved with the rackets. It seems Internal Security found out he's in debt big time with gamblers. That's probably why the shake down more than paying Champ support money."

Closing the cabinet drawer, he asked, "Is there something else you want to talk to me about?"

"No, boss, I just wanted to know what to tell them."

Leaving the office, Randy still had questions. Trying to put it all in perspective, he asked himself, *"Did Sergeant Howard pick up the gun because he really felt it was suicide, or to destroy fingerprints? He would have wanted her eliminated for two reasons. One would be keeping Champ from telling his wife that Lea was his child, and he's been paying support for 9 years. Number two, did she know he was involved with gamblers and threaten to expose him? Could Jimmy have enough of a motive because she threatened to tell his wife she's pregnant by him? What about Donna? Could her extreme jealousy and hatred of Champ for breaking up her family, be enough to warrant murder? Lastly, what about Eric? She had a restraining order against him. Did he finally get his revenge? There were so many unanswered questions. Maybe it was suicide. She was still in love with Jimmy and saw no resolve with his attachment to his wife and son's. Being pregnant by him, and not knowing what to do about it;*

also weighed heavy on her mind. Was it all too much for her to handle? Maybe she did the unthinkable by eliminating herself from all her problems."

Well, the official word was in, but in Randy's mind. *Was it?*

The End

The author writes in several genre, such as murder mysteries, paranormals and a historical fiction novel.

Other publications are:

Veronica – a fiction murder mystery which takes place on Long Beach Island, N.J.

New Hope – another fiction murder mystery which takes place in a Theatre in New Hope, Pa.

Mystery of the Windowed Closet – a paranormal haunting with an angry spirit.

Mist in the Blue Bottle – a sequel to Mystery of the Windowed Closet. The bottle used for the séance's has far more powers beyond the psychic's ability to control.

To be released in the fall of 2021.

Biloxi – a 35 chapter historical fiction novel, which takes place in the antebellum south, between 1855-1865.